WILDER GIRLS

YOU WILL CHANGE. YOU *MIGHT* SURVIVE.

It's been eighteen months since the Raxter School for Girls was put under quarantine. Since the Tox hit and pulled Hetty's life out from under her.

It started slow. First the teachers died, one by one. Then it began to infect the students, turning their bodies strange. Left to fend for themselves on their island home, the girls don't dare wander outside the school's fence, where the Tox has made the woods wild and dangerous. As it seeps into everything, they wait for the cure they were promised.

But when her best friend Byatt goes missing, Hetty will do anything to find her – even if it means breaking quarantine and braving the horrors that lie outside. And when she does, Hetty learns that there's more to their story, to the Tox and their life at Raxter, than she ever thought possible

Praise for *Wilder Girls*

"A staggering gut punch of a book" *Kirkus*, starred review

"Evocative, haunting, and occasionally gruesome" *Booklist*, starred review

"The perfect kind of story for our current era" *Hypable*

"An ode to empowering women and a testament to the strength of female bonds" *Shelf Awareness*, starred review

"Electric prose, compelling relationships, and visceral horror" *Publishers Weekly*, starred review

"*Wilder Girls* is so sharp and packs so much emotion in such wise ways. I'm convinced we're about to witness the emergence of a major new literary star" Jeff VanderMeer, author of the *New York Times* bestseller *Annihilation*

"The eeriness of Raxter Island permeates every scene, and Rory Power's characters are fierce and honest, blazing from the pages. This is a groundbreaking speculative story – brutal and beautiful, raw and unflinching. I adored this book" Emily Suvada, author of *This Mortal Coil*

"*Wilder Girls* is the bold, imaginative, emotionally wrenching horror novel of my dreams – one that celebrates the resilience of girls and the earthshaking power of their friendships. An eerie, unforgettable triumph" Claire Legrand, *New York Times* bestselling author of *Furyborn*

"A feminist, LGBT+, sci-fi-horror story with all the tantalizing elements of gore, mystery, war, and love you can ask for. Real, flawed, brave girls against a world gone mad. A shudderingly good read!" Dawn Kurtagich, author of *Teeth in the Mist*

WILDER GIRLS

RORY POWER

MACMILLAN CHILDREN'S BOOKS

First published 2019 in the US by Delacorte Press, an imprint of Random House
Children's Books, a division of Penguin Random House LLC, New York

This edition published 2020 in the UK by Macmillan Children's Books
an imprint of Pan Macmillan
The Smithson, 6 Briset Street, London EC1M 5NR
Associated companies throughout the world
www.panmacmillan.com

ISBN 978-1-5290-2126-4

5 7 9 8 6

A CIP catalogue record for this book is available from
the British Library.

Interior design by Betty Law
Printed and bound by C

To my mother,
and to me,
and to the versions of us
who never thought
we would arrive here
together

All things counter,

original,

spare,

strange

—Gerard Manley Hopkins,
"Pied Beauty"

HETTY

CHAPTER 1

Something. Way out in the white-dark. Between the trees, moving where the thickets swarm. You can see it from the roof, the way the brush bends around it as it rustles to the ocean.

That size, it must be a coyote, one of the big ones hitting shoulder high. Teeth that fit like knives in the palm of my hand. I know because I found one once, the end of it just poking through the fence. Took it back and hid it under my bed.

One more crash through the brush and then the stillness again. Across the roof deck Byatt lowers her gun, rests it on the railing. Road clear.

I keep mine up, just in case, keep the sight raised to my left eye. My other eye's dead, gone dark in a flare-up. Lid fused shut, something growing underneath.

It's like that, with all of us here. Sick, strange, and we don't know why. Things bursting out of us, bits missing and pieces sloughing off, and then we harden and smooth over.

Through the sight, noon sun bleaching the world, I can see the woods stretching out to the island's edge, the ocean beyond. Pines bristling thick like always, rising high above the house. Here and there, gaps where the oak and birch have shed their leaves, but most of the canopy is woven tight, needles stiff with frost. Only the radio antenna breaking through, useless now the signal's out.

Up the road someone yells, and out of the trees, there's Boat Shift coming home. It's only a few who can make the trip, all the way across the island to where the Navy delivers rations and clothes at the pier the ferries used to come and go from. The rest of us stay behind the fence, pray they make it home safe.

The tallest, Ms. Welch, stops at the gate and fumbles with the lock until at last, the gate swings open, and Boat Shift come stumbling in, cheeks red from the cold. All three of them back and all three of them bent under the weight of the cans and the meats and the sugar cubes. Welch turns to shut the gate behind her. Barely five years past the oldest of us, she's the youngest of the teachers. Before this she lived on our hall and looked the other way when somebody missed curfew. Now she counts us every morning to make sure nobody's died in the night.

She waves to give the all clear, and Byatt waves back. I'm gate. Byatt's road. Sometimes we switch, but my eye doesn't

4

do well looking far, so it never lasts. Either way I'm still a better shot than half the girls who could take my place.

The last Boat girl steps under the porch and out of sight, and that's the end of our shift. Unload the rifles. Stick the casings in the box for the next girl. Slip one in your pocket, just in case.

The roof slopes gently away from the flattop deck, third floor to second. From there we swing over the edge and through the open window into the house. It was harder in the skirts and socks we used to wear, something in us still telling us to keep our knees closed. That was a long time ago. Now, in our ragged jeans, there's nothing to mind.

Byatt climbs in behind me, leaving another set of scuff marks on the window ledge. She pushes her hair over one shoulder. Straight, like mine, and a bright living brown. And clean. Even when there's no bread, there's always shampoo.

"What'd you see?" she asks me.

I shrug. "Nothing."

Breakfast wasn't much, and I'm feeling the shake of hunger in my limbs. I know Byatt is too, so we're quick as we head downstairs for lunch, to the main floor, to the hall, with its big high ceilings. Scarred, tilting tables; a fireplace; and tall-backed couches, stuffing ripped out to burn for warmth. And us, full of us, humming and alive.

There were about a hundred girls when it started, and twenty teachers. All together we filled both wings off the old house. These days we only need one.

The Boat girls come banging through the front doors, letting their bags drop, and there's a scramble for the food. They send us cans, mostly, and sometimes packs of dried jerky. Barely ever anything fresh, never enough for everyone, and on an average day, meals are just Welch in the kitchen, unlocking the storage closet and parceling out the smallest rations you ever saw. But today's a delivery day, new supplies come home on the backs of the Boat Shift girls, and that means Welch and Headmistress keep their hands clean and let us fight for one thing each.

Byatt and me, though, we don't have to fight. Reese is right by the door, and she drags a bag off to the side for us. If it were somebody else, people would mind, but it's Reese—left hand with its sharp, scaled fingers—so everyone keeps quiet.

She was one of the last to get sick. I thought maybe it had missed her, maybe she was safe, and then they started. The scales, each a shifting sort of silver, unfolding out of her skin like they were coming from inside. The same thing happened to one of the other girls in our year. They spread across her whole body and turned her blood cold until she wouldn't wake up, so we thought it was the end for Reese, and they took her upstairs, waited for it to kill her. But it didn't. One day she's holed up in the infirmary,

6

and the next she's back again, her left hand a wild thing but still hers.

Reese rips open the bag, and she lets me and Byatt root through it. My stomach clenching, spit thick around my tongue. Anything, I'd take anything. But we've got a bad one. Soap. Matches. A box of pens. A carton of bullets. And then, at the bottom, an orange—a real live orange, rot only starting to nip at the peel.

We snatch. Reese's silver hand on my collar, heat roiling under the scales, but I throw her to the floor, shove my knee against the side of her face. Bear down, trap Byatt's neck between my shoulder and my forearm. One of them kicks; I don't know who. Clocks me in the back of the head and I'm careening onto the stairs, nose against the edge with a crack. Pain fizzing white. Around us, the other girls yelling, hemming in.

Someone has my hair in her fist, tugging up, out. I twist, I bite where the tendons push against her skin, and she whines. My grip loosens. So does hers, and we scrabble away from each other.

I shake the blood out of my eye. Reese is sprawled halfway up the staircase, the orange in her hand. She wins.

CHAPTER 2

We call it the Tox, and for the first few months, they tried to make it a lesson. Viral Outbreaks in Western Civilizations: a History. "Tox" as a Root in Latinate Languages. Pharmaceutical Regulations in the State of Maine. School like always, teachers standing at the board with blood on their clothes, scheduling quizzes as if we'd all still be there a week later. The world's not ending, they said, and neither should your education.

Breakfast in the dining room. Math, English, French. Lunch, target practice. Physicals and first aid, Ms. Welch bandaging wounds and Headmistress pricking with needles. Together for dinner and then locked inside to last the night. No, I don't know what's making you sick, Welch would tell us. Yes, you'll be fine. Yes, you'll go home again soon.

That ended quickly. Classes falling off the schedule as

the Tox took teacher after teacher. Rules crumbling to dust and fading away, until only the barest bones were left. But still, we count the days, wake every morning to scan the sky for cameras and lights. People care on the mainland, that's what Welch always says. They've cared from the second Headmistress called Camp Nash on the coast for help, and they're looking for a cure. In the first shipment of supplies Boat Shift ever brought back, there was a note. Typed and signed, printed on the Navy's letterhead.

FROM: Secretary of the Navy, Department of Defense
Commanding Officer, Chemical/Biological Incident
        Response Force (CBIRF), Camp Nash Director,
        Centers for Disease Control and Prevention (CDC)
TO: Raxter School for Girls, Raxter Island
SUBJECT: Quarantine procedures as recommended by
        the CDC

Implementation of a full isolation and quarantine effective immediately. Subjects to remain on school grounds at all times, for safety and to preserve conditions of initial contagion. Breach of school fence, save by authorized crew for supply retrieval (see below), violates terms of quarantine.

Termination of phone and internet access pending; communication to route only through official radio channels. Full classification of information in effect.

Supplies to arrive via drop-off at western pier. Date and time to be set via Camp Nash lighthouse.

Diagnostics and treatment in development. CDC cooperating with local facilities re: cure. Expect delivery.

Wait, and stay alive, and we thought it would be easy—together behind the fence, safe from the wildwood, safe from the animals grown hungry and strange—but girls kept dropping. Flare-ups, which left their bodies too wrecked to keep breathing, left wounds that wouldn't heal, or sometimes, a violence like a fever, turning girls against themselves. It still happens like that. Only difference is now we've learned that all we can do is look after our own.

Reese and Byatt, they're mine and I'm theirs. It's them I pray for when I pass the bulletin board and brush two fingers against the note from the Navy still pinned there, yellowed and curling. A talisman, a reminder of the promise they made. The cure is coming, as long as we stay alive.

Reese digs a silver fingernail into the orange and starts peeling, and I force myself to look away. When food's fresh like that, we fight for it. She says it's the only fair way to settle things. No handouts, no pity. She'd never take it if it didn't feel earned.

Around us the other girls are gathering in swirls of high laughter, digging through the clothing that spills out of every bag. The Navy still sends us enough for the full number. Shirts and tiny boots we don't have anybody small enough to wear them.

And jackets. They never stop sending jackets. Not since the frost began to coat the grass. It was only just spring when the Tox hit, and for that summer we were fine in our uniform skirts and button-downs, but winter came like it always does in Maine, bitter and long. Fires burning in daylight and the Navy-issue generators running after dark, until a storm broke them to bits.

"You've got blood on you," Byatt says. Reese slices off the tail of her shirt and tosses it onto my face. I press. My nose squelches.

A scrape above us, on the mezzanine over the main hall. We all look up. It's Mona from the year ahead of me, red hair and a heart-shaped face, back from being taken to the infirmary on the third floor. She's been up there for ages, since last season's flare-up, and I don't think anybody expected her to ever come back down. I remember how her face steamed and cracked that day, how they carried her to the infirmary with a sheet over her like she was already dead.

Now she has a lattice of scars across her cheeks and the beginning of an aura to her hair. Reese is like that, with her blond braid and the glow the Tox gave it, and it's so much hers that it's startling to see it on Mona.

"Hey," she says, unsteady on her feet, and her friends run over, all fluttering hands and smiles, plenty of space between them. It's not contagion we're afraid of—we all

11

have it already, whatever it is. It's seeing her break apart again. Knowing someday soon it'll happen to us. Knowing all we can do is hope we make it through.

"Mona," her friends say, "thank God you're okay." But I watch them let the conversation drop, watch them drift out into the last daylight hours and leave Mona stranded on the couch, staring at her knees. There's no room for her with them anymore. They got used to her being gone.

I look over at Reese and Byatt, kicking at the same splinter in the stairs. I don't think I could ever get used to being without them.

Byatt gets up, an odd little frown creasing her brow. "Wait here," she says, and goes over to Mona.

They talk for a minute, the two of them, Byatt bending so her voice can slide right into Mona's ear, the shine of Mona's hair washing Byatt's skin red. And then Byatt straightens, and Mona presses her thumb against the inside of Byatt's forearm. They both look rattled. Just a little, but I see it.

"Afternoon, Hetty."

I turn around. It's Headmistress, the angles in her face even sharper now than they used to be. Gray hair twined tight in a bun, her shirt buttoned up to her chin. And a stain around her mouth, faint pink from the blood that's always oozing out of her lips. Her and Welch—the Tox is different with them. It doesn't cut them down the way it did the other teachers; it doesn't change their bodies the

12

way it does ours. Instead, it wakes weeping sores on their tongues, sets a tremor in their limbs that won't go away.

"Good afternoon," I say to Headmistress. She's let a lot of things slide, but manners aren't one of them.

She nods across the hall, to where Byatt is still bent over Mona. "How's she doing?"

"Mona?" I say.

"No, Byatt."

Byatt hasn't had a flare-up since late summer, and she's due for one soon. They cycle in seasons, each one worse than before until we can't bear it anymore. After her last one, though, I can't imagine something worse. She doesn't look any different—just a sore throat she can't shake and that serrated ridge of bone down her back, bits of it peeking through her skin—but I remember every second of it. How she bled through our old mattress until it dripped onto the floorboards underneath our bunk. How she looked more confused than anything as the skin over her spine split open.

"She's fine," I say. "It's getting about time, though."

"I'm sorry to hear it," Headmistress says. She watches Mona and Byatt a little longer, frowning. "I didn't know you girls and Mona were friends."

Since when has she cared about that? "Friendly, I guess."

Headmistress looks at me like she's surprised I'm still standing there. "Lovely," she says, and then she starts across the main hall, down the corridor to where her office is hidden away.

Before the Tox we saw her every day, but since then, she's either pacing up in the infirmary or locked in her office, glued to the radio, talking to the Navy and the CDC.

There was never any cell reception here in the first place—character building, according to the brochures—and they cut the landline that first day of the Tox. To keep things classified. To manage information. But at least we could speak to our families on the radio, and we could hear our parents crying for us. Until we couldn't anymore. Things were getting out, the Navy said, and measures had to be taken.

Headmistress didn't bother comforting us. It was well past comfort by then.

Her office door's shutting and locking behind her when Byatt comes back over to us.

"What was that?" I ask. "With Mona."

"Nothing." She pulls Reese to her feet. "Let's go."

Raxter is on a big plot of land, on the eastern tip of the island. The school has water on three sides, the gate on the fourth. And beyond it the woods, with the same kind of pine and spruce we have on the grounds, but tangled and thick, new trunks wrapping around the old ones. Our side of the fence is neat and clean like it was before—it's only us that's different.

Reese leads us across the grounds, to the point of the island, rocks scrubbed bare by the wind and pieced together like a turtle's shell. Now we sit there side by side by side, Byatt in the middle, the chilled breeze whipping her loose hair out in front of us. It's calm today, sky a clear sort of not-blue, and there's nothing in the distance. Beyond Raxter, the ocean drops deep, swallowing sandbanks and pulling currents. No ships, no land on the horizon, no reminder that the rest of the world is still out there, going on without us, everything still the way it always was.

"How are you feeling?" says Byatt. She's asking because two mornings ago the scar across my blind eye bloomed wide. It's left over from the early days, a reminder of the ways we didn't understand what was happening to us.

My first flare-up blinded my right eye and fused it shut, and I thought that was all, until something started to grow underneath. A third eyelid, that's what Byatt thought it was. It didn't hurt, just itched like hell, but I could feel something moving. That's why I tried to tear it open.

It was stupid. The scar is proof enough of that. I barely remember any of it, but Byatt says I dropped my rifle in the middle of Gun Shift and started clawing at my face like something had taken hold of me, working my fingernails between my crusted eyelashes and ripping at my skin.

The scar's mostly healed, but every now and then it splits open and blood weeps down over my cheek, pink and watery with pus. During Gun Shift I've got plenty else to think about, and it's not so bad, but now I can feel my heartbeat in my skin. Infected, maybe. Though that's the least of our worries.

"Can you stitch it for me?" I'm trying not to sound anxious, but she hears it anyway.

"That bad?"

"No, just—"

"Did you even clean it?"

Reese makes a satisfied sound. "I told you not to leave it open."

"Come here," Byatt says. "Let me see."

I shift around on the rocks until she's kneeling and my chin's lifted to her. She runs her fingers along the wound, brushing my eyelid. Something underneath it flinches.

"Looks like it hurts," she says, pulling a needle and thread from her pocket. They're always with her, ever since my eye first scarred over. Of the three of us she's closest to turning seventeen, and at times like this you can tell. "Okay. Don't move."

She slips the needle in and there's pain, but it's small enough, the cold air wicking it away. I try to wink at her, make her smile, but she shakes her head, a frown hanging on her brows.

"I said don't move, Hetty."

And it's fine, Byatt and me, and she's staring at me like I'm staring at her, and I'm safe, safe because she's here, until she digs the needle in too deep and I buckle, my whole body folding in. Pain blinding and everywhere.

Around me the world's gone water. I can feel blood leaking into my ear.

"Oh my God," she says. "Hetty, are you okay?"

"It's only stitches," says Reese. She's lying back on the rocks, her eyes closed. Shirt riding up so I can see a pale strip of stomach, stark through the dizzy blur. She's never cold, not even on days like this when our breaths hang in the air.

"Yeah," I say. Reese's hand never gives her trouble, not like my eye does me, and I smooth a snarl off my lips. There's enough to fight about without picking at this. "Keep going."

Byatt starts to say something, when there's a yell from near the garden. We turn around to see if somebody's had their first. Raxter runs sixth grade through high school, or it did, so our youngest girls are thirteen now. Eleven when this whole mess began, and now it's started to take them apart.

But there's nothing wrong, just Dara from our year, the girl with the webbed fingers, waiting where the rocks start. "Shooting," she calls to us. "Miss Welch says it's shooting time."

"Come on." Byatt ties off my stitches and gets up, holds out her hand to me. "I'll do the rest of your eye after dinner."

––––––

We had shooting before the Tox, too, a tradition left over from the start of the school, but it wasn't like it is now. Only the seniors—and Reese, best shot on the island, born to it like she was born to everything on Raxter—got to go into the woods with Mr. Harker and fire at the soda cans he'd line up along the ground. The rest of us got a class on gun safety, which usually turned into a free period when Mr. Harker inevitably ran late.

But then the Tox took Mr. Harker. Took Reese's firing hand and changed it so she couldn't grip the trigger anymore. And shooting stopped being shooting and turned into target practice, because now there are things we have to kill. Every few afternoons, as the sun comes back to earth, one by one, firing away until we hit a target dead center.

We have to be ready, Welch says. To protect ourselves, each other. During the first winter, a fox got through the fence, just slipped between the bars. Afterward, the Gun Shift girl said it reminded her of her dog back home, and that's why she couldn't take the shot. That's why the fox made it through the grounds to the patio. That's why it cornered the youngest girl left living and tore out her throat.

We practice out in the barn, near the island's point, with its big sliding doors open on each end so the stray shots fly into the ocean. There used to be horses, four of them, but early in the first season, we noticed how the Tox was starting to get inside them like it got inside us, how it was pushing their bones through their skin, how it was stretching their bodies until they screamed. So we led them out to the water and shot them. The stalls are empty now, and we pile into them to wait our turn. You have to fire at the target, and you're not allowed to stop until you've hit the bull's-eye.

Ms. Welch keeps most of the guns locked in a storage closet in the house, along with the bullets the Navy started sending once they heard about the animals, so there's only a shotgun and a carton of shells out here for all of us, laid out on a table made from sawhorses and a thin plywood plank. Not like the rifles we shoot with during Gun Shift, but Welch always says a gun's a gun, and every time, it makes a muscle in Reese's jaw twitch.

I hoist myself up onto the door of a stall, feel it swing as Byatt jumps up next to me. Reese slouches between us. She's not allowed to shoot because of her hand, but she's here every day, tense and quiet and watching the target.

At some point the order was alphabetical but we've all lost things, eyes and hands and last names. Now it's the oldest girls who go first. We get through them quickly, most of them good enough to hit home in only a few shots. Julia and Carson both done in two, an endless, mortifying wait as Landry takes more than I can count, and then it's our year. Byatt makes it in three. Respectable, but there's a reason they pair her with me on Gun Shift. If she doesn't hit her target, I will.

She hands the shotgun to me, and I blow on my hands to work the feeling back in before I take her place, lift the

19

shotgun to my shoulder, and aim. Breathe in, focus, and breathe out, finger squeezing tight. The sound rattles through me. It's easy. It's the only thing I've ever been better at than Byatt.

"Good, Hetty," Welch calls. Somebody at the back of the crowd repeats it, singsong and laughing. I roll my eye, leave the shotgun on the makeshift table, and join Reese and Byatt again by the stable door.

It's usually Cat who goes next, but there's a little shuffle, a whimper, and someone shoves Mona out into the middle. She stumbles a step or two and then rights herself, scanning the faces of the girls around her for some ounce of pity. She won't find any—we keep it for ourselves these days.

"Can I have a pass?" she says, turning to Welch. There's a waxy calm on Mona's face but a fidget in her body. She almost made it, almost got by with skipping her turn. But the rest of us won't let it happen. And neither will Welch.

"Afraid not." Welch shakes her head. "Let's go."

Mona says something else, but it's too low for anybody to hear, and she goes to the table. The gun is laid out. All Mona has to do is point and shoot. She lifts the gun, cradles it in the crook of her arm like it's a doll.

"Any day now." From Welch.

Mona levels it at the target and sneaks a finger onto the trigger. We're all quiet. Her hands are shaking. Somehow she's keeping the gun aimed right, but the strain is tearing at her.

"I can't," she whimpers. "I don't . . . I can't." She lowers the shotgun, looks my way.

And that's when they slice, three deep cuts on the side of her neck, like gills. No blood. Just a pulse in them with every breath, the twitch of something moving under her skin.

Mona doesn't scream. Doesn't make a noise. She just drops. Flat on her back, mouth gasping open. She's still looking at me, her chest rising slow. I can't look away, not as Welch hurries over, not as she kneels at Mona's feet and takes her pulse.

"Get her to her room," she says. Her room, and not the infirmary, because only the worst of us wind up there. And Mona's been sicker than this before. We all have.

The Boat Shift girls, marked out by the knives they're allowed to keep stuck in their belt loops, they step away from the rest. Always them, and they take Mona's arms. Haul her up, lead her away, back to the house.

Chatter, and a break as we start to follow, but Welch clears her throat.

"Ladies," she says, and she drags it out like she used to do during dorm checks. "Did I dismiss you?" Nobody answers, and Welch picks up the shotgun, gives it to the first girl in the order. "We'll start again. From the top."

There's no surprise in any of us. We left it someplace and forgot where. So we line up, we wait, and we take our shots, and we feel the warmth—Mona's warmth—seeping out of the shotgun and into our hands.

Dinner is scattered and fraying. Usually, we manage at least to sit in the same room, but today we get our rations from Welch and then split, some here in the hall and others in the kitchen, crowded around the old woodstove, the last of the curtains burning to keep them warm. After days like this and girls like Mona, we peel apart and wonder who's next.

I'm by the stairs, propped up against the banister. The three of us were last to get food today, and there was barely anything good left: just the ends of a loaf of bread, both slimy with mold. Byatt looked about ready to cry when that was all I brought back—neither of us got anything for lunch, not when Reese won that orange fair and square—but luckily, Carson from Boat Shift gave me some expired soup. We're waiting for the can opener to come our way so we can eat, and until then, there's Reese on the floor trying to nap, and Byatt looking up to where you can just see the door that bars the staircase up to the third-floor infirmary.

It used to be the servants' quarters back when the house was first built. Six rooms branching off a narrow hallway, with a roof deck above it and the double height main hall below. You can only get there using the staircase off the second-floor mezzanine, and it's locked behind a low, tilting door.

I don't like looking at it, don't like thinking of the sickest girls tucked away, don't like that there isn't room for everyone. And I don't like how every door up there locks from the outside. How, if you wanted to, you could keep someone in.

Instead, I stare across the main hall, to the glass walls of the dining room. Long empty tables ripped apart for kindling, silverware dumped into the ocean to keep the knives away from us. It used to be my favorite room in the house. Not on my first day, when I had nowhere to sit, but every one after I'd come in for breakfast and see Byatt saving me a seat. She had a single our first year, and she liked to get up early, take walks around the grounds. I'd meet her in the dining room, and she'd have toast waiting for me. Before Raxter, I ate it with butter, but Byatt showed me jam was better.

Cat catches my eye from across the room, and she holds up the can opener. I push off the banister and pick my way toward her, skirting where a quartet of girls are arranged in a square on the floor, their heads resting on one another's stomachs as they try to make one another laugh.

"Saw you got Carson to cave," Cat says as I approach. Black hair, so straight and fine, and dark considering eyes. She's had some of the worst of the Tox. Weeks in the infirmary, hands bound to keep her from clawing at her skin as it boiled and bubbled. She still has the scars, pockmarks of white all over her body, and blisters that bloom and bleed fresh every season.

I look away from a new one on her neck and smile.

"Didn't take much." She gives me the can opener, and I tuck it in my waistband, under my shirt so nobody can steal it from me on my way back to the stairs. "You guys good? You warm enough?" She's only got the detachable fleece lining of her friend Lindsay's jacket. The two of them had bad luck in the last clothing draw, and nobody manages to keep a blanket around here for long unless you never take your eyes off it.

"We're all right," Cat says. "Thanks for asking. And hey, with your soup, make sure the can's not bulging at the lid. We've got enough to worry about besides botulism."

"I'll pass that on."

That's Cat, kind in her own way. She's from our year, and her mom's in the Navy like my dad. Raxter and Camp Nash are the only life for miles up here, and over the years they've twined so close that Raxter gives a scholarship to Navy girls. It's the only reason I'm here. The only reason Cat's here. We took the bus down to the airport together at the end of every quarter, her on her way to the base in San Diego, and me on mine to the base in Norfolk. She never saved me a seat, but when I sidled in next to her, she'd smile and let me fall asleep on her shoulder.

I'm just sitting down next to Byatt again when there's a commotion by the front door, where Landry's girls are clustered. You can break the whole of us into maybe eleven or twelve parts—some bigger, some smaller—and the largest group is centered around Landry, two years above me and from an old Boston family, older even than Byatt's.

She's never liked us much, not since she complained that there were no boys on the island, and Reese gave her the blankest look I've ever seen and said, "Plenty of girls, though."

It made something jump in my chest, something I can still feel at night when Reese's braid casts a rippling glow on the ceiling. A reaching. A wish.

But she's too far away. She's always been too far.

Somebody yelps, and we watch as the group shuffles and knits itself into a ring, clustered thick around a body laid out on the floor. I bend down, try to get a glimpse. Glossy brown hair, frame frail and angular.

"I think it's Emmy," I say. "She's having her first."

Emmy was in sixth grade when the Tox happened, and one by one the other girls in her year have crashed headlong into puberty, their first flare-ups screaming and bursting like fireworks. Now it's finally her turn.

We listen as she whimpers, her body trembling and seizing. I wonder what she'll get, if it's anything at all. Gills like Mona's, blisters like Cat's, maybe bones like Byatt's or a hand like Reese's, but sometimes the Tox doesn't give you anything—just takes and takes. Leaves you drained and withering.

At last, quiet, and the group around Emmy starts to clear. She looks all right, for a first flare-up. Her legs wobble as she gets to her feet, and even from here, I can see her veins in her neck standing out dark, like they're bruises.

There's a smattering of applause as Emmy dusts off her jeans. Julia, one of the Boat Shift girls, tears a chunk off her stale dinner roll and tosses it to Emmy. Somebody will leave a gift under her pillow tonight. Maybe a pair of bobby pins, or a page ripped out from one of the magazines still floating around.

Landry gives her a hug, and Emmy's beaming, so proud to have made it through so well. It'll hit her later, I think, when the adrenaline fades away, when Landry isn't there to watch. The real hurt of it. The change.

"I'm still bitter," I say. "Nobody ever gave me anything for my first."

Byatt laughs, her hands moving quick to open the soup can, and she gives me the lid. "There. My gift to you."

I lick off the layer of vegetable sludge, ignore the sparkling acidity. Byatt takes a sip from the can. When she hits a third of the way down she'll pass it to me. Reese always goes last. You can't get her to eat any other way.

"When do you think they'll post the new Boat Shift list?" Byatt says loudly. She's asking me, but she's doing it for Reese—Reese, who's been angling to get on Boat Shift since nearly the very beginning.

Her mom left before I ever came to Raxter, but I knew her dad, Mr. Harker. He was the groundskeeper and maintenance staff and handyman all in one, and he lived in a house off the grounds, on the edge of the island. Or he did, until the Tox, and the quarantine, and then the Navy sent him in to live with us. He doesn't anymore. Went out

26

into the woods when the Tox started getting to him, and Reese has been trying to go after him ever since.

Boat Shift's the only way to do that. The only way past the fence. Usually, it's the same three girls until one of them dies, but a few days ago the third girl, Taylor, said this was her last trip and she wouldn't go out anymore. She's one of the oldest still here, and she was always helping, always calming everybody down and stitching everybody up. We can't figure out exactly what made her stop.

There's a story going around it had something to do with her girlfriend, Mary, who went feral last summer. One day Mary was here and then she was gone—just the Tox left in her body, and no light in her eyes. Taylor was with her that day, had to wrestle her down and put a bullet in her head. Everybody thinks that's why she quit Boat Shift, but when Lindsay asked her about it yesterday, Taylor backhanded her across the face, and nobody's mentioned it since.

It hasn't stopped us from wondering. Taylor says she's fine, says everything is normal, but quitting Boat Shift isn't normal. Especially not for her. Welch and Headmistress will have to post a new third name soon, someone to take her place.

"Maybe tomorrow," I say. "I can ask."

Reese opens her eyes, sits up. Her silver fingers twitch. "Don't. You'll only piss Welch off."

"Fine," I say. "Don't worry, though. You'll get it."

"We'll see," Reese says back. These aren't the nicest things we've ever said to each other, but they're close.

That night Byatt finishes the stitches over my eye, and afterward I can't sleep. I stare up at the bottom of Reese's bunk, to where Byatt's carved her initials over and over. *BW. BW. BW.* She does that everywhere. On the bunk, on her desk in every class we had, on the trees in the grove by the water. Marking Raxter as hers, and sometimes I think if she asked, I'd let her do the same to me.

The quiet, on and on, until near to midnight two gunshots break the silence. I tense, wait, but it's barely a heartbeat before the shouts come echoing down from Gun Shift, yelling, "All clear!"

Above me, Reese is snoring on the top bunk. Byatt and I share the bottom, pressed so close I can hear her teeth grinding when she dreams. The heat went out a while ago, and we sleep as near as we can, in our jackets, in our everything. I can reach into my pocket and feel the bullet there, the casing smooth.

We heard about it soon after Welch assigned the first rounds of Gun Shift. The first girls saw something from the roof. They couldn't agree on what—one girl said it was hazy and gleaming, moving almost like a person in a slow, measured gait, and another said it was too big for that—but it spooked them enough that they gathered all the Gun Shift girls into the smallest room on the second floor, and they taught us how to crack a bullet open. How to ignore that shudder in our guts and how to swallow the gunpowder like poison, just in case we ever need to die.

Some nights I get to thinking about what it could've been, what they could've seen, and it helps to feel the casing in my hand, to know that I'm safe from whatever they saw and whatever they're afraid of. But tonight, Mona's all I can see—Mona holding the gun and Mona looking like she wanted to put it to her head.

I'd never held a gun before Raxter. There was one in my house, sometimes—my dad's Navy-issue pistol if he was home—but he'd keep it locked away. Byatt hadn't even seen one in person.

"I'm from Boston," she said when Reese and I laughed. "We don't have them down there like you do here."

I remember it because she almost never mentioned home. Never slipped it into conversation the way I always found myself doing with Norfolk. I don't think she ever missed it. Raxter didn't let us have cell phones, so if you wanted to call home, you had to line up to use the landline in Headmistress's office during afternoon rest hour. I never saw her there. Not once.

I roll over to look at her, stretched out next to me and already dozing. I'd have missed home if I were from a family like hers, all blue blood and money. But that's the difference with us. Byatt's never wanted anything she doesn't have.

"Stop staring at me," she grumbles, and pokes me in the ribs.

"Sorry."

"Such a creep." But she hooks her pinkie around mine and slips under again.

I must fall asleep after that, because there's nothing, and then I'm blinking, then a creak in the floorboards, and Byatt isn't in the bunk with me anymore. She's at the threshold, closing the door behind her as she comes inside.

We're not supposed to leave our rooms at night, not even to go to the bathrooms at the end of the hall. The dark is too thick, Welch's curfew too strict. I prop myself up on one elbow, but I'm covered in shadows and she must not see. Instead, she pauses at the foot of the bed, and then she climbs the ladder up to Reese.

One of them sighs, and there's a rustle as they settle in, and then the yellow-white of Reese's braid is hanging from her bunk to swing gently above me. It drifts like feathers, covers the ceiling in faded patterns of light.

"Hetty asleep?" she says. I don't know why, but I slow my breathing, make sure they won't know I can hear.

"Yeah."

"What is it?"

"Nothing," Byatt says.

"You went out."

"Yeah."

The hurt of it twists in my gut. Why wouldn't she take me with her? And why is it Reese who gets to hear about it? Byatt isn't supposed to find things in Reese that she can't find in me.

One of them moves around, probably Byatt tucking into Reese. She sleeps close, Byatt. I'm always waking with her fingers hooked in pockets of my jeans.

"Where'd you go?" Reese whispers.

"For a walk." But I know how a lie sounds. No way she risked sneaking out just to stretch her legs. We get enough of that every morning. No, there's a secret buried in her voice, and usually, she shares those with me. What's different now?

Reese doesn't reply, and Byatt keeps going. "Welch caught me on my way back."

"Damn."

"It's fine. I was only downstairs, in the hall."

"What'd you say?"

"Told her I was getting a bottle of water, for a headache."

Reese's silver hand pulls her braid out of view. I can picture the shuttered gleam of her eyes, the strong set of her jaw. Or maybe she's easier in the dark. Maybe she breaks all the way open when she thinks you can't see.

The first time I met her was the day I got to Raxter. I was thirteen but not real thirteen, not thirteen with a chest and hips and bared teeth. I'd met Byatt already, on the ferry from the mainland to the island, and that had been fast and tight. She knew who she was and who I should be, and she fit right into all the places in me I couldn't fill. Reese was different.

She was sitting on the stairs in the main hall, her uniform too big, her knee socks sagging around her ankles. I don't know if they were afraid of her already or if it was something else, if maybe her being the groundskeeper's daughter meant something to them it didn't to me, but the other girls in our year were clustered by the fireplace, as far away from her as they could get.

Byatt and I passed her on our way to the others, and the way Reese looked at me then, already angry, already burning—I remember it like nothing else.

For a while after that there wasn't anything between the three of us at all. Just class and a nod here and there in the hallway on the way to the showers. Then Byatt and I needed a third for our group project in French, and Reese was at the top of the class—had muscled past Byatt a few tests back—so we picked her.

That's all it took. Reese next to us at dinner, Reese next to us at assembly, and if I remembered how she looked at me that first day, if I noticed the way my stomach clenched any time she said my name, it didn't matter. It still doesn't. This is as close as I'll ever get to her—a bunk above me, her voice soft in the dark as she talks to somebody else.

"Do you think," she says after a while, "that it's getting worse?"

I can practically hear Byatt shrug. "Probably."

"Probably?"

"I mean, I don't know," Byatt says. "Sure. But not for everyone." A beat of nothing, and then her voice again, so quiet I have to strain to hear. "Listen, if you know something—"

I hear the scrape of Reese's boots as she rolls over. "Get down," she says. "You're crowding me."

I wonder, sometimes, if she was different before her mother left. If she was easier to reach. But I can't imagine her like that.

I stir when Byatt gets into our bunk, but I pretend not to wake, just turn over so my back is to her. I think she watches me for a moment, but she slips under soon after. I only follow once light is starting at the bottom of the sky.

CHAPTER 3

Dawn breaks quick and cold. A new layer of frost on the windows. Ice collecting in sheaves among the reeds. Byatt and I get out of bed, try to leave Reese sleeping as we head outside for our walk.

The walks were just Byatt's at first. Her, alone, making slow circuits of the grounds. The other girls used to whisper about it. Homesick, they said, lonely, and it was all pity and laughter. But I know it gave her a glow, made her someone to get close to. By the end of our second month here, I was wandering after her and hoping it would rub off on me.

Today the main hall is empty as we pass through, except for the girl keeping watch at the front doors. The school is shaped like a bracket, a newly built wing branching off each end of the old house. On the second floor it's dorms and a handful of offices, and here on the ground floor it's classrooms, and the hall, and Headmistress's office at the corner of the bracket, Headmistress probably inside tallying supplies, checking the numbers.

I reach out as we pass the bulletin board and tap the note about the cure, right on the letterhead. That's where the luck is best, and you can see how the color's worn away where a hundred girls have touched it a hundred times. I smile, think of me and Byatt in some sun-soaked city somewhere, free of the Tox.

"Hey," Byatt says to the door girl, who's one of the youngest we have left, thirteen. "Everything good?"

"Yeah." The girl tugs on the door without Byatt asking. People are like that for Byatt, no matter what she's like for them.

The door's barely an inch open, too heavy for the girl to move on her own. We start them young on Door Shift—if there's anything really wrong, the Gun Shift girls will take care of it, but the responsibility of manning the door molds the younger girls into the right shape. I step up and lay my hands over hers. Pull, feel the give under the rust, newer and thicker every season. This will be our second winter with the Tox, my third at Raxter altogether. How many more will I have here?

"Thanks." I knock my arm against her shoulder so she won't realize I don't remember her name. "See you later."

Out on the porch I wait while Byatt buttons her jacket. The grass is long dead, and there, stamped into the frost that covers it, is a trail of footprints. Could some of them be Byatt's from last night?

"So," I say. "Cold out."

She doesn't answer. She's fussing with the top button of her jacket, hidden under her chin, as we step onto the flagstone path to the gate.

I try again, hope I don't have to dig too deeply. If only she'd just tell me where she went. "Sleep well?"

"Sure."

"Was I restless?"

"No more than usual."

I wait, give her another chance to come out with it, but she doesn't. "Because I woke up, right in the middle of the night, and you weren't there."

Byatt veers off the path, to the left. It's the way we always go. "Yeah?"

"Yeah."

At first I think she won't explain—she doesn't always with me, even though I do with her—but then she stops, looks me full in the eye, and says, "You talked in your sleep."

It's so far from what I'm expecting that my jaw drops. "I did?"

"Yeah." There's a delicate sort of hurt creeping into her expression, like she's not sure she wants to let me see it. "I don't know what you were dreaming, but you said . . . something."

I didn't. I know I didn't, but I don't understand this enough to say so. "What did I say?"

She grimaces, shakes her head. "It wasn't something I'd want to hear again. Let's leave it at that."

For a moment I feel just the way she wants me to. Too anxious, too guilty to keep pushing. But it's not real. I was awake, and I saw her. "Oh," I say. "Are you sure?"

It's the closest I can get to confronting her. Lean too hard and she'll let herself snap. I've seen her do it a hundred times, with teachers when one of us forgot their homework, with field trips when Welch caught her forging my mom's signature. Byatt lies so well. But usually, she's lying for me.

"Yeah," she says, with just the right tremble. "It's fine, okay? I just climbed up to bunk in with Reese."

That, at least, is true. But what secrets are there to keep at Raxter? We all have the same horrors in our bodies, the same pains, the same wants.

"I'm sorry," I say. There's nothing for it but to play along. "Whatever it was. You know you're my best friend."

Byatt brightens immediately and throws her arm around my shoulders to draw me close. We start walking again, steps matching steps. "Yeah," she says, "I know I am."

Above us, the house looms, and the voices of other girls spill through cracked windows as they start to wake. Arguments over clothes and bedding, and a few sharper than that, but mostly the same conversations every day. The same magazines passed around and around, quizzes taken and retaken, the same memories told like stories until they belong to everybody. Parents sliced up to share, first kisses exchanged like gifts.

I never had anything to add—couldn't conjure up enough of my dad, couldn't bear thinking of my mom all alone in our house on the base. And I've wanted boys, and I've wanted girls, but I've never wanted anyone enough to miss them, enough to pluck them from the slideshow of my old life and bring them here.

Sometimes if I close my eye, I forget what's changed. And Raxter isn't a rush of gunpowder and hunger anymore. It's boredom, an idleness burrowing deep.

We're at the fence now, the house behind us and the woods stretching out ahead, branches evergreen. Road slicing through, worn flat and narrower each year. A few feet past the fence, I can see what the gunshots must've hit last night—a deer, hours dead, flesh too contaminated to eat. Worms crawling in its open mouth, blood stiff in its fur.

Besides the deer there's more out there. It's something we all know but don't talk about. If you're outside at the right time, you can feel the ground shake every now and then, like my house on the base whenever a jet flew too close overhead. Early in the Tox we used to leaf through the earth science textbooks, look at the lists of flora and fauna and wonder what might be out there. But then we had to burn the books for warmth, and wondering wasn't as fun anymore.

"Come on," Byatt says.

We don't look up to the roof, where two girls are aiming rifles over our heads. Instead, we trail our fingers along the bars of the fence, follow it until it meets the water, where frills of rock pile and stack, catching the spray in pools that won't freeze through until the deep of winter. Folds of gray, the algae a sharp green, and the ocean rolling into the distance, black and heaving.

I climb onto a spear of rock, lean onto my palms so I can look into the biggest pool. No fish—barely any come near the island since things changed—but this time I see something. Small, no bigger than my fist, and a bright, uneasy sort of blue. A crab.

"Hey," I say, and Byatt clambers over to balance next to me. "Look."

They showed up a few years before I did. A sign of the times, that's what our biology teacher said when she took us out here to observe them my sophomore fall, during our climate change unit. Used to be they never came north of Cape Cod, but as the world changes, so does the water. We call these ones Raxter Blues, and they grow different up here.

Mr. Harker helped us catch a few, and we took them back to the classroom, took turns holding the scalpel. Salt thick on the air, and two girls nearly fainted as we cracked the shells, lifted them like lids. See, our teacher said. How they have both gills and lungs, to breathe in the water and on land. See how a body will change, to give you the best chance it can.

We watch the crab for a while as it trundles across the floor of the tide pool, and then Byatt shuffles forward and nearly knocks me into the water.

"Careful," I say, but she's not listening, her arm outstretched, fingers breaking the surface. Something thin and long darts under a shelf of rock.

"I want to see it again," she tells me. She's sweeping circles in the water, lifting the crab with the current.

"Don't," I say. "It's awful. And if you keep putting your hand in there, you'll get frostbite sooner or later."

But she's not listening. Quick like one of the herons that used to live here, her hand darts in, ripples splashing at her elbow, and when she comes up again, it's with the crab pinched between two fingers, dangling by a claw. It nips at her, but she pins it to the ground.

Keeping it still with one hand, she fumbles with the other for one of the loose rocks at the rim of the pool. Gets a good grip and slams the rock down on the crab. It writhes, limbs twitching frantically.

"Jesus, Byatt."

She stares down at the shattered crab. Starting at the very tips of its claws, the blue shell is darkening, turning black like it's been dipped in ink. The sight of it is what sent those girls reeling in biology, what left them dizzy and gasping.

"Why do you do that?" I ask, looking away. If we'd already had breakfast, I might be throwing it up right now.

"Because," she says. She picks up the crab, still moving

but only just, and tosses it back into the water. "It's how you know they're real Raxter Blues."

"You can't just pick a flower?" The irises do it, turn black as they're dying. They have since before the Tox, and now we do too. Every Raxter girl, fingers black up to her knuckles as the Tox takes her.

"It's not the same," Byatt says.

She stands then, leaves me behind and picks her way out to the last of the rocks, her feet sure, boots slick as the tide pushes in. She told me once that it was her favorite thing about Raxter, the way the edges of it change. Earth dropping away and slipping under and there, Byatt with her eyes closed and her chin lifted.

"Can you remember?" I call suddenly, the winter breeze tearing my voice from my mouth. "What it was like, before?"

She looks over her shoulder at me. I wonder if she's thinking of the same things I am. Of watching from the porch while the seniors gathered on the beach in their white graduation dresses, of linking fingers during assembly and squeezing hard to keep from laughing. Of standing in the dining room, the last echoes of sun drifting through the paneled windows, and singing an off-key hymn before sitting down to eat.

"Yeah," Byatt says. "Of course."

"And you miss it?"

For a second I think she won't answer, and then her mouth splits wide, and she's smiling. "Does that matter?"

41

"I guess not." Above us the clouds shift, let a little warmth through. "Let's go in."

We meet Reese at the kitchen threshold, waiting as two girls wash their hair in the sink with a bucket of rainwater. Every few days Byatt and I share a turn, my hair too short to need much more than a scrub at the roots, but Reese's braid scatters the water like stars, beautiful and hard to look at, and she gets the whole sink to herself.

"They're taking forever," Reese says as we come up beside her. She's got her braid gripped tight in her silver hand, and I can see the tension in the other girls, see them looking at the door like they might make a run for it.

"Sorry," one of them says. "We're almost done."

"Well, hurry up."

They look at each other, and then the girls are wringing their hair out and hustling past us. The second one has shampoo suds still glistening at her temples.

"Thanks," Reese says, like she gave them a choice.

Byatt and I stand in the doorway as Reese undoes her braid and dunks her hair into the bucket of water. It takes a few minutes. By the time she's done, her sleeves are drenched, and she's still dripping as the three of us find an empty couch in the main hall and settle in to wait. If the shifts are going to change, Welch tells us early, right when the youngest ones have finished their breakfast.

I slump against the armrest, drop my legs into Byatt's lap. On the other side of her, Reese is bent forward, damp head ducked down as she rebraids her hair.

She isn't nervous. There's just something winding tight in her. It's always there, but some days it feels closer to the surface, and today's one of those. We don't say anything when Reese starts picking at the upholstery with her silver hand.

I've never wanted anything the way Reese wants Boat Shift. I can still see her at the gate that day Mr. Harker left, reaching through to him. I can still hear her yelling as Taylor pulled her away. Of course she wants to go out, past the fence, past the curve of the road. To see if there's anything left of him.

We couldn't sneak her out, not without breaking the quarantine, like the letter says. And it's too dangerous, anyway, for a girl on her own, but Byatt and I did what we could. Took her up on the roof deck, just to see if we could find the outline of her old house in the trees. It only made her angry.

"I don't know," she said as we climbed inside. "Just, fuck." And then she didn't speak to us for two days after.

The door to Headmistress's office swings open, and Welch comes down the corridor with a sheet of paper in her hands. Reese stands up.

"Ladies," says Welch, "please take a look at the revised schedule. Some of you will have changed rotations." She switches the old out for new, tacking the paper next to the note above the fireplace. "Girls on the Boat Shift, find me when you can. I'll be by the south storeroom."

I expect Reese to rush up there just as soon as Welch is gone, but she's halting when she approaches, her legs moving like machinery. There's talk, still, in the hall, but nobody else has come up to check, and that's how I know they're watching.

Reese gets close. I tense up, waiting for the small smile that means she's got what she wants. Except it doesn't come.

Wheeling around, Reese is by the couch in a few strides, and her silver hand locks around my ankle. Jesus, it's cold, and then she gives one tug, hard, and I'm on the floor.

"Reese," I say, shock jolting through me, and I start to sit up, but she's already moving. Straddling me, her knees pinning my arms, the heel of her hand pushing at my chin, laying my neck bare.

I'm trying to say something, and my feet are thrashing, and I try to twist my hips, maybe that'll help, I just need to breathe, just one breath, but she's pressing harder, landing a silver punch on my chest.

"What happened?" I can hear Byatt yelling louder and louder. "Reese, stop. What happened? What is it?"

Reese turns her head just a fraction, and I manage to fight one of my arms free. I reach around her for her braid and yank her head back. She howls, and there's a slice and a burn across the blind side of my face. She lays her forearm across my windpipe. Leans.

I try to push her off, but she's strong—strong like she's

something more than herself, and there's Byatt behind her, screaming, screaming. One last ragged gasp before the world goes black, and I say her name.

Reese scrambles away, staggering to her feet.

"Oh my God," Byatt says, color drained from her face.

I can't move, hurt hollowing out my chest. We've fought before, but only over rations. It always ends there. That's the line we stay behind.

Reese blinks, clears her throat. "She's fine," she says gruffly. "She'll be fine."

She must leave after that, because Byatt kneels next to me, and she's the one who helps me up when I can find my feet again.

I almost don't check the schedule. I almost just go upstairs to rest. But we pass close by, and I squint, skim past the new Gun Shift pairs and the new guard rotations and find my name. And there it is. That's why. I'm the new Boat Shift girl.

I'm smiling. I don't mean to be, but I am, and there are whispers coming from behind me, and I have to stop, right now, or Reese will hear about it and she'll hate me even more.

Byatt lays her hand on my shoulder. "You should go find her. Talk to her."

"I don't think that's a good idea."

"I mean, I know it wasn't right, what she did," Byatt's

saying, and she's smoothing my hair off my face. "But she's—"

"I have to check in," I say. "With Welch." I can't help the brightness in my voice. I didn't want this—I know it wasn't supposed to be mine—but I'm proud now that I have it. I'm a good shot. I can carry my weight. I know why my name is on that list.

"Fine," Byatt says. She pulls back, crosses her arms over her chest, and I can tell she has something else she'd like to say. Instead, she gives me one last look before making for the stairs.

Around me the other girls are waiting. Watching me, new attention in their eyes now that I'm Boat Shift. They're waiting for me to show them, to tell them what to do, and it's more than I thought I'd have to carry. But I have to remember that for all the rules that have fallen apart, there are new ones, stronger and more rigid than anything we had before. Nobody goes past the fence—that's the first rule, the most important, and now I'm one of the girls allowed to break it.

I give the nearest girl a smile that I hope is mature and responsible and then hurry out of the room, still feeling the stares. Welch said to meet her so I go, along the south corridor to the storeroom, where I find her taking inventory.

"Hetty, great," she says. She looks so tired, and for a second I'm grateful. The Tox doesn't hurt her as badly as it hurts us girls, but at least between flare-ups, we can count on a moment or two of peace. "Come and help me for a minute."

She dumps a stack of blankets into my arms, and I hear her counting softly. I drop my forehead against them, make sure I'm breathing slowly. I think the stitches over my eye have opened up.

"We'll probably go out again tomorrow or the day after," Welch says, taking the blankets back from me. "Yesterday's shipment was small, so with any luck they'll supplement it."

The best we can hope for is some extra food, and maybe a blanket or two. In the early days there was more. Contact lens solution, so Kara didn't have to wear her glasses. Insulin for Olivia, and Welch's birth control, to manage her hormones. But they stopped coming after a month or so, and even Headmistress couldn't get them back. Left Kara without her lenses, Welch without her pills, and Olivia dead.

"So where do I meet you?" I ask. "And what do I bring? Is it—"

"I'll come fetch you." Welch gives me a once-over. "Make sure you're getting some good rest. And try to avoid displays like that fuss in the main hall, if you would."

"Tell that to Reese," I mutter.

"Oh, sorry," I hear from behind me. I turn, see Taylor shifting from foot to foot in the doorway. At first I think she's here to give me a hard time about taking her spot on

47

Boat Shift, even though she's the one who gave it up, but she's focused on Welch.

"Didn't mean to interrupt," she continues. "Welch, can I catch up with you later?"

A look passes between them—quick, almost nothing, and gone before I can pin it down. "Sure," Welch says lightly.

Taylor ducks down the hall. I stare after her, trying to spot whatever the Tox did to her. Nobody's sure what her flare-ups have left her with, not even the other girls in her year. Whatever the changes, they must be hidden under her clothes.

"Remember, Hetty," Welch says as she finishes tallying the blankets. I snap back to her. "Rest and hydration, and no fuss. Away with you now."

Out in the corridor I'm just in time to see Taylor disappearing into the kitchen. Welch wouldn't tell me what to expect past the fence, but Taylor might.

I follow her, sidle into the kitchen to see her kneeling by the old fridge, one arm wedged behind it.

"Um," I say, and she jumps, free hand flying to her belt where she used to keep a knife during her Boat Shift days.

"God, Hetty. Make a noise, won't you?"

"Sorry." I inch closer. "What are you doing?"

Taylor glances over my shoulder, still holding herself coiled and tight, and then smiles a little. I watch the tension drain out of her. She sits back on her heels and pulls a plastic sleeve of crackers out from behind the fridge. "Want a snack?"

Hiding food is strictly forbidden. A few girls tried it near the beginning, and it wasn't the teachers who came down hard but the rest of us. Boat Shift took them outside to have a talk and left them bloodied in the courtyard. Taylor, though—she's earned some leeway. I can't imagine anybody punishing her.

"Sure," I say, and sit down next to her on the checkered tile. She hands me a cracker. I feel her watching me as I take a bite. "Thanks."

"I put these here sometime last summer. Figured one of you girls would've found them by now."

"Nobody's gonna look back there," I say. "Too many gross cobwebs. And, like, mice or something."

Taylor scoffs. "When was the last time you saw a mouse around here?" She swallows a cracker down in two bites and wipes crumbs off her mouth. "So? Ask what you want to ask."

"What?"

"Your name shows up on the Boat Shift list and you're in here talking to me by accident? Okay, Hetty."

I take another cracker, but my mouth is dry, and I wind up just holding it in my clammy palm. "I guess I'm wondering what I should be prepared for. I mean, what, we go pick up the stuff and come back? It can't be as easy as that."

Taylor laughs, and it's the kind of thing where you

hear it and laugh along with her because if you don't, she might cry. "They use the lighthouse at Camp Nash to tell us they're coming. Morse code or some shit. I don't know. But Welch'll come in and wake you if they give the signal. She likes to leave early so you can get home before sundown. It'd be nice if they could just drop the stuff here, save us a trip."

I'd never even thought that was a possibility. "Why don't they?"

Taylor takes another crumbling bite of cracker. "They say it would risk contamination," she tells me, mouth full. "Really, I just think they can't get around the rocks off the point. Not like they're the Navy or anything. Not like the Navy's supposed to be good at that whole sailing thing."

It's startling, hearing this hallowed process rendered in bitter words. But then, she's been a lot closer to it than I have.

"Is it . . ." And I have to stop, find the right words. "Is it as big as it looks out there?"

"Big?"

I think of the grounds, the way the pines have gotten taller, the way they seem nothing like what I've seen from the roof. In the woods the Tox is still wild. No girls for it to pick apart, so it got into everything else. Out there it blossoms and spreads with a kind of joy. Unbridled and vicious and free.

"Yeah," I say. "I guess."

Taylor leans forward. "Do you remember what it was like? That first day?"

A year and a half back, in early spring sun. I was out in the jack pine grove when it happened, in the tangle of trunks and limbs, Reese and Byatt watching as I walked out on the lowest branch as far as I could go. And I fell, which wasn't strange; we were all of us covered in scabs and nicks then, some of us turning a corner too fast, some of us sewing our hems too short, some of us pressing sharp things into ourselves just to see what it would feel like. It was what came after.

I stood up, laughing, but then blood started dripping out of my right eye. Slowly at first, and then faster and faster, running down my cheeks and pooling in my mouth. Hot like it was about to boil, and I started to cry because I couldn't see.

Byatt swore and grabbed my elbow. Reese took the other, and they rushed me to the house. I kept my eyes closed. I could hear other girls, hear them talking and giggling and falling silent as we passed by. Byatt tucked her body in close to mine. She was the only thing that kept me on my feet.

In the main hall, Byatt sat with me on the stairs while Reese ran to get the nurse. We sat there for a while, I don't know how long. Byatt held my hand in both of hers while I leaned on her shoulder and bled on her shirt. When Reese came back, she had Welch with her, and they pressed gauze to my right eye until it dried. Until they could see the skin of my eyelids fusing together.

The nurse was gone. Three other girls were sick. Everything was starting.

They quarantined the island the next morning. Helicopters overhead, military issue. Days of doctors in hazmat suits swarming the house, tests and tests and no answers, just a sickness spreading through every one of us.

"Yeah," I say. I have to clear my throat. "I remember."

"It's still like that outside," Taylor says. "Here at the house you have it so easy, but out there it's like the first days. Like we don't know a damn thing."

Maybe she'll tell me the truth. Maybe I've earned it, now that I'm Boat Shift. "Is that why you quit?"

It's the wrong question, and Taylor's face changes the second I ask it. Eyes cold, mouth a flat line. She gets to her feet. "You're welcome for the crackers. Put them back when you're done."

Reese doesn't find us for dinner. She's made curfew, that's all Welch tells us when we ask, but we don't see her, not when I pick up our rations from the kitchen, not when Lauren and Ali come to blows over a fresh pack of hair elastics and Julia has to pull them apart. That's my job now too, I remind myself. I'm Boat Shift—I'm that girl.

Her bunk is empty when we get to our room, and I think I see the flash of her silver hand out of the corner of my eye, heading farther down the hall. I force myself to look away.

"I should be the mad one," I say to Byatt as we settle into bed. "She strangled me, not the other way around."

"You took something from her," Byatt says. "That's how she sees it, anyway."

I hold my breath, tip my chin up to keep the prickling in my eye from turning to tears. She can't really think I did this to hurt her. But that's Reese—always protecting herself from some threat I can't see. "I didn't ask for this."

"I don't think she cares about that."

There's a moment as we adjust, me with my back tucked against the wall, and Byatt flat on hers, taking up most of the bunk. We've slept like this since the start of the Tox, first to stay warm, and then just because we got used to it.

"You could refuse the spot," she says once we're settled.

"I might've," I say sharply, "if she'd asked." But the anger doesn't last. I sigh, shut my eye. "I just don't know how, with her."

Byatt makes a small noise. "Thank goodness I'm here, huh?"

"You have no idea." Some days it's fine. Others it nearly breaks me. The emptiness of the horizon, and the hunger in my body, and how will we ever survive this if we can't survive each other? "We're gonna make it. Tell me we're gonna make it."

"The cure's coming," Byatt says. "We're gonna make it. I promise."

CHAPTER 4

Taylor was right. When Welch wakes me the next morning, it's before sunup. My eye's gummy with sleep, leaving me blind, and it takes me a beat to put her together.

"What's going on?" I say. She gives me an extra shake.

"Downstairs, quick as you can. We're heading out."

The door clicks shut behind her. Reese is still asleep up on her bunk, but Byatt rolls over and pushes up onto her elbows.

"You're going?" she says, voice heavy and hoarse.

"Yeah."

"Okay. You'll be careful."

It's an order, and I smile a little in case she can see. "I'll try."

Welch is waiting with Carson and Julia by the time I get to the closet outside the kitchen. Carson's missing three fingernails after a flare-up had her scratching at the infirmary door, and Julia's deep brown skin is spattered with bruises that grow every day. Nobody's sure what puts them there, only that their color never fades.

Julia and Carson aren't the first Boat Shift girls. Taylor, whose place I took, was the last left of the original team. She got picked with Emily and Christine, twins from some school down near DC who were here on exchange. They were only supposed to be here for a semester. They chose the wrong one. About three months into the Tox, they came back from the woods with their names torn out of their heads. The Tox took who they were, took everything except how to hold a knife. It made them stick each other in the main hall during dinner, made them watch themselves bleed dry.

Carson smiles at me as I get close. She's wearing a second jacket, this one heavy and lined with flannel, and she's got her hair tucked up under her hood. Next to her, Julia is bent in front of the closet, pulling out things for her and I guess for me.

"Here." She stuffs a bundle of clothes into my arms and sits, kicking off her boots to pull on more socks. "Get that on."

The coat is somewhere between black and navy, with big brass clasps across the front, like on some kind of steamer trunk. It fits pretty well, and with the collar flipped up, I won't feel the wind on my neck. There's also a red hat, the kind with flaps over the ears, but I'm not convinced it'll fit, so I look up at Welch, and she's got a red scarf.

So does Carson. And Julia, standing now and frowning impatiently, has a red puffy vest on over her jacket.

"The color's easy to spot," Welch says. She's fiddling with a walkie-talkie hooked on her belt, one that must connect her back to Headmistress's radio. "So we can find one another, just in case."

Julia snorts. "And everything else can find us too. Come on, Hetty, put it on. We have to go."

It shouldn't, but it surprises me when Welch presses a bowie knife into my hands and shows me how to slip it through the belt loops on my jeans just like Julia and Carson do with theirs. The knife is all I'll get for now, but like Welch, Julia has a gun. Not a rifle like we use on the roof, but a snug little pistol that she seems to know her way around.

"All set?" Welch says, and nods at me. "Behind Julia. Stay close."

We go out the front doors and onto the path. I turn around just to see the house, to remember, and it's like I'm thirteen again, climbing out of the van and coming up the walkway with Byatt half a step behind me. The big doors, the porch, and everything feeling like it's about to be something.

At the fence we stop and wait for Welch to pull it open. It's wrought iron, the bars close enough together that you can't slide through, not even if you suck in hard, and it's been up since the school was built some hundred years ago. Built to keep the manicured grounds separate from the wildwood, built to keep the animals from finding their way into the trash. Built, too, I suppose, to keep the girls inside, on the grounds. As if there was anywhere else on this island to go.

But since the Tox, the trees have crept closer, new saplings springing up, stretching through the fence like they're reaching for us. Pines, some of them, dead needles dusting the frozen ground, and others, too, scaled and gnarled like nothing else. They grow right up against the iron, and their branches reach up and over the fence before dipping low, loaded with berries the color of blood. Nobody will eat them. When they break open, their insides are black and oozing.

There's only one place where the trees pull away from the fence, and that's on the north side of the island, right where the shore drops off at a twenty-foot cliff. Everywhere else we've hacked back what we could and built up the fence with everything we could get our hands on, everything we could spare.

The woods are bad enough—I'd swear they want us for their own—but when the animals come, they come fast. The coyotes, grown bigger than wolves. The foxes that hunt now in vicious packs. Too fast for the Gun Shift girls sometimes, and so we've studded the fence with glass shards and the lids off used soup cans. Boarded up the gaps with bulletin boards torn off classroom walls.

We don't keep a girl stationed at the fence. Too close to the woods, too tempting for any of the animals, and we don't need one anyway. Instead, the gate opens easy and locks behind you as you leave. The only way back in is with the matching iron key dangling from Welch's belt.

The gate inches open and we sidle through the narrow gap. When Welch shuts it again, you can hear the lock slide home, and it sounds so flimsy, like I could break it just by thinking about it. Is this really all that's keeping us safe?

"Ready?" says Welch. She doesn't wait to see if I am. We start walking.

The road is dirt, with roots and weeds bleeding through the edges, and potholes filled in with rocks by Reese's dad, Mr. Harker. I've spent a year and a half staring at it from the roof, but I forgot what it feels like under my feet, frozen through, crunching like spun sugar. My breath in clouds, a snap in the air, and it was fall a week ago, but today it's nothing but winter.

Above us the pines stumble up to the sky. Taller than they should be, trunks broader, branches splitting a thousand times and the canopy filtering what sun there is, turning the light muddy and clinging. It all feels forgotten, like we're the first people here in a hundred years. No tire tracks left on the road, no sign this was ever anything but what it is now.

We shouldn't be here. This place isn't ours anymore.

I don't think I ever realized how much sound we make at the house, but I figure it out after a few minutes on the road. It's so quiet that you can hear the woods; you can hear them growing and moving and you can hear the things growing and moving inside them. Deer, small before the Tox and so big now they could feed us for weeks, if their meat weren't rotten and dying. Coyotes, and I've heard wolves, though I've never seen one. Other things, too, that never show themselves. The Tox didn't just happen to us. It happened to everything.

Moss layering thick carpets across the ground, vines spiraling high. Here and there, patches of flowers growing strong, even in the cold. They're irises, vivid indigo petals coated with frost, a cluster in the middle gathered close with a skirt of petals draping down. They grow all over the island, all year round, and we used to have a vase of them in practically every room of the house. Raxter Irises, special for the way their petals darken once they're picked. Like Raxter Blues. And now like us.

Before the quarantine it wasn't like this. The animals felt practically tame, even if we did get lectures about storing food properly to keep it from them, and the woods felt different, felt like they were ours. Pines, growing in ranks, but the soil so thin and their trunks like needles so that if you stood in the right place, you could pretty much see from one end of the island to the other. You never forgot the ocean because the air was always tangy with salt. Here in the thickness, you only get a spark of it now and then.

The way it happened is that the woods got it first. That's what I think, anyway. Even before the wilderness reached inside us, it was seeping into the earth. The trees were growing taller, new saplings springing up faster than they had any right to. And it was fine; it was nothing worth noticing, until I looked out the window and couldn't see the Raxter I knew anymore. That morning two girls tore each other's hair out over breakfast with an animal viciousness, and by afternoon the Tox had hit us.

This part of the road runs arrow-straight, footprints dotted across it from a year and a half of Boat Shift girls making the trip. On either side there's nothing. Nothing left of the small paths that used to scurry off into the trees. No sign of anybody else. All I can find are long, raw stripes ripped in the tree trunks. Claws, maybe, or teeth.

I expected it to be different. I watch the trees attack the fence, the dark between them thick and reaching. I know what the Tox does. But I thought something of my old life would still be here. I thought something of us would have survived.

"Come on," Welch says, and I realize I've slowed down, the others a few yards ahead. "We have to keep moving."

I wonder what's left of Reese's house. It would be off to the right somewhere, tucked in among the reeds. I never learned the way myself, always let Reese lead. It took her a long time to invite us over, and even once she had, it never quite felt like we were supposed to be there. Reese and her dad, laughing and talking as Byatt picked at her food, and I didn't know what to do so I smiled the whole time.

Somewhere behind us there's a crash and then a kind of bleating, high and quick, and I can't help the curse that drops from my mouth. Welch throws herself against the nearest tree, dragging me with her to lie flat between the roots. Across the road, Carson and Julia press into a hollow in the thicket, crouch low, heads bent together.

"What—"

"Shhh," Welch whispers. "Don't move."

On the roof it was different, just branches and the sight of my rifle. But I can feel the shake in the earth. Heavy, churning steps. My mouth goes dry, fear shivering through my body, and I bite my lip to keep quiet.

Pressed to the ground next to Welch, the pine tree's sprawling roots twisting around us, I catch a glimpse. First a hulking mass of shadow, and then as it prowls into view, I see it. Fur rippling like long grass. Too big for a coyote, too dark for a bobcat. A black bear.

I know what I'm supposed to do if it sees us. Grizzlies are different, but with a black bear, you make noise, stare it down. Don't run. Fight back. That's the lecture we got after Mr. Harker saw one digging through his trash. They're faster than they look, he said, and they can spot a flash of color in the brush.

I snatch off my red hat and smother it under my coat,

sweat freezing on my scalp. Count the beats of my racing heart, try not to breathe too loud.

Next to me Welch smiles, just a smudge of one, like she can't help it. We stay there for I don't know how long. Wait until the footsteps have passed, the trees stilled, the noise faded, and then she stands up, pulls me with her.

"It's gone," she says. "You can put your hat on again."

She calls out to Carson and Julia. They come jogging through the branches looking like they didn't just have the life scared out of them, like they see this kind of thing all the time.

"Having fun?" Julia asks. I think she might be serious.

Raxter is only about five miles long, give or take, shaped like a bullet with the tip pointing west, but we're moving slow so it takes us a while to get to the other end. You can tell as we start getting close; all the trees rear back from the shore like they're afraid of it. Up ahead somewhere, hidden from view by the last of the woods, is the visitors' center. It was built even before the school, used to be the headquarters for some local fishing company until the lobsters disappeared and it got converted. Before the Tox it was always empty and closed up except during summers, and even then it was just Mr. Harker, sitting behind the counter and listening to a Sox game while tourists passed by on ferries, headed to other towns, other islands.

At last the woods start to thin, and ahead I can see the

open stretch of the salt marsh. In the distance, maybe a half mile out, the ocean is gray and rough, the horizon empty like it always is.

"Oh," I say, before I can stop myself.

Welch frowns at me. "What?"

"I just thought they'd be waiting for us."

Nobody answers me, so I swallow my disappointment and fall into single file with them, me between Carson and Julia, as Welch leads us out of the cover of the trees. Immediately, the wind is stinging, so strong it just about knocks me over. I shove my hat in my coat pocket and edge closer to Julia, hope she'll take some of the worst of it for me.

The road here is scrubbed flat, and on either side the ground drops off into reeds and soupy pools of mud. To the right I can see the remains of the boardwalk that used to lead from the pier to the visitors' center, winding through the marsh and the woods, dotted with informational plaques that don't seem to be there anymore. I want to ask what's happened to them. But the answer would be the same as everything else: the Tox.

We stay on the road, and it's a slow walk until we hit the start of the ferry pier, ragged old red tape fluttering across the entrance. Everybody said at the beginning that they were planning a wall, a real one, with metal and plastic to see through, but this was the most they ever did. Some tape and a sign that says "Wait until area has been cleared."

We stop here, and Welch drops her bag on the ground and digs around in it. She comes up with a pair of binoculars, stares through them at the horizon.

"What do we do now?" I say, knocking one foot against the other to shake off the cold.

"Usually," Carson starts, "we have to wait a while. But so—"

And then a bird chirps. I whip around, checking the trees, my depth perception slipping as my eye fights to adjust. "What the hell was that?"

The birds stopped singing right when we got sick, went quiet like they'd never been there at all. As the days passed we watched them fly away, herons and gulls and starlings flying forever south. I haven't heard one in so long I'd forgotten what they sound like.

"Oh, good," Welch says. "They're almost here."

I'm still wondering why the bird doesn't seem strange to anyone else when a foghorn kind of noise blasts from out on the water. I jump, my heartbeat ratcheting up, breath sharp in my lungs.

"Where is it?" I say.

It's a clear enough day, the sun up somewhere behind the gray sky. You can see the shore from here, a smear way out across the waves. And in between, no boat, no ship.

"Just wait."

"But I don't see."

Another foghorn, and the others look ready, like this is the way it's supposed to be, and then, out of the gray, like it's pushing through some great fog, the prow of a ship.

It's a tug with a blunt nose and a faded hull. Too big to get close on our side of the island, but the ferry pier is just right, jutting out over deep water. I recognize the ID stamp as the tug swings closer, the white number and the stripes of yellow and blue on the stack. I saw these sometimes in Norfolk. Navy-issue, they mean, from Camp Nash on the coast.

The wake is just hitting the shore as the ship turns, and if I squint, I can make out two people, bigger than they should be in bright-colored suits, moving around on the flat tail of the deck. The ship is turning, the motor getting louder and louder until Carson crams her fingers in her ears. There's a big orange crane near the back—I can make it out now—and it's lifting, extending, and we watch it hoist a pallet from the deck, over and out across the water, to the end of the pier.

The crane releases and the pallet crashes down. Under us the pier boards shudder. I take a step forward, but Julia throws her arm across my chest.

"They have to give the all clear," she says.

The hook has released and the crane's retracting, and the two people are just standing there on the deck, looking at us, and I'm waiting for one of them to wave or something when the horn goes off, and it's so close and so big that we just stand there, mouths open, let it wash over us.

Eventually, it stops, and I take a gasping gulp of fresh air.

"Now we can go," Julia says.

The water's slapping against the supports as the wake gets bigger, now the tug is moving fast again. Two seagulls land noisily on the railing of the pier. They're watching us, watching the supplies the boat left. Here to scavenge, to get what they can. They must follow the tug from the mainland.

Now that we're closer I can see that there's a lot in this delivery. And I mean a lot, more than what they usually carry back. The pallet is covered with wooden cartons, all nailed shut, and on top of those are five or six bags, the kind Boat Shift always come home with.

"What is all this?" I ask. I know the push of Byatt's ribs too well. She needs this food. We all do.

"It's between us," Welch says. "That's what it is."

"It's okay," Carson is saying, and I fight to tear my eye away from the pile of cartons. "It's a lot to take in, I know."

"Is this all food? This could feed us for a week."

"Longer, probably," Julia says dryly.

They're all watching me, waiting for something, only I don't know what. "Is it always like this?" Maybe this is the first time, maybe they're as surprised as I am, but Welch nods calmly. "I don't understand. Where does it all go? Why doesn't it come back to the house?"

Welch steps toward me, her body between me and the

food. Julia and Carson slot in alongside her, their faces solemn save the anxious frown blooming on Carson's brow.

"Listen to me very carefully," Welch says. "I picked you for a reason. This job is about protecting those girls back at home. Even when it's hard. Even when it doesn't look the way you expect it to."

I shake my head, take a step back. This isn't right. I can't make sense of it. "What are you talking about?"

"Some of the food is off," Welch explains. "They send a lot, but maybe only half of it's unspoiled. All sorts of bad things in there. Expired products. Pesticides."

"Pesticides?" I say, incredulous, but Julia and Carson are nodding, grim expressions to match Welch's. "We're starving because of pesticides?"

"Your systems are so compromised already. I'm not sure you can afford to take risks with what you eat."

"So instead, we eat barely anything at all?"

"Yes," says Welch. Her voice even, her gaze considering and cool. "I told you, Hetty: I picked you because I thought you could handle it. Admittedly, sometimes I'm wrong about people. And if that's the case, we can take care of that just fine." She moves slightly, and I watch as her hand rests on the butt of her revolver where it's tucked in the waistband of her jeans.

I can picture it. One shot right between my eyes, and Welch watching as my body collapses into the sea. Easy enough to explain a missing Boat Shift girl to everybody at school.

"But I hate to be wrong," Welch goes on. "And I don't think I am. I think you can handle this, Hetty. Am I right?"

At first I can't answer. We've all fought one another for the smallest scrap of food, and the whole time there was so much more. What makes Welch think she has a right to keep this from us?

But it's my life on the line if I pick this fight. Welch will have no problem killing me. She won't lose a second of sleep. After a year and a half of the Tox, we've all learned to do what we have to. And honestly, I can't pretend it doesn't mean something that they picked me. Me and not Reese.

"Well, Hetty?"

Whatever's wrong here—and something is, I'm sure of that—it's nothing I can fix right now. I stand up straighter, look Welch in the eye. I can't lie like Byatt, but I can try. "Yeah," I say, "you're right."

Welch clasps my shoulder, her smile wide and genuine. "I knew we made a good choice."

"Well done," Julia says, and Carson darts in to smack a chapped kiss on my cheek. I jerk back in surprise—Carson is freezing to the touch, her lips even colder than the air around us.

"Good to have you," she says. Both of them with relief tingeing their smiles, as if they were prepared to go home without me.

And of course they were.

Welch slings her arm around me. "Obviously, we don't tell the girls," she says, ushering me toward the cartons, "but just so you know, we also try to keep this off Headmistress's plate."

"Off her plate?" I can't keep from sounding surprised. As strange as all this is, it's stranger still that Welch and Headmistress could hide anything from each other.

"She's got a lot going on. No need to bother her with specifics about food delivery." Welch smiles. "Simpler just to handle it ourselves. You know how she likes to micromanage."

"Sure," I say. It seems like the right answer, and she's made it perfectly clear what she's willing to sacrifice to keep this secret.

"Great." She lets go of me. "We'll get started. It's a lot to take in, so how about you just watch this time? You'll pick it up as we go along."

Carson starts passing the bags to Julia, who loosens the ties and lets the contents spill out onto the ground.

Vegetables, fruit, even a pack of bacon. Everything packed up like it's straight from the grocery store. Except when I look closer, some boxes have been opened, some bags slit and resealed using tape stamped with the Camp Nash crest. A compass and a globe, and a banner with text too small to read.

My stomach growls as Welch picks up a bag of carrots and holds it up to her nose.

"No good," she says, and throws it over the edge into the ocean. I have to stop myself from diving after it.

The bacon goes next, and then a bag of grapes, and

then a bushel of bell peppers, until two bags are empty and the waves around the pier are full of food.

"Here we go," Welch says. She's at the third bag now, and inside are cases of water, the labels on the bottles fresh and blazing with the same brand name as always. That's all we drink now—the school used to run on well water, but after the Tox, the Navy told us to stop, said it might be contaminated.

Carson starts counting the cases of water. Next to her, Julia is sorting out the matches and the soap into piles. I can see the shampoo bottles peeking out of her bag, all pearly and pale and completely unnecessary.

It takes them a while but eventually, they've emptied the bags and packed away what they want to keep, food still in its regular packaging, crackers and jerky and even a sleeve of bagels turned hard as rocks, and that's when Julia pulls out her knife to pry the first of the cartons open. Shavings of paper come flying out in the wind, dusting across the surface of the water like ash.

There are four cartons in all. One is full of medical kits, bags for biohazard material, those masks doctors wear over their mouths, and we chuck about half of it and take the rest. The second is filled to the brim with ammunition, and the third holds a pair of pistols, neatly packed in foam. Welch takes the guns and tucks them away in her bag, passing some of the boxes of bullets to each of us.

And then we open the last box. It's mostly paper and straw, but buried in the middle is a bar of chocolate, real chocolate, and dark, the good kind. We crowd around Welch as she lifts it out of the carton.

"Is that . . . ?" I say, but I don't get to finish because Welch is tearing the foil and you can smell it, and I'd forgotten what it was like, the way the sugar climbs out into the air like a vine growing, and before I know it I have my hand outstretched.

Carson laughs. "Hold on, you'll get some."

"Have you had this before?" I ask, and Julia nods. I know I should be angry. But jealousy is all I can manage.

It makes the best sound I've ever heard when Welch snaps off the first two squares, a thick sound, a real sound, like it's actually there.

"They send one every time."

"Well, not every time," says Welch. The second two squares are in Julia's hands now. "But often enough."

And it's my turn, and it's already melting against my skin, and I cram it into my mouth so fast I think I might choke, but who cares, honestly, who really cares because it's so damn good.

When we're finished, and it's after a while because I keep licking at my fingers, trying to get every last bit of chocolate, we pick up the bags and carry them back to the road. The pallet is clear. Welch pushed the cartons into the water, too, and when I asked her why, she said it was because if we left anything there, they'd send us less next time. We leave it bare, even though we're only taking maybe a third of it.

I know it's the same road that we took on the way out, but the farther we get from the pier, the more different it looks. Maybe it's the light, which is more yellow now than it was in the morning, but maybe it isn't, maybe it's something else. The seagulls have taken off, and they're wheeling overhead, cries feverish and sharp. I'm pulling the flaps of my hat more firmly over my ears when Welch stops, so suddenly that Carson stumbles into her.

"Sorry," she says, but Welch isn't listening.

"What is it?" says Julia.

Welch turns around to look at us, something pinching at the corners of her mouth. "Something's coming." The gulls are gone, leaving a brittle silence in the air. "Split up," she says. "Pairs. Stay off the road and meet back at the gate. Hetty, you're with me."

Julia and Carson exchange a look and then disappear into the brush, until I can't see the red on their clothes anymore.

Welch leads me into the forest, our pace quick, bark catching on our clothes as we wind our way between the pines. Over my shoulder, the gloom thickening, and every sound an animal prowling through the trees. Deeper and deeper we go, the bag I'm carrying starting to slip in my clammy palms.

"Welch," I say, but she doesn't answer, just reaches back to grab my jacket and haul me along.

At our left, a crack in the brush. Welch jerks to a halt. Stock-still, her arm thrown across my chest. Around us the pines hemming in, scattered in broken ranks, slicing the horizon into slivers. I can't see anything moving. Maybe we misheard, I think, maybe we're home free. But it comes again, and I catch a flicker. Movement. Eyes glassy and yellow before they disappear.

"What was that?" I whisper. My heart stuttering in my chest, and I can feel my lungs tighten as panic clutches them closed.

"Not sure." She fumbles at her waistband for the pistol she's carrying, holds it at her side, finger off the trigger. "I didn't see—"

Something cuts her off, a soft rumble from behind us. A growl, and the snap of a branch. I turn.

It's a bobcat, gray fur, body long and crouched low. Pointed ears lying flat, teeth glinting as it snarls. Maybe ten yards out and coming closer in careful, stalking steps, the frost crunching underneath it.

Before the Tox they were small and skittish. You could scare them off with a gunshot. This one, though. I can see its muscles rippling under its fur, its massive shoulders nearly up to my waist.

"Get behind me," Welch whispers. "Slowly."

I can barely breathe, my eye locked on the bobcat, but I slip in behind Welch, feeling the ground with my boots before I take each step. The cat lets out another growl, drops its chest to the ground. It's closer now, and I can see dark spots on its back, dried blood crusting where its skin has fallen away in patches. Sores bubbling along the inside of its front legs, bile staining the white fur on its neck.

A step forward, and another, its tail flicking from side to side. Welch pushes me back, and my foot snags on a root. I stumble with a curse. The cat hisses and darts forward. Lets out a grating scream.

Welch fires her gun into the air, the sound exploding into my head, and the bobcat springs back with another growl, circles us with its tail lashing.

"On my signal," Welch says, "make for the house. I'll catch up if I can."

Turning, turning, the gun shaking in Welch's hand, and I can't tell anymore which way we came from, which way I should go. But it doesn't matter. The beat of my pulse telling me run, run, run.

"Ready?" Welch says. The bobcat is still growling, snapping its jaws as she aims the pistol between its eyes.

No, I think. But it's too late. A squeeze on the trigger, and a scream from the cat as a bullet rips along its side. Welch shoves me away. "Go!" she's yelling. "Now!"

She's muffled by the ringing in my ears, but my body hears it. I hoist my bag over my shoulder and break for it. Feet thundering against the earth, and I'm gasping into the cold air, throwing myself forward, pushing as hard as I can. Another gunshot behind me. I don't look back.

The pines rush past as I weave through them. Fear like a veil, and everything looks like something else, like danger, like hurt. A path opens in front of me. I follow it, the hair on my arms prickling. I'm too exposed out here, too vulnerable, but I think this is one of Mr. Harker's trails, on the south side of the island. At least I'm heading the right way.

My lungs burning, a cramp starting to set in my leg, my bag thumping painfully against my hip. Ahead I can see a stand of spruce trees, their branches ducking low to the ground. If I get inside, I'll be hidden from anything following me, and I can wait for Welch.

I shoulder through the thicket of branches and find myself in a small, sheltered space, the air green and spiced, the whole world shredded by a crosshatch of needles. Beyond, the woods look still, nothing moving. No flash of red on Welch's clothing. I search through my bag for my hat and balance it on one of the branches, so that Welch will see it if she passes by.

If she doesn't come in a few minutes, I tell myself, I'll keep moving. But the thought of going out there again turns my stomach. I never spent time out here alone before the Tox. I always had a class of girls with me, all of us on a nature walk for biology, or I had Reese and Byatt as we tramped through the forest to Reese's house for dinner. And it wasn't like this, then. The trees didn't grow so close. There was more air to breathe.

I crouch down at the base of one of the spruces and push some of the dead needles into a pile to sit on, to keep me farther from the frosted ground. But there's something here, hidden under the brush, something hard and hollow.

I scrape off the dead leaves, ignore the scattering beetles that cascade like glossy black beads. Something tangy and rotten tickles my nose the more dead foliage I move, until what's hidden underneath is clear—a cooler, vivid blue plastic and folded handle, like someone's left it behind after a picnic.

I glance over my shoulder before prying the cooler open with my dirty fingernails. Probably just an old tackle box of Mr. Harker's, but worth checking.

I'm expecting moldy bait, a bundle of hooks and some fishing line, but it's not that at all. The outside of the cooler is covered in grime, but inside is clean, as though it's been wiped down. And sitting there at the bottom, in a clear plastic bag sealed with bright red tape, is a vial of blood, labeled "Potential RAX009" in handwriting I almost know.

"Hetty?" Welch's voice drifts through the trees, urgent and clipped.

I slam the cooler shut and pile the leaves back onto it. Whatever this is, I don't think I was ever supposed to see it.

"Are you there?" Welch calls again, and I get to my feet, hoist my bag back up over my shoulder.

"Here," I say, pulling my hat from the branches and climbing from the spruce stand.

She comes hustling through the trees, all noise and

frantic steps. Blood on her cheek, a rip in her jacket, her hair coming out of its braid. In a second she's in front of me, and she grabs my shoulders, gives me a shake.

"What the hell, Hetty?" she says, and she's not Miss Welch, scolding me for missing curfew. She's just another girl left threadbare by the Tox, left worried and worn. "You were supposed to keep going."

"I'm sorry," I say. "I just . . . I was worried about you." I was scared to be on my own, that's the truth, but I'm not about to tell it. "What about the bobcat?"

"It's dead," she says. "But, Hetty, I gave you an order. Next time you have to follow it, okay?"

I nod quickly. "I will."

She checks over my shoulder, eyes lingering on the spruce trees, and I shift a little. I want to ask if she knows about the cooler, if she knows what RAX009 means, but I remember the way she looked at me on the dock. The way we know things we're not supposed to talk about. Is this another test? Is keeping this secret part of my job, too?

Welch frowns. "You okay?"

Better safe than sorry.

"Yeah," I say, and paste on a smile. "Let's get home."

We cut back to the road, move quick toward the house. Here the beginning of a path, there an open patch of grass, rubble scattered like gravestones. I blink hard, feeling the blindness in my right eye.

Sweat turning cold in the late fall air, and I'm shivering by the time we near the gate, deep in the afternoon. I forgot what it was like to see the white crest rising over the trees. Up on the flattop roof the Gun girls are two silhouettes. I wonder what I look like to them.

There's a dead coyote by the gate, flies swarming around its bloodied face. Julia and Carson are waiting just beyond it, sitting propped up against the fence, and they get to their feet as we approach, weaving around the carcass.

"Remember," says Welch, low and close to my ear. "Big smile. It's our job to show the girls inside that everything's fine."

My lungs are still tight from running, my hands heavy with the food we threw over the side, but I stand up straight and do my best to put it all away. These secrets are mine to keep now. They picked me because they thought I could handle it, so I will.

Welch unlocks the gate and we slip through single file, and through the front doors of the house. I set down my bag, look pointedly away from the girls clamoring around to get their shot at what's inside. There's Byatt waiting at the bottom of the stairs for me. And tilting her head, and not saying anything.

"Where's Reese?" I ask once I'm close enough.

"Haven't seen her all day." Byatt reaches for me. I want to sag against her, to let her hold me up, but I'm not supposed to let anybody see. "Okay?"

"Tired."

Behind me, a set of measured footsteps, and when I turn it's Headmistress, concern shaping her face into something almost motherly.

"Are you quite all right?" she says.

I nod, ignore the building pressure in my chest. "I'm fine. It's just a lot to take in."

"Why don't you head upstairs?" Headmistress lays her hand on my shoulder, fingers trembling like the Tox is alive inside them. "Some rest will do you good."

"She's right," Byatt says. "Come on."

"But the food . . ." A rest is all I want, but I'm supposed to wait until the girls have taken their share, then help carry what's left into the pantry. It's my job.

Welch comes up alongside me and eases me away from the crowd. "We'll take care of it," she says. "You go sleep."

I don't have the energy to argue. "Okay." I reach for the bowie knife, to give it back to her, but Welch shakes her head.

"You earned it," she says. A knife in my belt like Julia, like Carson. I guess it's official.

I let Byatt lead me up the stairs, and after a step or two I shut my eye. Behind us I can hear the girls scratching and clawing for the food, and I think of the ocean at the pier, of everything we threw overboard. Of the chocolate I ate without a thought for anybody stuck here.

Finally, our room, and I climb into our bunk, lie on my side. Byatt sits on the edge of the mattress, my body curling around her.

"Do you want some water, maybe?" she says.

"I'm fine, really."

"What happened out there, Hetty?"

And I want to—oh, I want to—because if anybody knows what to say, it's Byatt. But I swallow hard, fold a little more into myself. Everything is fine, I hear Welch say. "Nothing."

She's quiet for a moment, and then she leans back against me, the knobs of her second spine pressing hard into my hip.

The lines of her face are lit with the last of the sun. Sloping nose and long neck so familiar I could trace them in my sleep, rich chestnut hair hanging down around her shoulders. Mine used to be long like hers, until she cut it for me during freshman spring. The two of us out on the porch, Byatt quiet and methodical as she trimmed it so the ends brush my jaw. She still does it, every few months, the ends splitting and fraying against the blunt blade of whatever knife she's managed to borrow from the Boat girls.

I nudge her a little, and she glances down at me. "You okay?" I ask. I forget to, sometimes. I forget she's like the rest of us. But she just smiles fondly.

"Get some sleep. I'll be right here."

And I did what I did, and I saw what I saw, but Byatt is here, and I fall asleep like it's the easiest thing in the world.

CHAPTER 5

Reese isn't at breakfast the next morning. It's been nearly two days since I saw her last, since I got Boat Shift, but Byatt says she's seen her on the grounds, seen her holed up in what used to be a teacher's office at night.

We're sitting by the fireplace today, sharing one of the couches with Cat and Lindsay. They started the same year we did, and I never used to talk to them much outside of class. After the Tox we started drifting together, trading food and blankets. Everybody needs more help now than they did before.

Usually, I'm the one who goes for food, but I still feel sick when I think about yesterday, about the rations we tossed into the water. Byatt went today instead, and she managed to wrangle a bag of croutons. Now she takes a handful, nudges the bag in my direction.

"You have to eat something," she says.

"Later." I can't. I know, I know, we threw that food away

for a reason, but that doesn't make it any easier to watch Byatt counting every bite she takes.

"Hetty, a word?"

It's Welch. I twist around on the couch to see her. Her mouth is flat, a tight, thin line, but she seems almost nervous, like she did before the Tox when she'd catch you breaking curfew.

"Sure," I say, and get up, start toward Welch.

"I'll save you some food," Byatt calls. "Whether you like it or not."

I wave over my shoulder. "Thanks, Mom."

Welch leads me to the mouth of the hallway. This close I can see frown lines setting in her forehead, and her eyes look bright, like she's on the edge of a fever.

"What's up?" I say.

"Byatt is right. You should eat something."

"I'm not hungry." I can't. I can't take more than what I've taken already.

Welch lets out a breath. "Hetty." And she sounds serious. "I need you to work a little harder, please."

"What?" Just the fact that I'm in the main hall is already more than I can take.

"I told you it was your job to show everybody here that things are fine. But instead, you're sitting there looking, quite frankly, ready to vomit."

"I'm trying, okay?" I say, frustration bleeding into my voice.

"Not hard enough." She looks over my shoulder, to

where I know Byatt is sitting. "There are usually three of you. Where's Reese?"

"That's not related."

Welch scoffs. "Everything is. After that stunt she pulled when you got Boat Shift, the two of you are on the radar." She leans in. "The girls are watching you, Hetty. So whatever your little fight was about, I need you to fix it. Kiss and make up. Anything that gets the three of you back to normal. Normal, Hetty."

"It's Reese. Sulking is normal for her."

"I'm not asking," Welch says sharply. Her jaw set, her eyes glinting.

"Yeah." I hold up my hands in surrender. "Okay. I'll talk to her."

"You won't tell her anything you shouldn't."

I barely tell her anything on a good day. "I won't."

Welch smiles, or gets close to it, and rests her hand on my shoulder. "Thank you," she says. "Sometime today would be good."

She makes it a few steps away before it slips out of me. "Doesn't it bother you? Lying to everyone?"

For a second she doesn't answer, and then she turns. I can see it in her face, how she wants to do it right, how she wants to say the adult thing. "Yeah, it does." And she shrugs. "So?"

So doesn't that mean something? I want to yell. *So doesn't that matter?*

"So nothing, I guess."

She nods. "Today, Hetty."

When I get back to Byatt I can tell she's been watching us. Fingernails freshly bitten, frown lingering.

"I have to talk to Reese," I say. "You better come find us in about five minutes in case she tries to kill me again."

"It was only choking," Byatt says, but she nods, and hooks her fingers in my belt loop to stop me as I pass. "Careful, yeah?"

I give her a smile. I'm always careful with Reese, even though she rarely is with me. "Sure."

It was easier with Reese when her dad was here. Right when they set up the quarantine, they brought Mr. Harker to our side of the fence, stuck him in the wing with the teachers, and we all pretended like it wasn't the strangest part of what was happening, having a man in the house with us.

He was here for maybe a month. We kept track of things like that, then, but now it feels so long ago I can barely remember. All that's left are flashes. Reese and her father eating breakfast in the dining room, back before we trashed the furniture for burning. Reese and her father rigging up the generator out back. The two of them on the porch tracing constellations in the sky, Reese laughing in a way she never did with me and Byatt.

And other things too. How he started to change— slowly, at first, just an eagerness in his hands, to scratch and tear apart. The Tox, though we didn't call it that yet. All we really knew was that one day Mr. Harker was safe and the next he wasn't. One day he was himself, and the next he was throwing up a black sludge, grainy like dirt, and looking at us with empty eyes.

Reese ignored it, pretended it was fine, picked a screaming match with Byatt, and then the next day Mr. Harker was gone. He left a note tucked in Reese's jacket while she was sleeping, saying he had to go. Saying it was safest that way for everyone.

She ran to the fence that morning, I remember that. Cut her palms to ribbons clawing at it, trying to get through. But Taylor held her back, and me and Byatt, we watched Reese fall apart. When she came back together again, there was something gone.

It was never like that for me. Goodbyes at airports and watching the news, but my dad always came back.

I find Reese in the jack pine grove by the water, in the same spot where we were sitting the first day of the Tox. She's there, now, on that same low branch of that same tree, and the only thing different from that day to this one is the glint of her silver hand as she shivers in her thin jacket.

I come up slow, in front of her where she can see, which is always safest. In the nearly two days since I last saw her, circles have darkened under her eyes. She looks hungry,

I think. And cold. But it was never her who needed us. Always the other way around.

"Hi," I say. She doesn't look up, and I bite my lip to keep from saying something I shouldn't. Remember what Welch said, I remind myself. Remember this is important.

"About Boat Shift." I lean against the trunk, leave plenty of room between us. "I didn't know I'd get it. I thought it would be you."

"Me too," she says, voice gritty and hoarse like it was her throat that got crushed, not mine. And I want to scream, want to wring an apology out of her. But then she looks at me, frowns. "You okay?"

It's something. Maybe the most I can expect. "Fine. Really, fine."

"Are you sure?" She tries for a smile. "Because you look terrible. Like, that's a Beth in *Little Women* face."

"Oh no," I say flatly. "Do you think I might be sick?"

"At Raxter?" She raises her eyebrows, face stamped with fake surprise. "Never."

We fall quiet, both of us I think in shock that we've managed to make even the weakest joke. Byatt needs to get here, and quick, before we ruin it.

I twist around to peer through the trees, and when I face front again, Reese is swinging her feet. She looks almost shy. But Reese doesn't do shy. Even when she came out to me, it was like a weapon. "Queer," she said then, as though she was daring me to disagree.

"You went on Boat Shift yesterday," she says now. And waits.

"Yeah."

"What's it like?"

"It's different." I barely get the words out.

"Different how?"

"Um." Remember Welch, remember my job. Everything is fine. "There are more trees," I say stupidly.

"Look, Hetty, I have to know. I have to. Did you see him? My dad? My house? Anything?"

I shake my head. "I'm sorry, Reese." She looks away, but not before I see the tears she's blinking back. I clear my throat awkwardly, wish more than anything I could just disappear. "Where is Byatt? She was gonna come find us."

Reese doesn't answer, so I start toward the house. But I'm only a few yards out of the grove when Cat comes running, breathing hard. I try not to look at the blisters scattered across her hairline, each of them torn and bleeding.

"Hey," she says. "You better get inside."

Dread, creeping and bitter. I swallow hard. "What for?"

"It's your girl. She's having a flare-up."

At first there's nothing. Just a tingle in my fingers, a dull ache behind my blind eye. And then a dizziness, and I sway as my knees buckle.

"No," I say. "No, I just saw her."

"Sorry," Cat says. "I came as quick as I could."

It's impossible. I was with Byatt barely ten minutes ago, and she was fine. She has to be fine.

I turn, searching for Reese, but she's jumped down from the branch, followed me out of the grove and is right there behind me, mouth drawn in a tight line. Without a word we run for the house, faster and faster, until I'm tearing into the main hall.

Mostly empty this time of day, with only a few girls clustered by the fireplace. No Byatt. I should've asked Cat where she was, I should've, I should've.

"Easy," Reese says quietly, and I reach out, fumble for her hand, squeeze tight.

I've been there for them all, for the flare-up that stole Byatt's voice for nearly a week, for the one that sliced a line down her back and left her with a second spine. I have to be there for this one.

A shuddering whine breaks the air. Fear crashing over me, cold and fresh, and I tear away from Reese. That came from the back of the house, down the south wing toward the kitchen.

I elbow my way through the group by the fireplace and sprint along the hallway, classrooms and offices rushing past. Each one empty, and no Byatt, no Byatt, no Byatt. Until at last, there she is. Sprawled on the kitchen floor, her dark hair covering her face.

Please. This can't be happening.

I crash to my knees next to her. Twin lines of blood trail from her nose, streaking across her teeth as she gasps for air. She's crying, I think, but it's hard to tell. One hand gripping a packet of crackers, the other clawing at her throat.

"What happened?" I say, words tumbling frantically over one another. "What hurts? What is it?"

She mouths something, and it looks like my name, but then her eyes roll back. She convulses, her muscles snapping tight as a curve sweeps up her body like a wave.

I think I'm screaming, but it sounds like nothing. Hands on my shoulders pulling me back. I bat them away, feel for a pulse on Byatt's neck.

"Hey," I say as she opens her eyes, both of them bloodshot. "It's me. You're okay."

"I sent someone to find Welch," Reese says. She sounds calm, deliberate, but I know Reese, and I know that means she's panicked. She comes to stand on the other side of Byatt's body, only she's not watching Byatt. She's watching me. "Hold on, okay?"

Last time there was so much blood. Blooming underneath her, pooling in the cracks between the floorboards. This time there's only her nosebleed, smeared across her mouth, dripping onto the floor. I push up her sleeves, search for marks or wounds, anything.

"I need your help," I say, kneeling over her. It empties me out to see her like this. "You have to tell me what's wrong."

She reaches up, her hand shaking, and hooks her

fingers in the collar of my shirt. I bend so close I can feel her saliva sticking to my cheek.

"Hetty," she says. "Hetty, please."

It's the worst thing I've ever heard. Her voice sounds like metal on metal, like a million people all together, a scream and a whisper and everything in between, and it hurts, a real hurt reaching all the way to my bones. Like they're cracking, like they're glass.

I curl in on myself, press my hands to my ears. It feels like it lasts forever, until finally the rattle is gone from my body and I can think again.

"Shit," Reese says, airy and weak like it hit her too. "What was that?"

I ignore her and crawl back to Byatt, who's nearly hyperventilating, trying to sit up. And she looks afraid. A year and a half of the Tox. I've never seen her afraid until today.

"You're all right," I say, reaching out. But she shakes her head and presses her hand to my cheek. Like she's asking, *What about you?*

Down the hall I can hear voices getting closer. Welch and a few others—probably Julia and Carson. This is what Boat Shift does. Clean up the mess, put it away. Except now the mess is Byatt, and I won't let them take her from my sight.

"I'm fine," I say when Byatt tugs on my earlobe, pulling my attention back. "Welch is coming, okay? She's gonna look after you."

91

Byatt takes a breath, ready to say something, and Reese is there in a second, her hand clapped firmly over Byatt's mouth.

"Don't talk," Reese says. "It'll hurt."

Welch jogs into the room, Julia and Carson a few steps behind. They're watching Byatt, Julia's hand lingering too close to the knife in her belt, but Welch turns to me. "Can she walk?"

I know what Byatt would say—that she's right here, that she can speak for herself—but I don't ever want to feel the way I did when she spoke. "I think so."

Welch nods to Carson and Julia. "Take her up."

I scramble to my feet, swaying a little. "I'll help."

"Absolutely not," Welch says, shaking her head.

"It's Boat Shift's job. I'm Boat Shift."

"Not for this you aren't."

Julia and Carson come closer, boots squeaking on the checkered tile. They keep from looking at me as they crouch on either side of Byatt and grab her elbows, help her up.

She doesn't fight it. I think she knows there's no point. She just looks at me as they take her past, and at the last second, she reaches out and smacks something into my palm.

The packet of crackers. Broken to pieces, now. She must've found Taylor's stash.

I clutch them to my chest, try not to cry. She wanted me to eat. She said I shouldn't go hungry.

"You're going to have to put those back," Welch says, and I swing around to look at her. She can't be serious.

"Excuse me?"

She nods to the crackers. "Food is food."

I hardly know what to say. But I don't have to.

"No, thanks," Reese says. "I think we'll keep them."

She looks at me, and my heart feels too big for my chest. So this is what it's like to have Reese go to bat for you.

Welch glances between us and then shrugs. Nobody is here to see her give in, and she's still got a soft spot for us, when she can afford to let it show.

She's almost out of the room when it bursts out of me. "Is Byatt going to be okay?" My voice is about to crack, and it would be embarrassing if I cared about that at all. "Will she come down soon?"

Welch stops. Doesn't turn around. Just the line of her shoulders against the dark, and then she keeps going. Leaves me in the kitchen with my vision blurring. And even though I can still feel her hands around my neck, Reese is all I want.

"I bet it's nothing," I try, like it'll make more sense if I say it out loud.

"That's right," Reese says.

She's watching me from the top bunk. I'm underneath on mine, flat on my back, arms folded across my chest. I thought maybe she'd stay away, like she has been since I got Boat Shift, but she followed me upstairs as if none of that ever happened. And I tried to sleep—we both did—but halfway into the night I let out a sigh, and Reese leaned over the side of her bunk to look down at me.

"I'm sure she'll be fine."

But we both know only the sickest girls go up to the infirmary. And most of them never come down again.

I wrap myself up tighter in my jacket. "I'm worried."

"I know."

"She's all I have."

A heartbeat of quiet, and I realize how it must sound to Reese. Reese, who is right here.

"Sorry," I say.

"It's okay."

I know this is the part where I'm supposed to tell her I didn't mean it. But the truth is I never think of Reese as mine. As if someone like her could belong to someone like me, to anyone at all.

"Really, though," Reese says. "Byatt will be fine."

"You can't promise that."

She frowns, rolls back over onto her bunk so I can't see her anymore. "I'm not promising."

"Okay," I say, and hear her squirm around to get comfortable.

"What about the time we went to that museum?" she says slowly. "The one in Portland."

Byatt and I used to do this, for the first little while after

94

the Tox. Trading stories from before, the two of us on the bottom bunk, and Reese above, never saying anything but listening. I know now she was listening.

"Oh, yeah," I say. "I remember that."

"I'd never been to Portland before."

"You'd never been anywhere," I say with a laugh.

"And we got lunch in that food court, with the soda machines. We kept mixing them all in one cup."

"It was a fun field trip," I say.

"My favorite part was when you got sick in the planetarium."

It's almost what Byatt would say. Reese is trying, but she can't get it quite right, because nobody's Byatt but Byatt, not even the girl in these memories. There's this place in her, somewhere nobody can touch, not me or Reese or anyone. It's just hers, and I don't even know what it is, really, just that it's there, and that she takes it with her when she goes.

CHAPTER 6

I don't want the morning, but it comes anyway. Hard and bright, sun out from the clouds. I bury my face in my pillow, dreading the sight of the emptiness where Byatt should be.

The top bunk creaks, and I hear Reese whisper my name. I roll over, ease my eye open, my blind one pulsing with hurt like it always does when I wake. There she is, peering down at me over the edge of her bed. Her hair's coming loose from her braid, fine wisps of gold falling in her eyes. Small rounded nose and low, flaring cheekbones.

"Hey," she says, and my mouth goes dry. Have I been staring? "Did you know that you snore?"

Oh. I swallow down what tastes almost like disappointment. "I don't snore."

"Sure you do. It's this little whistling." She tilts her head. "Like a bird. Or a kettle."

My cheeks are hot, and I shut my eye tightly. "This is really nice. I like being bullied first thing in the morning."

She laughs. I look up just in time to see it. Her hair full of shine, her head thrown back, throat bared to the sunlight. She's in a good mood this morning. I can't understand why. Doesn't she remember what happened to Byatt? Doesn't she care?

She might not care, but I do. And I'm not letting this go until I know Byatt's all right.

"Where are you going?" Reese asks as I get to my feet.

"The infirmary." I bend down, do up my boots. We sleep with them on to keep the cold from setting too deep, but I always loosen my laces before bed. "I'm visiting Byatt. You coming?"

"No," Reese says, her chin propped on the edge of her bunk, "considering Headmistress will never let you up there."

Maybe not, but I'm Boat Shift now, and I have the knife in my belt to prove it. If there's an exception to be made, Headmistress will make it for me. "She's my best friend," I say. "It's worth trying."

Reese is quiet for a moment, and when I look up she's watching me with an expression I can't quite place. Not anger—I know that on her too well—but something softer. "I don't know, Hetty," she says. "Is it really friendship with you and Byatt?"

I've wondered. Of course I have. And I love Byatt more than anything, more than myself, more than the life I had before Raxter. But I know the warmth in my heart when I look at her. How it burns smooth and even, without a spark.

"Yes," I say. "She's my sister, Reese. She's part of me."

Reese frowns and sits up, swings her legs over the edge of her bunk. "Look, I get it's not my business—"

"You apparently feel the need to comment on it anyway."

"Because it affects me," she says, and I'm taken aback by the sting in her voice, by the snarl of her lips. "I like Byatt, okay? But I don't want you to be with me the way you are with her."

"You don't want us to be friends?"

Reese sighs like I've said something wrong, like there's something more I'm supposed to understand. "No," she says plainly, "I don't."

I can't pretend it doesn't send me reeling. "Well, that's—" I start, but there's nothing after, just an emptiness, and not as much surprise as I'd like. "Okay," I finish at last, and head for the door. I can hear Reese saying my name, but I don't listen, just yank the door open and hurry out into the hallway.

It shouldn't matter to me. I have Byatt to worry about, and besides, I wrote Reese off years ago. Too closed, I remind myself, too cold. She's only with me because she has nobody else.

The hallway opens onto the second-floor mezzanine, and talk drifts up from the girls gathered below in the main hall, their voices soft with sleep. A few of them will go back to bed once they've eaten breakfast. Sometimes that's all there is to do.

But across the mezzanine is the door to the infirmary staircase, and up there somewhere is Byatt. I'm wondering if I can work the lock with the point of my Boat Shift knife when the door jerks open, and there's Headmistress, stepping off the last of the rickety, narrow stairs.

"Excuse me," I call, hurrying over. Headmistress looks up from the clipboard she's carrying. As soon as she sees me, she shuts the door behind her. "Is Byatt all right? How's she doing?"

"I think perhaps there's another way you might begin this conversation," Headmistress says. She's dressed the same as always, slacks and a button-down shirt, her sturdy hiking boots the only concession to what's happened at her school. In her slacks pocket I can spot the edge of a bloodstained handkerchief, the one she uses when the sores on her tongue burst. " 'Good morning,' for instance."

I stop and take a deep breath, fight the impulse to push past her. "Good morning, Headmistress."

She smiles brightly. "And good morning to you. How are you today?"

This is torture. That's what this is. "I'm good," I say, through gritted teeth, and she raises an eyebrow. "*Well.* Sorry. I'm well."

"I'm very glad." She peers down at her clipboard and

then, when she realizes I'm not leaving, clears her throat. "Can I help you with something?"

"Byatt's up there," I say, like she doesn't know. "Can I go see her?"

"I'm afraid not, Miss Chapin."

"I won't even go into her room," I plead. "I'll just talk to her through the door or something." I don't care if I don't see her. I just have to know that she's okay. That she's still her.

But Headmistress is shaking her head, giving me that smile adults always have in their pocket, the one that says they feel sorry for you in a way you can't understand yet. "Why don't you go downstairs for breakfast?"

This isn't fair. This is my home as much as hers. I should be able to go where I like. "It'll only take a second," I say.

"You know the rules." She locks the door to the infirmary stairs with one of the keys on the ring she always has hanging from her belt. I clench my fists to keep myself from ripping it off her. What does any of this matter? We're all sick—it's not like seeing Byatt will make either of us worse. "I'm sorry. I know you must miss your friend."

My friend. My sister, that's what I told Reese. I should've called her my lifeline. "Yeah," I say. "I do."

It's clear Headmistress won't change her mind, and I'm about to turn and leave, to think of some other plan, when she presses the back of her hand against my forehead, the way my mom used to, to check for a fever. I reel back, startled. She only makes a disapproving sound and does it again.

"How are you feeling?" she says. "You don't seem warm."

It takes me a minute to remember, but she's talking about when I got back from Boat Shift. That was the day before yesterday, but it feels like ages ago.

"I'm fine," I say, inching away uncomfortably. Headmistress doesn't usually like to let you know she cares.

Before the Tox it was different. I remember the first time I met her. How nervous I was, coming up here from Norfolk all by myself. Thirteen and alone, and I missed my mother, and when Headmistress saw me getting teary during the school tour, she told me her door was always open if I ever needed someone to talk to or even just a little space away from the other girls.

"Well," Headmistress says, plucking a piece of lint from the collar of my jacket, "I'm glad to hear you're feeling better. I'm sure your friend Miss Winsor will follow suit. And in the meantime she's lucky to have you looking for her."

It runs through me like a current. "Looking for her?" Like she's missing, like she's gone, and I heard Headmistress right, I know I did.

For a moment her expression freezes, and then she smiles, strain showing through. "Looking *out* for her," she corrects me. "Now why don't you go down to breakfast? You must be hungry."

I linger for a beat longer, enough to see Headmistress's knuckles turn white where she's gripping the clipboard, and that does it. I back up, give her my best smile, and head down to the main hall. There are the other girls, dotted in clusters, taking small, controlled bites of molding bread and breaking the edges off stale crackers.

It punches back into me. Everything that's happened, everything I've seen and the secrets I've kept. The others are rationing food and starving themselves through breakfast, and I held what they needed in my own two hands.

I can't do this. Not now.

I pick my way through the others, to the double doors at the front entrance, and slip outside. My jacket is too thin to keep out the cold, but it's better here than in the main hall. At least this way nobody can remind me of what I've done.

I spend the rest of the day out by the water, at the point where the stones are bleached and smooth. I count my fingers as I lose the feeling in them, let the weak sun scatter across my numb skin. When I get back to my room for the night, Reese is already there, sprawled on her top bunk. Asleep, or pretending to be. This distance between us is getting too familiar. But at least this time she's not avoiding me. At least this time she's here.

I don't know if Byatt ever will be again. And I can't let that stand.

I wait until the moon is high. My mattress groans as I get out of bed, and I hold my breath, wait to make sure Reese hasn't heard. Nothing from her bunk. I edge toward the door, and she's still, her hair burning in the black as I slip into the hallway.

It's empty; only a few snatches of talk from the dorms breaking the quiet. The youngest girls are whispering about something, laughter here, a hush there, and they don't hear a thing as I tiptoe past to crouch where the hallway opens to the mezzanine.

There's the door to the infirmary staircase, shut tight as always. Without a key, there's no way past it for me. So the best way to get to the infirmary rooms, then, is the roof. It slants up from the second floor to the roof deck, with dormers for each window poking out. If I get up there, I can sneak around the back side, climb through one of the windows without Gun Shift or Headmistress catching me.

I count to ten. Even steps so the floorboards don't creak.

I never minded the dark before Raxter. Never had it, really, not on the base with the steady glare of the floodlights. Here, it feels different, somehow alive.

I tug my jacket around me tight. And go, across the open mezzanine, past the top of the staircase and into the mouth of the north wing. There's no one here as I make my way down the corridor. Just empty rooms. A handful of faculty offices, papers long since burned. Bare bed frames in teachers' dorms. Chairs broken up for kindling. At the end is the Gun Shift room, the admissions sign still on the door. The open window, chilled fall air gusting through. My way out.

It's easy, hoisting myself up like I did every day for Gun Shift. Strange without Byatt behind me to swat at my heels, but soon enough I'm crouched low on the slope of the roof, shingles wet with melted frost under my hands. On the deck above me, I can see the silhouettes of two girls with their guns aimed. They're looking straight ahead, out at the woods as they talk softly to each other. Good. As long as I'm quiet, they won't notice.

I crawl forward, toward the nearest dormer. Through it I can see one of the infirmary rooms, just a bed and bare mattress draped in shadow, door closed to the hallway. No Byatt, but no Headmistress either. I notch my shoulder in under the window frame and start to work it up.

The wood's warped after a year and a half without maintenance, and I have to stop every few shoves, make sure the girls on Gun Shift haven't heard me. Feet slipping on the shredded shingles, and below me the night swallows the ground, but I don't look. One, two, three, and the window shudders up, opens maybe a foot.

I don't go through. I wait, crouched on the sill, and I watch as Headmistress's candle lights up a strip at the bottom of the door and fades out. Footsteps tapping on the stairs as she heads down to the second floor. And then quiet.

I go in headfirst, scramble up to standing. There are six rooms on the third floor, three at the front and back each. I'm in the one closest to the stairs. Five more to check before someone catches me.

Cross to the door, test the latch. It's unlocked. These doors have bolts on the outside, left over from the house's earliest days and put to use after we got sick, but with nobody here, Headmistress must not bother doing them up. I pull it open with both hands.

Out in the narrow hallway I stop again and listen. The house is never silent, not one this old and not now that everything's changed, but I don't hear Headmistress or Welch anywhere. Don't hear Byatt either, but I tell myself she's probably just asleep.

I try the opposite door. Unlocked, too, and the room empty just like the other.

It's fine. Four more rooms. Four more places she could be.

But the third one's empty, and the fourth, and by the time I get to the fifth room, I'm breathing hard. I can hear my heart beating in my ears, and she's not here, she isn't, she isn't.

Sixth door. Swinging wide. The bed empty, mattress askew and dipped in moonlight. And there, amid a set of scuff marks on the floor, a needle and thread. Byatt's. The ones she always carried in her pocket, the ones she used to fix me.

She's gone.

Dread, cold and spreading, but I push it away. Something happened, but whatever it was, she got through it, like she gets through everything. She's somewhere, and she's alive. I should check the offices on the second floor, and every classroom, and hell, maybe the big storage closet just to be—

A sound on the stairs. Someone's coming.

I freeze, then snatch up the needle and thread and hurry back to the first room. The open window still waiting, air gusting through. No time, can't climb out without making too much noise, and there's a light, Headmistress's candle, closer, closer—here. It stops in front of the door to this room.

Can't move. Can't breathe. If Headmistress comes in, if she catches me, I don't know what she'll do.

And then something I haven't heard in a year and a half, not since Mr. Harker left. The crackle of static, the filter and hiss of a walkie-talkie, and a voice. A man's voice. It's like cold water in my veins, and a shiver scrapes over me.

"Raxter, call in, over."

There's a beep, and then a hitch in the static. "This is Raxter, over."

I jerk with surprise and narrowly miss hitting my head against the window frame. It's Welch, not Headmistress like I was expecting. Welch doesn't come up here much, if ever.

"Requesting status report," the man says. "Over."

It must be someone from the base on the coast—the Navy or the CDC. They're the only other people in the world who know what's happening here. Even our parents don't know the whole truth. Influenza, I think that's what they were told. I wonder if they knew it was a lie.

"All well," Welch says. "Did the replacement arrive safely? Over."

Silence, and then the man says, "Confirming receipt. Over."

Receipt? And replacement for what? Nothing leaves the island, not even our bodies. When one of us dies, we burn her out back, as far from the house and the fence as we can manage. A whole square of earth scorched, the smell unbearable, bones and fillings buried under stone cairns.

"There's something else," Welch says, sounding almost reluctant. "We have to make a return. Over."

The supplies, that's what I think of first, but we've done that already. She has to mean something else.

For a long moment no answer. Welch starts to pace, and I track her movement as the steady light under the door shifts. She won't come in here, I tell myself. I'm safe, I'm safe, I'm safe. Finally, her walkie chirps back to life.

"This time tomorrow," the man says. "Drop her at the Harker house. Over."

Her. Not the body, but *her*, and that's Byatt. It has to be. And they're talking about her like she's still someone. I feel my heart bloom with relief. But if she's not here, where is Welch keeping her until tomorrow? And what for?

Welch stops pacing. "Confirmed, over."

"Over and out."

The air goes quiet. A moment later the light under the door fades, and I hear Welch's footsteps heading farther along the hall. I ease out the window, heave it shut. Settle on my hands and knees and slowly, slowly, inch across the roof. The Gun Shift girls still have their eyes on the trees, and they don't see me as I lower myself over the edge and swing in through the second-floor window.

I sneak down the hallway, across the mezzanine. Check the rise of the moon, mark it in my head—this time tomorrow, that's what the man on the walkie said—and go back to my own room, to my own bed. To Reese, sitting up in her bunk and waiting for me, because of course she knows I left.

"Something's happened," I say. "She's not in the infirmary."

Reese frowns, and I can see it already, the disbelief building in her. "What are you talking about?"

"And there was this man, on the walkie." I'm practically out of breath, tumbling over myself to get it all out.

"Slow down. Start from the beginning."

I tell her everything, about the empty rooms, about the needle and thread. About Welch, about the walkie-talkie and the man's voice on the other end, about the plans they made to take Byatt to the Harker house.

"I don't know where else Welch could be keeping her," I finish, leaning against the ladder. I can feel a shake setting in my muscles. "She has to be holding her somewhere if they're not leaving until tomorrow."

The classrooms on the ground floor aren't private enough, and there aren't any outbuildings on the grounds besides the barn. Just an old toolshed, but we've torn that apart for firewood. "What do you think?" I say, looking to Reese.

At first she says nothing, the light from her hair showing me her widened eyes. And then she lets out a shuddering sigh.

"My house," she says. A strange contortion of her face, like she's trying not to laugh, or maybe cry. "You're sure he said my house?"

Of course that's what she's focusing on. I guess I can't exactly blame her. "I'm sure," I say. "For real, Reese, we have to find Byatt. She's still here somewhere."

"I'm sure she is," Reese says. Words light and easy, a deliberately blank expression on her face, and that means she's holding something back.

"But what?" I say. "Byatt's here somewhere, but what?"

I should be expecting it, but it's still a surprise when Reese says, "Is she dead or alive?"

A hot rush of anger, bright and shattering, because I've been pushing that thought back since the infirmary, and couldn't she let me? "What kind of question is that?"

"An important one," she says. "You're not an idiot, Hetty. You know what usually happens to girls like us."

"None of this is what usually happens." I take a deep breath, clench my fists. Don't let it in. She's alive, she's alive, she's alive. "Girls don't usually disappear like this. That has to mean something."

"Yeah," Reese says. "I think it means she's already dead."

I push back from the bunk, ignore the panic swelling in my gut. Reese is wrong, and Byatt is fine. "Then how come we haven't burned her? She's alive. I have to find her. I just do."

"And then what? We can't help her."

She's right, of course. But it doesn't matter. "We can get through it with her," I say. "That's all we have left. And I'm not giving it up. I might not know where she is right now, but I know where she'll be tomorrow night. I'm going out there after her."

"You can't do that." Reese's voice is low, urgent as she leans closer. "You know you can't. It's breaking quarantine."

"So what?" I say. "I'm Boat Shift. Boat Shift is allowed past the fence."

She rolls her eyes. "I think they meant that for going to pick up supplies and not sneaking after your friend."

I wave it away. They've always told us the quarantine is the most important thing, but if I'm choosing between it and Byatt, it's no choice at all.

"And even if you did go out there," Reese continues, "how would you get back in past the fence?" She pulls at the end of her braid with silver fingers, her split ends starting to fray. "The gate locks and—"

"I'll climb over it," I say hotly. "I'll figure it out. I'm not worried about that."

"I am," she says, but she's looking at me, her face open and unsure, and there it is, that kick in my chest, that reaching I've been trying to ignore since we met.

"Come with me," I say. "We'll go together."

It's magic. One second she's in it with me, her head bent close to mine, and then she's settled back into that posture I know so well. Arms crossed, jaw clenched, eyes emptied of heart.

"No," she says. "No, you do what you want, but I won't go with you."

For once I'm not willing to let it lie. This is too important, all of it. "Why not?"

She makes an exasperated sound. "Hetty—"

Whatever patience I had left is gone. I'm gripping the edge of the bunk so hard I can feel a splinter bite deep into my palm. "What is wrong with you? Byatt's our friend. Don't you want her to be okay?"

"Wanting has nothing to do with it," she says, but it's pouring out of me, louder than I should be, angrier than I expected.

"Because I know you don't care." I keep on, a bitter twist to my words. "I know that makes you better than me, but I can't just write the whole world off like you do."

"I don't care? Are you—" And then she breaks off like

111

it hurts. For a second I can see it all laid out across her. The longing and the resignation and the betrayal, the sting of watching the island she loves steal the people she pretends she doesn't.

"Oh," I say. My voice thick, lodged in my throat. I've spent every day since I met her telling myself the wrong thing. Telling myself over and over that she was cold, when maybe she was burning the whole time. "I'm sorry. Jesus, Reese, I'm sorry."

Her parents both gone, and this is what it did to her. This is the wreck it left behind. I should have seen it. I should have seen how she loves as hard as I do. Only I think it pins her down where it picks me up.

"I wish I could," she says, not looking at me. "I wish I could be like you. But I can't go looking for her if I couldn't go looking for him. I thought Boat Shift was the only way past the fence, but here you are, ready to tear it down with your bare hands." She lets out a shaking breath, and then softly, "Why couldn't I do that for my dad?"

For once I think I know what to say. It's what people used to tell me when I was small, when my father was deployed. "You're his daughter," I say. "You're not supposed to be the one protecting him."

She doesn't answer. Still she has to be listening. "But Byatt's our girl." I'm watching Reese's face, and I have her. I know I do. "We are supposed to protect her. Just like she'd do it for us." I take a deep breath. "Just like I'd do it for you."

A flicker of surprise on her face, one that lights an answering spark of shame in my stomach. Is that really news to her?

But she reaches out then, and I feel something catch in my chest as her palm slides against mine. "Yeah," she says. "Okay."

There's nothing more to be done tonight, and the adrenaline is draining from me, leaving me about ready to keel over. I smile at her and let go, duck into my bunk.

I lie on my back, still leaving room next to me for Byatt like always. Above me I can hear Reese taking off her jacket to use as a blanket. It's too quiet, and as easy as it just was with her, suddenly, I want more than anything for the ground to swallow me up so we don't have to listen to each other pretend to be asleep.

"Hey," Reese says suddenly. "It wasn't my dad, was it? On the walkie?"

"Um." I'm not sure how to let her down.

"Never mind." She sounds gruff, embarrassed, and I can picture her shaking her head. "I just . . . I thought if one of my parents was gonna come back, it would be him."

A rustle, and a creak in the wooden ribs of our bunk beds as she gets comfortable, ending the conversation. I'm surprised she started it to begin with.

But then, she's different without Byatt here. Or maybe we both are. I clench my fists, try to work up the courage. I've wondered this since I met her, but when Reese doesn't want to talk, nothing can make her.

"You don't have to tell me," I start. There's a tremor in my voice. I keep going. "But, Reese, where did your mom go?"

I can't see her, so instead, I watch the patterns of light her braid throws onto the ceiling, trace their soft, blurring glow. "It's complicated," she says at last. "Or maybe I just wish it was."

"I don't understand."

"Last I heard, she was still in Maine. Portland, maybe."

"What?" That's barely two hundred miles away. I'd always assumed she'd gone far, or even that Reese didn't know where she was.

"Yeah," Reese says. She doesn't sound sad. Or angry. Or anything. "She didn't want to leave Maine. She just wanted to leave me."

I don't know what could soothe that sting. But she's talking to me. That has to count for something. "I'm sorry," I say. "You know you could have told me about it before."

"Some things don't belong to other people," she says, tired and drifting. "Some things are just mine."

As if I needed more proof that we're built from different things. Reese holds herself so apart, and all I've ever wanted was to be half of someone else. Coming to Raxter, it was like I hadn't found my place until I got here. Like I didn't know who I was until Byatt told me.

And I know what Reese would say. I know she'd say that's not healthy, say that's not how it's supposed to work.

But the whole world is coming down around us every day, and don't we have bigger problems?

No, Reese isn't Byatt, but I like her. I like how she talks without talking. I even like that she doesn't always like me.

BYATT

CHAPTER 7

Trying to blink but what
    Slow thick like my tongue hot and dry   here a
sliver of something here the world sneaking back under
my eyelids here I am   I am I am

Awake.

Heat running through my head like a current. Light
pricking at my eyes until I'm in a bed in a room. And I
don't hurt, but I feel my whole body at once.

The room is big. Built for something different than
this. Peeling linoleum floor. Curtain half drawn around
me, and through the gap a bulletin board on the wall,
hanging at an angle, and three other beds, all empty. I
reach out to touch the curtain, to pull it back, to

Can't move. Hands strapped down, held by my wrists,
IV needle slipped in through my skin.

Somewhere a door opening   heavy, muffled
steps   a suit, plastic and pale sleepy blue, I can see

it through the curtain as it approaches. Pushing in and shaking an arm to keep the curtain from clinging and it says

Feeling okay?

He is a boy, he says.

His name is Dietrich.

He's just joking. He doesn't know why he said that.

His name is Teddy and he's nineteen. He's only a Seaman and this is his first day. He was barely at Camp Nash for a week before they sent him here, and he is still not sure why they did because all he does is move equipment and look out of windows. He is sorry, he is rambling, but it's only that he doesn't know what the CDC doctors are saying most of the time, and medicine is confusing and he is very nervous.

Look hard, try to remember how a boy is built. Can only see his eyes above his surgical mask, the rest of his body blurred by the plastic suit. Hair brown like mine, skin golden but faded, like it's missing the sun.

Teddy asks me questions. Teddy asks me what day it is. He asks me my birthday, my last name, the price of milk. I don't answer   I want to but the words won't line up on my tongue.

Jack fell down and broke his crown, he says. Jill Jill   Come on you know this.

Jill came tumbling I say but that's all   can't   and oh god I forgot   I forgot how it hurts like a shock like bile stinging in my throat like a shiver in my bones   shaking and screaming and if I don't stop I'll just break apart and   eyes wet   stomach heave

Quiet Teddy says please be quiet   that hurts us both

Tells me it's okay. Tilts a cup of water to my lips, drip, drip and swallow. Locks the door behind him when he goes.

Alone, awake, all of me here in my body. Nobody around, just the whir of a fan somewhere beyond my curtain. Tug and tug but the straps around my wrists have no give.

I think I have been a problem all my life. Here I am where problems go. First Raxter and now here, and I have always been heading here, haven't I, haven't I. Too bright and too bored and something missing, or perhaps something too much there.

It was my mother's idea and my father just nodded and went to sit in another room. Silence all that summer until they put me in a car headed for Raxter. Nobody there will know, I told myself. Nobody will know what you do when you're bored. What you do just because you can.

———

Teddy comes back with the sun, tells me they're figuring it out. Quiet for now, he says, and I don't mind. I remember the hurt. And he lays out a packet of forms, unbuckles my wrists and moves the IV stand and helps me write the answers down.

Byatt

Byatt Winsor

16 almost 17

January 14th

No allergies

Elizabeth and Christopher Winsor

Beacon Hill

What street?

West Cedar

House?

Number 6

You're getting anxious, Teddy says. Don't get anxious.

I almost forgot, I write.

But you didn't.

Wake up before I'm supposed to   IV still full   a haze I can't blink away   and when I close my eyes I am back back in the woods   that night   the night I came here

Cold   damp   irises   crunching   under my boots and Welch holding me tight   for the best she says for your friends   like there's a choice I

122

made   but it wasn't I didn't and   pulled me from the infirmary marched me down the stairs   no guards no nothing   Hetty asleep somewhere Hetty alone

She needs me I said and Welch   said no   said she needs you to do this

Through the gate into the trees   sounds in the brush animals moving their eyes like torches   Welch's breath warm on my ear and then   people   waiting

They took me even though I fought   even though I ran   dart in my thigh and a fog in my brain and Welch leaning over me

I'm sorry she said and I think   the worst part is I think she meant it

Something blue out in the bigger room, and I notice, my eyes clear, world firm and real around me. Barely time to see it all, barely time to check my IV and see it's empty before the curtain's sliding back, a rustle of plastic pushing through, and then it's a person, a woman in a suit like Teddy's, standing at the foot of the bed, holding a patterned hospital gown.

"Hello," she says. She sounds like she's smiling. "Time to change."

She undoes every strap holding me down and helps me to my feet. My limbs are weak and shaking, so she undresses me, her heavy fingers working slowly at the buttons on my shirt and the laces on my boots. For a second I'm shivering in my bra and underwear, and I see her staring at me, at my back where that extra ridge of bone erupts through my skin, and then the gown is slipping over my head. I can't even lift my arms to get them through the holes. She has to do that for me.

Her suit is thick like Teddy's. Rubbery and stiff. They must be afraid of me, of what I have. But it stops at her neck, and I can see the beat of her pulse. Count it—one, two—and it feels better that way.

"Does that feel all right?" the woman asks as she straps me back in. "Comfortable?"

I open my mouth, but she lays one gloved finger across my lips before I can get anything out.

"Let's stick with nodding for now. Teddy tells me we've had some trouble with talking." She pulls back the curtain a little more to show a sink tucked into the counter against the wall. It doesn't look quite like a hospital. There's something sad and ordinary about it. Like the kitchen in a back room of a church, or the break room in an office building.

The woman fills a plastic cup of water for me and holds it to my mouth until I take a sip. "We'll get you something to write with," she says. "In the meantime it's probably best to let you rest. You've been through a lot."

I keep drinking until the cup is empty. She dumps it in a trash basket by the foot of my bed and comes closer. "I'm

Dr. Paretta," she says, bending over my right arm. "Should I call you Byatt? Or is there something else you like to go by? A nickname, maybe?"

I shake my head.

"Byatt it is. All right, you might feel a pinch."

I don't see exactly what she does. There are too many folds to her suit. But when she comes away it's with a tube of blood. She holds it up to the light. Squints, like she can tell what's happening inside, and then fetches a small red cooler from the foot of the bed and slots this vial of blood inside, next to another one. "Potential RAX," I think it's labeled, but she closes it before I can read the rest.

"One last thing, before I forget, and then I'll leave you to sleep." She takes my hand in between hers, curls my fingers and bends my wrist so that I can feel the side of the bed frame. There's a button there, round and raised.

"This is your call button. In case the pain gets too bad, or you need something. Do you feel it?"

I nod. She looks at me, and then she straightens back up. Waits another second or two. Then: "Do you remember my name?"

My lips peel apart. "Paretta."

I wanted to say it, to say something, to have my voice again, and I didn't think it would hurt that bad. Just one word couldn't hurt that bad. But it does, like something's trying to rip my spine out through my throat.

"Well," says Paretta. She sounds out of breath. "We won't be doing that again."

CHAPTER 8

Gone, until I'm not. Flat on my back, the world moving around me as four suited figures wheel my gurney into a dark room. I test the restraints at my wrists, but they hold firm, nylon rubbing my skin raw.

"Good morning," one of them says to me. I almost don't recognize her, but there, the eyes, and the curling brown ponytail. Paretta.

High ceilings, no windows. An operating room, with something makeshift about it. The table in the middle is shrouded in paper, lit stark and hard. They line the gurney up alongside it and begin to undo my restraints. I could fight, I know, but the door's shut and locked behind us, and I don't know, really, what I'd even be fighting for.

I barely have a second once the buckles are undone before they're gripping me tight and lifting. They swing me onto the table and stretch my arms out, strapping them back down. I wince, the ridge of bone that runs like a second spine grinding uncomfortably against the table. One of the doctors wraps a blood pressure cuff around my left arm, and as it tightens, the other settles an oxygen tube under my nose and adjusts it. After that come sensors, stuck to my forehead and chest, and I watch as the screens start to show slices of me, to record the beat and wave of my heart.

"It's all right," someone says, and it's Paretta, bending over me. She pushes my hair off my face. "You're here to help us figure out what's happening, and how to fix it."

The other three doctors are stepping back slowly, until I can't see them anymore. It's just me and Paretta.

"We've been working with some of your friends," she says. "And we think we're nearly at a point where we can make real progress here. But I need your help. Can you do that for me, Byatt?"

My friends? Have there been others here? I open my mouth to ask, to say something, but Paretta claps her hand over my mouth.

"Remember?" she says. "Stay quiet. This will be over before you know it."

After a moment she lets go, grabs a nearby tray, and wheels it over. Silver on silver. Bouquet of scalpels, wrapped in plastic. I start to struggle, the sight of the blades sparking a gut-deep fear. Something writhing in my stomach. It takes everything in me not to yell.

But it's not the scalpels she reaches for. It's something

else, lying small and innocuous next to a bottle of water. A round yellow pill in its own clear sleeve.

"This is all it is," she says, tipping the pill onto her palm. "Nothing to worry about."

"RAX009" I see, labeled clearly on the discarded sleeve, before Paretta takes hold of my jaw and pries it open. The pill is on my tongue then, dissolving bitter and slow.

009. The ninth version of that pill, maybe. Or the ninth girl strapped to this table.

I swallow, gagging as the taste hits the back of my throat. Paretta watches me carefully before reaching for the bottle of water, the brand the same as we get back at Raxter. She undoes the cap and props my head up as she pours a little into my mouth. There's a clump of powder stuck on my tongue, and it takes a few tries to get it down.

I was expecting something to happen right away—for the bones down my back to melt, for my voice to be back like it was. But one minute, and then another, and another. Paretta disappears, and I crane my neck to watch her join the other doctors leaning against the wall. They're waiting. Just like I am.

More time slipping by, and I drift off, come in and out. I'm so tired. My whole body aching, second spine tender and bruised. Maybe this whole thing isn't so bad if I'm getting a chance to rest.

And then. A sparking. I know this feeling.

Just before a flare-up, there's a moment. Hard to

describe, hard to pin down, but for me it almost makes it worth it. The pain and the loss, all of it a fair price for this. This strength, this power, this eagerness to bare my teeth.

I wait for it to fade, the way I'm used to, wait for it to turn into blinding pain. Instead, it builds, ricocheting through my body, shredding my insides, and I feel my hands clench into fists, nails biting deep into my palms. The heart monitor starts going haywire, the room full of beeping and alarms.

"What's going on?"

"Get a readout from the monitor."

The doctors are rushing to gather data, their silhouettes blurring around me. I shut my eyes. This is my body. It will do what I ask it to.

Calm down, I think. Hold it in.

Only part of me doesn't want to. I can hear it, snarling and low, telling me to let go. Telling me this has always been inside me and that these doctors are trying to take it away.

My back arches, eyes slamming open. Thrashing against the straps pinning me, throwing my weight from side to side. Paretta, at the foot of my gurney, saying my name, but she's the one who did this to me. I scream.

Blood dripping from my nose, agony lancing down my back. Paretta clamps her hands over her ears and falls back, and so I scream again, pull with everything I have against my restraints. Still the strength thrumming through my body, still the gift the Tox gave me. One of the restraints rips free.

I scrabble at the other buckle and leap from the table, but the other doctors are there. They grab hold of my arms. Drag me back, and I kick, scratch tears down the front of their hazmat suits.

"Byatt!" Paretta yells. "Byatt, you need to calm down."

And I want, suddenly, not to escape, not to be free. I want to hurt her.

I only make it a step before they stick the syringe into my neck and the world goes dark.

HETTY

CHAPTER 9

I wake up with a headache. Throbbing at my temples, sharp behind my blind eye. It leaves me clutching at the edge of my bunk, body braced for a flare-up. Since my first, they've all led with a pain like this, and followed with something worse. Last time it was wet webs of tissue, so thick in my throat I couldn't breathe, each fresh with blood, like they'd been ripped from the inside of my stomach.

A headache like this could mean my next flare-up is coming. Or, I know Byatt would say, I could just have a headache.

Above me Reese's bunk creaks, and I remember everything from last night, all at once. Welch's voice, and the plans she made with the man on the walkie. The needle and thread, now tucked safely into my pocket. Byatt is somewhere in this house. And if I can't find her today, I'll find her tonight. Past the fence, after midnight in the last of the dark. Reese and I will follow Welch to Reese's house, and Byatt will be there. And she'll be alive.

"This lying in silence thing is fun," Reese says suddenly from above me, "but can we go eat?"

On the days without a supply delivery, meals are quiet, almost orderly. Anything good goes fast in that first rush after Boat Shift. All that's left is what nobody really wanted. Most of the girls wait in the main hall, but there's one from every small constellation of us that heads down the southern corridor to the kitchen where Welch doles out the food and bottled water, ready to carry something back to her friends.

This has been my job since the start. Byatt said people would feel the worst for me and let me have the best of what was there. They're scared of Reese, and that works for Boat Shift day, but the name of this game is pity, and I'm how we win.

I leave Reese in the main hall and follow Cat down the south wing corridor. At the corner where the hallway hooks to the left, there's Headmistress's office, one of the last places left we're still not supposed to go. I've only been there twice before: once on my first day at Raxter and then again a semester later, when I got reprimanded for talking during assembly.

Maybe that's where they're keeping Byatt, I think. I

have my hand on the latch before I realize I'm doing this in plain daylight, and Cat is waiting for me.

I hurry to catch up with her. She gives me a smile, doesn't ask how I am or what the hell I was doing, and I'm grateful for that. After we put in an appearance at breakfast I'll circle out around the house, peer through the windows of Headmistress's office. And then keep searching if I don't find what I'm looking for.

Together Cat and I turn the corner and continue on to where the kitchen opens, with its skylights and checkerboard tile. The last time I was here, Byatt was on the floor, coming apart. The last time I was here, the whole world ended.

Enough, I think. I'm doing what I can. Soon I'll have her back.

A handful of other girls are already there, waiting for Welch to come in and unlock the pantry, where we keep the food. I'm dreading having to look her in the eye, but there's no way she knows what I overheard last night.

"Hey," says Emmy, barely up to my shoulder, her sleek hair still baby-fine. After her first flare-up the other day, she was bouncing off the walls, excited to be like the rest of us even if her flare-up left her coughing up teeth from somewhere deep inside, but today she's got on an affected solemnity. Of course she does—she's here for Landry, probably bursting with pride at representing the girl at the top of what's left of Raxter's social ladder.

"I just wanted to say," Emmy continues, "I hope you're okay. After what happened with Byatt."

"Thanks," I say, and I hope that's it, but she keeps talking.

"She's in our prayers." Emmy says it just the way Landry would, the same polished tone and rounded corners.

"I'm sure she appreciates it," I say, rolling my eye. None of this is helping my headache, now dulled to a constant hum of pain. I'm used to it, but that doesn't mean I wouldn't rather have quiet than Emmy playing at being Landry.

Footsteps pull our attention to the door, and finally, there's Welch, hastening into the kitchen, already fussing with the ring of keys on her belt. Where did she come from? Was she with Byatt? She doesn't look any different than she did yesterday, doesn't look like she's hiding something. But after the pier, I know she's better at that than I expected.

"Sorry," she says as we crowd around her. There's a crust at the corner of her mouth, something yellowing, the smell sour. Probably from one of those sores she and Headmistress get. "Bit of an issue. All right, who's first today?"

Passing out food used to be oldest first, the way it is at every other school, the way it was before. And then we realized the oldest would always be the oldest. None of us could leave. Now we rotate through, year by year, day by day, and it's youngest first today, which is why Landry's sent Emmy. She picks it just right, so she always eats first.

Cat and I are near the middle, with Julia and a few girls from Carson's year behind us.

It comes to my turn, and I duck under the lintel into the pantry and step aside to make room for Cat as she joins me. She seems okay today, her skin mostly healed. For the first season we thought maybe that meant she was better. But the blisters keep coming back, bigger and deeper each time, a flash of bone visible at the bottom of them.

The pantry is built off the back of the kitchen. Boat Shift carry everything that isn't taken immediately, back here after each trip, unpack and unload it into the trash cans for storage. Every day Welch drags one to the middle of the narrow room for us to root through. She counts what we take and writes it down.

Cat brushes some cobwebs off her jacket and sighs, looking at sugar cubes spilled on the floor from where Emmy probably snuck some out with her.

"We'll get ants."

"We've got worse." I lean over the trash can, root through to the bottom where some girls try to bury things for themselves. There's a pack of jerky—just what we need, but I hesitate. I watched the rest of Boat Shift throw away enough food for all of us. I shouldn't take anything. I don't deserve it.

But it's not just me I'm here for. It's Reese too. And we both need to eat if we're going to make it to the Harker house tonight. "I'll take the jerky, and that thing of honey mustard nobody wants."

Cat grabs a box of melba toast and a packet of rice. She waits a moment before sneaking a minibox of raisins into her pocket.

"It's Lindsay's birthday," she says quietly. "Please don't tell."

I check over my shoulder, to where Welch is leaning against the doorway, fiddling with the keys. She doesn't seem to have heard.

"Sure," I say. It's the least I can do after the pier.

I show my pickings to Welch as I leave the pantry, do my best to keep my hands steady. How can she just stand there like nothing's wrong? Like she's not keeping my best friend locked up somewhere? I put on a smile, try to keep from wondering what's happening to Byatt while I stand here in the kitchen, flecks of her blood still dotting the floor.

"All right," Welch says absently. "You're fine."

I bite back the urge to rip the answers out of her, hurry out of the kitchen, back to the main hall, where I'm startled to find Reese sitting with Carson. She's staring at her boots, and Carson is watching helplessly with that look I recognize, the look of someone beaten almost into submission by Reese's impassive silence.

"Hi," I say as I approach. "Carson, this is a nice surprise."

"'Surprise' is the right word," Reese says. I frown at her—it isn't fair to snipe at Carson, who never knows it's happening—and she shrugs.

"Morning" comes Julia's voice from behind me.

"Oh, good, another one," Reese says, but she sounds a bit gentler, looks almost rueful as she smiles at me.

I sit down next to her, try to keep from raising my eyebrows as Julia takes a seat opposite me. We keep mostly to our own circles, but now that I'm Boat Shift, are Julia and Carson part of mine? Or are they here to make sure I'm keeping all the right secrets from Reese?

It's a stifling quiet as we eat. I have nothing to say, and I know Reese certainly doesn't, and every minute we spend here is one I'm not looking for Byatt.

Carson sits up straighter, opens her mouth to start a new conversation, and Reese levels her with a look. "We don't always have to be talking, you know."

"Sorry," I say, giving Reese a sidelong glare. She has the decency to look a little guilty. "We're just tired."

"No problem," says Julia. If anything, she seems relieved to not have to make any more conversation. There's a fresh bruise peeking out from under the hem of her shirt, and she looks exhausted, like it's sucking the life from her as it grows. I watch as she spits out a mouthful of blood, and leaves it there on the floor, not bothering to wipe it up.

I can't finish my half of the jerky. Just the smell of it's making me sick, and if I pay attention, if I think about it too hard, I can feel a tingle starting behind my blind eye, breaking through the low haze of pain. Reese doesn't say anything, just takes the jerky from me and stuffs it into her pocket for later.

She looks like her dad in this light. Like the way he looked before. The same strong chin, the same eyes, all washed over with gold.

I wonder what she thinks of when she looks at me. Not my parents—I never kept a photo of them pinned to my wall like some of the other girls did.

I don't think of them much, my parents. I know I should. I did right after the Tox, for the first month or two. I lined up for my radio call and we had short, stilted conversations. But then they cut off our access, and things got worse, and then it didn't matter anymore. Because if I see my parents again, they will want to hear how I missed them, how it was the worst thing that ever happened. And I'll be lying, if I can say it at all.

Part of me really thought it would be that simple. A locked door, somewhere deep in the house, and Byatt on the other side of it.

Part of me really was an idiot.

After breakfast Reese followed me outside, and she kept watch as I peered through the window into Head-mistress's office. Nothing—just the bulk of her old desk and a stack of cardboard boxes in the corner.

"Byatt's not there," I told Reese, and I told her the same thing as I checked every classroom and every office. Every storage closet, every bathroom. The whole house unlocked like it was waiting for me, like it had something to prove.

Eventually, I couldn't stand it anymore, couldn't think past the throbbing in my head, couldn't feel anything but the guilt of failing Byatt like this.

And Reese took my hand, like she did last night, and she led me back outside. The air bracing and quick, waking the blood in my skin and thinning the pain in my head until it was barely there anymore. "There's still tonight," she said quietly. "It's not over yet."

Now we're on the north side of the house, wandering aimlessly toward the point. Off to the left, the cliff tapering to nothing on our side of the grounds, and up ahead, a tetherball pole and a rusted swing set, both listing to one side, the dead grass around them covered in frost. I can feel the cold pricking in my lungs, points like knives, and my nose has gone numb, but I don't mind. Out here I can breathe. Out here I feel awake.

The grounds are so open, nothing like the clustered press of the woods, and I'm thinking about that when I say, "We should get a gun," so suddenly that Reese nearly trips.

"What for?"

My body remembers the shake and the fear as I ran for my life that first time I was out beyond the fence. "Trust me, we want one."

"Sure," Reese says, frowning, "but it's not like we can steal one from the supply closet without Welch noticing."

A set of girls rambles by, on their way to wash their hair or steal some blankets or just be bored someplace new, and we give them a nod, a tight smile. Two are from the year below us, and the others are Sarah and Lauren from ours. I like Lauren, but Sarah's the girl who stole my last clean uniform skirt and got me a dress code violation my third week here. I can't stand the way she brags about her flare-up, either. One heart, two heartbeats—fantastic. She thinks it means she'll live longer. I think it just means she's that much more fucked.

"Hey, Hetty," Lauren says, slowing down. "Do you know if we're having target practice today?"

Welch would have said so at breakfast, and part of me wants to remind them of that, but I'm Boat Shift now. I'm the girl they come to with questions.

"Not today," I say. "Have a good one."

"'Have a good one'?" Reese repeats under her breath, and I know if I look at her, I'll see her holding back a smile.

Lauren looks a little disappointed, but she shrugs. "Thanks. See you, Hetty."

"Look at you," Reese says once they're gone. "You're like a politician. Or a mall greeter."

It's the way she'd tease me when Byatt was here, the same words, the same amused expression. But it's softer somehow. Or at least, I don't mind it.

I'm about to suggest we go back inside, maybe keep an eye on the storage closet and hope Welch leaves it unattended during the day, when Reese tugs on my sleeve. She nods over my shoulder, to where the barn is standing, empty and dark.

"Target practice," she says. "There's a gun we can take."

"How?"

But she's already walking, leaving a trail of footprints through the frost.

The barn's empty this time of day. Just vacant stalls and dust drifting, and the sliding doors open to the sea, chilled wind whipping through. I follow Reese to the back, behind the bales of hay stacked to make a target, to a long-locked chest meant for saddles and stirrups. Now it's where Welch keeps the shotgun we use for our lessons.

"Here," Reese says, crouching in front of the chest. It's only got one padlock, the kind with a dial and a combination, and it looks rusted, like it might be easy to break. Welch would notice if we smashed it, but I'm about to say that some things are worth the risk when Reese starts turning the dial, spinning to a set of three numbers: 3–17–03. Her birthday.

The lock clicks open, and she looks up at me with a grin. "My dad set the combo," she says. "I figured Welch wouldn't have changed it." Reese lifts the lid and pulls the shotgun out from a pile of old tack, fishing for any loose ammo. "Now what?"

"We should hide it somewhere," I say, still surprised at our luck, as she slips a pair of stray shells into her pocket, the metal clinging to her skin in the cold. We'll only have two shots between us. "Near the fence, maybe, so it's easy to grab on the way out." There's a copse of spruce trees off to the left of the gate, where some of the older girls used to bring their mainland boyfriends on visitor days. My face burns at the thought of going there with Reese, but we should be able to hide the gun there safely until tonight.

"All right," Reese says, and holds the shotgun out to me. I take it, unsure, only for her to turn around and shrug off her jacket. I'd be shivering if I were her, but all she's got are a few goosebumps down her arms. "Stick it in my waistband and we'll run it up my back."

It'll work, but I can't help a burst of nervous laughter. She looks over her shoulder at me. "What? You have a better way?"

Maybe it's her willingness to do this with me, to risk her life for Byatt's because I asked her to. Maybe it's the line of her jaw or the lure of her hair. But she's given me something, and I owe her something back. "Hey," I say. "You want to learn to shoot?"

I'm expecting her to snap at me. Instead, she sounds carefully bland when she says, "I know how."

"I mean on your other side." A heartbeat of silence, her expression curdling to something doubtful, but it's not a no, so I try again. "I shoot righty. I could teach you."

"Okay," she says. Nervous. Determined. Just like me.

I hand the shotgun back to her and lead her to the front of the barn, point her toward the patch of floor where the sawdust is ground. Reese takes her spot, drawing her jacket around her again, and I come up next to her.

"Show me how you normally stand."

She bristles. A week ago I'd have said it's because she hates to be told what to do. And she does, but I think she hates, too, to be seen as anything but strong.

"Just show me," I say gently.

Reluctantly, she snugs the butt of the shotgun in against her left shoulder, barrel cradled in her right hand. She starts trying to hook the fingers on her silver hand around the trigger. But her fingers are too fine at the point, and they won't catch and pull.

"See?" she says.

"Right," I say, "but that's okay. Now switch your position. Put your left foot forward and angle your hips."

They teach us to shoot in what Welch calls a bladed stance, with the support shoulder to the target and the trigger shoulder to the back. She says it's to make sure we hit right the first time, just in case the bullets stop coming on the boat and we have to make them count.

Reese adjusts, sets up with the shotgun lifted in her silver hand and her other hand waiting near the trigger. She's holding her shoulders the right way, but you can tell it's not how she likes it by the way her hips are still square.

"You gotta commit," I say. "Come on."

"I can't really see this way."

I laugh. "If I can see with one eye, you can see with two."

She's fussing, trying to get the gun to sit right, but she won't be able to if she's standing like that. I come up close behind her, reach out, my hand hovering over her hip. "Can I?"

She turns her head, baring the delicate skin along the nape of her neck, and my breath catches. A moment ago it was nothing, this was nothing, just me and her the way we've been a hundred times before. But it's not the same. Byatt gone, nobody between us.

"Yeah," she says quietly. "You can."

I rest one hand on her hip, the other sliding to her waist. She's warm through her jacket, alive and here with me, and if I couldn't feel it myself, I wouldn't believe it, but she's trembling. Reese, stoic and sharp and steel, shaking under my touch.

"This way," I say, turning her parallel to me. Her body learning the shape of mine, and I swallow hard. "Keep your form, though."

She lifts the shotgun again, and together we guide it into place, my touch keeping her hips bladed, my head ducked close to hers. Her lashes are dark against her skin as she shuts one eye to focus her aim.

"There," I say unsteadily. "Perfect."

We hold there, her frame inside of mine, and then she relaxes. Just barely, and not all at once, but it brings her back flush against my chest. My heart hammering, beat after shaking beat roaring in my ears. I've never been this close to her before, never seen the scar on the side of her nose or the spot behind her ear where her hair sweeps away. It looks soft, tissue-thin, and I don't mean to, don't realize I'm moving, but I reach up and brush my fingertip over the vein that's just showing, barely blue.

Her head whips around. I snatch my hand away. Mouth open, panic rising. I can't believe I've ruined it. Pushed too far, and got too close, right when we were just starting to figure out how to be friends.

"Sorry," I choke out. Anything to get us back somewhere safe. "I shouldn't have."

She's just staring at me, breathing shallow and quick. The cold catching in clouds around her, shotgun dangling from her silver fingers. "What was that?" she says at last.

I managed three years without giving it a name. But there she is, Reese with her starlit hair and her wildfire heart, and I knew what to call this last night in our room, her face beautiful and strange in the dark. I knew the day I met her, when she looked at me like I was something she didn't understand. I've known every minute in between.

"Nothing," I say firmly. Nothing, nothing at all. I can close this door. I've had plenty of practice. "You don't have to worry about it."

"No, Hetty, you have to tell me what that was." She sets the shotgun on the makeshift table, never taking her eyes off mine. "You have to, because I feel like I'm losing my fucking mind."

"What do you mean?" I say, keeping my voice as light as I can. I can do this—I can pretend, explain everything away.

She's not falling for it.

"I mean you've been different with me," she says, and

I could swear she's blushing, but there's the stubborn push of her jaw, the fierce resolve that I know so well. "I mean, you've been looking at me like you finally noticed I'm here."

Like I finally noticed her? God, she has no idea. She really has no idea. "That's not—"

"So," she presses, ignoring me, "I need you to tell me what that was just now." A step closer, the cool shine of her braid washing over my skin. "I need to know if you're where I am."

My breath catches. She can't mean it, can she? I'm not used to this, to the tight bloom of my heart. It's been too long since I hoped for anything. "And where is that?"

"Here," she says. She reaches out, tangles our fingers together. Watching me the whole time, and she sounds so sure, so confident, but I can feel her shaking, just like I am. Like she's spent as long wanting this as I have.

And maybe she has. Every time she cut me down, every time I couldn't reach her, all because she wanted me, and she thought I'd never want her back. And if there's anything Reese does well, it's self-defense.

But I can see through it, now, and I know what we've done for each other, the concessions we've made, the slights we've swallowed. Neither of us able to let go, no matter how much the holding on hurts.

"Yeah," I say. "Yeah, I'm here too."

For a moment we don't move, and all I can hear is my heart marking time. Until Reese lets out a shaky breath, and then we're both laughing, leaning into each other, practically giddy with relief.

"Okay, good," she says, her silver fingers careful as she traces the line of my jaw. So soft I barely feel it, but I do, I do, and it lights me up like a match to paper. Our laughter falls away as the curve of her body fits to mine. She's still smiling when she kisses me.

So am I.

CHAPTER 10

Evening, and we're back up in our room. After leaving the barn we snuck the shotgun out to the spruce copse by the fence, buried it there under a layer of rotting leaves. Reese next to me like always, nothing different between us but the look in her eyes and the heat in my veins.

Now she's sprawled on my bunk, watching me as I pace from one end of the room to the other. Every inch the sun sets is another notch of dread, a spring coiling in my gut. Closer and closer, the gate swinging open and Welch taking Byatt out into the woods.

Out in the hallway the other girls are drifting upstairs, back to their rooms in time for bed check. We stayed in the spruce copse clear through dinner, neither of us speaking, the iron bars of the fence looming larger and larger. I'm not hungry—just thinking of food still makes me sick with guilt—but Reese's stomach picks that moment to grumble so loudly I can hear it from across the room.

I stop pacing and watch as Reese sits up, takes the leftover jerky from breakfast out of her pocket and crams most of it into her mouth.

There should be more food here for us, I think, trying not to flinch. And there would be if I hadn't helped Welch on the pier.

When she sees me watching, Reese swallows thickly and holds out what's left, barely a bite. "Sorry," she says. "Did you want some?"

I let out a wheezing laugh. This is ridiculous. Welch took my best friend from me, and here I am still keeping her secret. "There's something I need to tell you," I say.

And then I describe it as simply as I can. The bags, overflowing with food in its strange packaging, and the way Welch rested her hand so casually on her gun as she asked whether she'd made the right choice. Reese's mouth goes slack as I talk. Dark eyes looking up at me from the bed, wide and incredulous.

"You're serious," she says when I finish.

I nod. I haven't told her about the chocolate, but I can't see what good it would do. And some part of me wants to keep it for myself. "Yeah," I say. "And we just tossed it over." She doesn't say anything, just stares out the window, fists clenched, and I feel a gnawing in my gut. I can't have ruined things with us. Not already, not before it's barely even started. "Are you angry?"

She scoffs. "Of course I'm angry."

"But I mean with me."

She looks at me then, and tentatively hooks her fingers through one of my belt loops. How could I have missed it? The warmth in her eyes, just mine and nobody else's. "You didn't have much of a choice, did you?"

It shouldn't, but it makes me feel better.

Outside I can hear Julia making her way down the hallway, stopping at each room for bed check. Reese and I exchange glances, and by the time Julia pokes her head inside our room, we're side by side on my bunk. Right where we should be, two girls following the rules.

"Three," Julia says, and then she coughs delicately. "Sorry. Two."

I stare at the floor after she goes, let my world narrow down to the slivers of dark between each floorboard. Welch will go out to the Harker house in a few hours, and so will we. Picking our way through the woods, breaking the quarantine. Fighting for our lives and Byatt's too.

I can do this for her. I have to.

Reese's cold, scaled fingers close around my wrist. The dark deepening around us, and when I turn to her, the aura of her hair is skimming over our skin, the pattern of her braid playing on the ceiling.

"You should get some rest," she says, so gently I barely recognize her. "You'll need it out there."

"I can't." Out the window, the moon is rising, and I only have the memory of how it lit the sky last night to mark the hours. I choke back the worry throttling me. "What if we miss it?"

"I'll stay up." The mattress shifts as she moves, and she drapes her jacket over my shoulders. "Go on."

At least if I'm asleep, I can't worry over what we're about to do. I let her urge me back, toward the wall, and stretch out on my side, leaving half the bed open for her. They're narrow, the Raxter bunks, built only for one, but I've shared one with Byatt since the first day of the Tox. I'm used to it.

Or I thought I was. Reese lies down next to me, her shoulder pressed to my chest, and it's nothing like that. Nothing like Byatt, whose body felt almost like my own. I can feel even the slightest spot where I'm touching Reese, can hear every breath she takes like it's the only sound in the world.

"Okay?" she says.

"Yeah."

I settle in, tuck my face against her neck. Close my eye, hope I dream about Reese, about this afternoon in the barn.

Instead, it's Byatt waiting for me, and I take her by the hand, lead her into the woods. There's no light, but somehow I can see as I stitch her into her shroud.

BYATT

CHAPTER 11

I told a story when I was ten years old.

It was just after summer break. My best friend was a girl named Tracy, whose clothes were always freshly ironed, and when Tracy got back from summer break, she told me she'd met a new friend at camp.

I didn't go to camp. I didn't meet a new friend.

So I told Tracy something else. I told her I'd met a girl named Erin, Erin who rode horses and swam all year round. She goes to a different school, I said, and she lives on my street, just a few houses down.

And I wrote letters and told Tracy they were from Erin. And I had my picture taken with my horrible cousin, and I showed Tracy, told her it was Erin. And then one day I told her Erin wasn't at home anymore. I told her Erin's mother had said Erin was sick. And the day after that, I dressed in black, and I told Tracy that Erin was dead.

Tracy cried. And she cried to her mother, and she cried to our teacher, who took me to the counselor's office and asked what had happened. And I told the whole story over again. Because I liked—I *like*—to see what I can do.

I blink, and my mother is at the window, there is a window, and my mother is there in blue like morning.

"I thought we were past this," she says.

We were and sometimes we still are, but there is a gnawing in my heart I cannot get out. The window shuts and disappears, and my mother gets taller and taller.

"We're very disappointed," she says, her head brushing the ceiling. "Disappointed disappointed disappointed."

Usually, it was an accident. A lie I never set out to tell. A trick I never meant to play. I'd open my mouth, and something strange would come out, new and not mine. Like there was someone else inside.

I'm sorry, I'd tell my parents, whenever something I'd made came crashing down. I never wanted to hurt anyone. And sometimes I meant it.

But sometimes I didn't. Anger, depthless and black, and I couldn't cut it out of me. Growing and growing until it was all I had room for.

Go to Raxter, my mother said. Start again.

And I tried. But we all have things we're good at.

I don't miss talking. I thought I would, but it's so easy this way. The smallest word written down, and they'll build a version of me in their head. Sounding just the right way, meaning just the right thing. Half my work done for me.

When Paretta comes back I see her shape through the curtain around my bed. I see her stop in the doorway, and I see her hesitate. Like she's remembering what I did. But then she's pulling back the curtain, and it's the same patched-up blue suit, the same faintly patterned mask. I wonder if they have any spares, or if the other doctors had to stitch up the tears I scratched in theirs.

"Good morning," she says.

My hands are strapped down. Can't reach for the whiteboard Paretta props against the bed, can't do anything but give her a thumbs-up, and I certainly won't be doing that.

"Do you know what a resonant frequency is?"

I raise my eyebrows. What a way to start the day.

"It's the frequency at which a particular object vibrates," Paretta explains. She sounds uncomfortable, like she's not used to putting anything so simply. "When you match an object's resonant frequency, it can break. Like a glass, if you sing the right note."

I clench my fists, wishing she'd let me use my whiteboard. I don't understand why she's telling me this.

"Most everything has one." She looks at me for a long moment. "Even bone, Byatt."

I swallow hard. Remember the pain shattering through me, shaking me apart. Me, and Paretta, and anybody else who heard me scream.

"There's nothing," Paretta says softly, "that ever hits that frequency hard enough to make it hurt. Nothing but you and your voice." She reaches out and rests one gloved finger against my throat. "What is it doing to you, sweetheart?"

I don't know, I want to say. *You tell me.*

Instead, she steps back, the sadness sweeping out of her eyes as I hear her clear her throat. "I'd like to show you something," she says, waiting briefly for an answer I can't give. "But I think you can understand why I'll need your word that we won't have a repeat of the other day."

I nod, because what else is there to do, and she bends over me to unbuckle my wrists. This close she smells like sweat, like salt. I can see patches of dry skin at her hairline, a mole at the corner of her eye.

I'm not strong enough yet to stand on my own, so Paretta has to help me into a wheelchair. Shivering out from under the blankets, legs bruised, toenails broken. Our bodies never seemed odd at Raxter, but here, I pull down the hem of my hospital gown, sit up straight to hide the second curve of my spine.

She tucks the whiteboard in alongside me, folds my fingers around the marker, and then pushes me out of the ward. I try to hang on to everything, every turn we take. The small lobby we pass through, pale squares on the wall where something must have hung, and the hallway Paretta wheels me down, shabby carpet and stale air. But they slip in and out of my head, and I'm not   I'm not I'm not   as here as I thought I was.

I think I might throw up. Fold over, press my hands to my forehead, and I feel the brush of Paretta's suit against my shoulder, but it's barely anything. I shut my eyes, try to disappear.

When I open them again I'm somewhere else. At first I don't know what I'm looking at, and then I blink and it separates out, floor from ceiling. Stacks of boxes, carts of folding chairs, and everything covered in thick plastic tarps. The floor is the same peeling linoleum as everywhere else, but carved into the walls are two deep alcoves. Empty, but lit like something used to be displayed inside.

I reach for the whiteboard, hold it up in front of Paretta to get her attention before I write.

What is this   where are we

"Some of it's storage," Paretta says, which doesn't really answer my question, but I think it's all I'll get. She wheels me down a narrow path between two shelving units, each draped over with clear plastic so thick it looks cloudy. Here, another part of the room, this one almost like a lab, two tables set up with equipment I don't recognize. On one table I think I spot the remains of a Raxter Blue, shell broken up in bits, but we turn away, and Paretta wheels me up to another alcove cut into the wall, one I didn't see from the doorway.

This one is layered with earth, built up more than a foot deep, and blooming there, in this room, in this building, is a quartet of Raxter Irises.

Tears prick at my eyes, and I blink, startled. But I miss it. I miss Hetty and Reese, but more than anything, I miss the dawn coming through the trees. I miss the north side cliff and the waves below, and I miss the way the wind steals your breath like it never belonged to you in the first place.

I'm reaching out to touch one of the flowers before I realize it, and Paretta snatches me back, her suited fingers catching my wrist.

"That," she says, "would be being a bit silly, I think."

Why do you have these, I write.

Paretta spins my wheelchair around so I'm facing her. I wish she wouldn't. I miss the sight of the irises already, the familiar indigo, the satin drape of their petals.

"We've been studying them," Paretta says, crouching down in front of me. "The irises, and the blue crabs too. All of this is something we're calling the Raxter Phenomenon."

A phenomenon. Not a sickness, not a disease. It burns through my heart—that's the word I've been looking for—but there's something about the way she says it. The name too familiar, too easy on her tongue.

"Did they teach you about Raxter Blues at school?" she asks. "About what makes them special?" I nod.

You mean the lungs

"And the gills," Paretta says. "It's pretty amazing, right? So it can survive anywhere. And I think it's pretty amazing, too, that you girls are part of it now."

Part of it. The way our bodies alter and bend. The way our fingers darken just before we die, pure black spreading up to our knuckles. I used to stare at my hands in the dark, Hetty asleep next to me, and try to will them to change color.

"Imagine how we could use this." Her voice is urgent, confiding. "Imagine the people we could help."

I think of the bodies we've burned, of the pain we've endured.

I don't think it's helping anyone right now

"Right." She rests her gloved hand on my knee. "You're absolutely right. To help anybody with this, we have to be able to cure it, to control it. And to do that, we need to understand why it's happening."

Good luck with that

She shakes her head, and I think I can make out the shadow of a smile through her mask. "I know," she says. "I've been studying this for years now, Byatt. First the Blues, and the irises, and now you girls, and I'm not any closer."

For years, I think, as she stands up and starts wheeling me over to the table where the crab is laid out in pieces.

She must mean she was here before the Tox found us. We learned in bio that the Blues were worth studying; it never occurred to me that somebody actually was.

She positions me in front of the table, still talking about something, but I don't hear her. There's the Raxter Blue splayed out, limbs snipped from its body, shell carefully set to one side to lay the inside bare. I wait for my stomach to turn, but instead, all I can feel is the sea spray from that day on the rocks with Hetty, the crab turning black in my hands. It was still alive as it broke apart.

I wonder if I will be too.

"I have something special for you," Teddy says. The clock tells me afternoon but not the day. Same blue plastic suit, the same surgical mask. I like his eyes, I think. They look like mine.

First the left strap undone, then the right. Whiteboard in my hands, a cramp in my fingers.

Good special?

"Is there any other kind?" he says. "We're going outside."

Seriously

"Seriously."

Why outside

"Dr. Paretta wants a little more color in your cheeks." Teddy draws back the curtain. Ward awry, beds pushed to one end. "She suggested a walk. Outside was my idea. Close your eyes, though. I want it to be a surprise."

Teddy, eager and happy to help, and invisible to the doctors here, with their world narrowed down to my charts and me. Breaking rules, because nobody's told him what they are.

I start to push myself up, but he rests a hand on my shoulder. "I'll help you."

He lifts my legs. Swings them around to hang off the bed. Hands cold through the suit, hair on my legs static and standing.

My jacket is stuffed in the cabinet against the wall, and Teddy helps me into it, does up the clasps before crouching down to lace my boots.

"Right," he says once he's finished. "We're all set. Need some help getting up?"

I shake my head and stand up. I think I'm getting stronger. Even if I'm not, I don't need help.

I carry the whiteboard, marker in my pocket. Teddy takes my hand. Guides me out and around three corners. I memorize them, lay them out in my head. When he says I can open my eyes, it's in front of a narrow, dented door. Not all the way closed, and through the gap at the bottom I see grass just starting to die.

"Go ahead," he says, and helps me lift my hand to open it.

Wind pulling at me, whipping the hem of my hospital gown. So cold I know it'll steal the feeling from me, but I won't mind.

"Deep breaths. Nice and easy."

I nod. Try not to gulp it down, the air, the spice and sweetness. Together we step out and let the door creak shut behind us.

A fence, the kind with wire across the top to keep you from getting out. Trees pressed up against it, their branches curling through. Between it and me, the ground is restless, cresting and breaking in small hills, splitting where the cold has reached deep. Turning brown and brittle.

"Come on," Teddy says. "Let's walk."

My bare legs prickle with goosebumps, sweat chilling me to the bone, but we keep going. The closer I get, the clearer the fence is. Step, and step, and a give in my knees, and Teddy wraps his arm around my waist. At last, there with the forest encroaching. I wind my fingers around the chain link.

Camp Nash. It must be. If I squint, I can make it look like Raxter, like home.

Teddy says something. World too loud. I prop the whiteboard against the fence.

Can't hear, I write.

He tries again—fuck, he says, it's freezing—but I pretend I don't hear, shake my head. Reach out, flick the fabric surgical mask over his face. I want him to take it off.

"No way."

We can go inside
If you want

"Hey, don't be like that. We're having fun out here, right?"

I learned when I was little. Quiet. That's how to get what I want.

"You know I'm really not supposed to." He waits. Then a sigh, probably, and he backs up a few steps. "Okay, but you stay over there."

Because he is nineteen, because he isn't thinking. Because I've practiced this smile enough times to know what it can do.

Teddy reaches behind his head, to where the mask ties, and fumbles with the knot until it drops. And there he is. Full lips. Jaw cut sharp. Teddy.

"Byatt."

I wave, and he grins. I lift the whiteboard, prop it on my hip as I write.

Can't I come say hi

"No," he says immediately, holding out a hand to ward me off. "You promised."

I didn't actually, and I make sure I look just right, a little shy, a little curious.

"Look," he says, "I know it must be lonely in that ward all by yourself. I'll try to come hang out more, but I—"

I hold up my hand, and his voice falls away. *Not the same,* I write. And then, when his eyes widen just that little bit, I add:

You can't catch it

He lets out a bark of laughter. "Is that true?"

Of course not. But I want what I want. *No boys allowed*

He's thinking, biting his lip as he frowns at me, and then I see his shoulders drop like he's let out his breath. Whether he knows it or not, he just gave up.

I take a step. Take another. He doesn't say a word. Watches me, and when I see his fingers flex—they look ridiculous through that suit, but I won't tell him that—I know I have him.

His mouth is slick and dark. I can see a nick on the slope of his jaw, can see the speckled blood he must've forgotten to wash off. I close the distance between us, lean my face in close to his. A piece of my hair slips loose, blows forward. Sticks to his bottom lip. I watch his eyes flutter shut.

It's simple. It's nothing at all. I inch that little bit closer, tilt my head up, brush my fingers against his chin, and guide his mouth to mine.

He kisses like he's afraid of me. And he is, but I don't think I mind it.

When he steps back it's not far, and he wraps my hair around his fingers, his other hand brushing my hip. I can tell he wants to ask. It's in every glance, every touch that's barely there.

I lean the whiteboard up against his chest, and he laughs as I try to write upside down, so he can see without letting go of me.

Go on

Ask

"Ask what?"

I give him a look, roll my eyes, and he smiles sheepishly.

"I'm just wondering about what exactly it does to you."

I take his hand from where it's resting on my hip and slide it around to my back, where the ridges of my second spine are clear even through my jacket. His eyes go wide as he feels the curve and spike of new bone.

"Shit," he says, and I smother a laugh. "Do all of you have that thing?"

I shake my head. *Some of us just die*

"But I mean—"

I know

I write a list. Mona's gills. Hetty's eye. Even try to draw Reese's hand, and there are a hundred more flare-ups I can't remember from a hundred other girls. It startles me, seeing it all laid out. How the Tox models us after the animals around us, tries to change our bodies, push them further than they're willing to go. Like it's trying to make us better, if only we could adapt.

"That sounds scary," he says when I finish, his eyes wide, face solemn, and I can't help laughing.

I guess   hard at first

"And then?"

And then. Hetty and Reese and someone needing me. A wilderness in everyone, like the one I've always felt in me. Only real this time. In my body, and not just my head.

Not so much

"They'll figure it out." He touches my cheek, plastic

169

glove catching on my skin. "Whatever the Tox is, they'll fix it."

Movement in the woods, a bird taking flight. He jerks around to look. I can't see anything but blood, flaking off his skin in the wind.

Let's go back in

Back in the ward, in my bed. Curtain drawn, jacket and boots off. Hands free, whiteboard wiped clean.

"Dr. Paretta will be by in a minute," he says. Winks as he draws his mask up, ties it tight. "If she asks, you thoroughly enjoyed doing laps of your room."

When she comes it's in that same blue suit, and she's carrying a stack of files and a pad and pencil, along with a tripod and a camera. Her hair is all dark and shine, and there are deep lines around her eyes. I wonder if there are matching ones under her mask, at the corners of her mouth.

"How are you this afternoon, Byatt?"

Shrug. *Fine*

"We've been easing back on your dosage of diazepam. I hope you haven't been in pain."

Shake my head. Point to the whiteboard.

"It was very helpful talking to you yesterday. I'd like to ask you some more questions, if you'll let me." She rests the camera on my bed and begins to set up the tripod. "Now, I know this will be a little unconventional. Normally,

I'd take notes in an interview like this. But since you'll be writing things down, this might be easier." The tripod stable, she slots the camera into the stand.

What do I do

"I'll ask you some questions, and you just answer me and show the board to the camera. Simple as that."

Screen flips out, red light blinks on. Paretta sits down on the bed by my feet and props her notepad up on her knee.

"Before I get to the disease in particular, I noticed something in your chart—a bit of missing information. Can you tell me about your cycle? Has it been regular during the quarantine? I know stress and nutrition can have a big impact on these things."

We lost them after the Tox

Paretta leans forward. "That's very helpful, actually, Byatt. What about those of you who hadn't hit puberty before the quarantine?"

It never occurred to me, really, to wonder. But nobody ever complained when the supplies came without tampons or pads.

I don't think they ever got it

"But they exhibit symptoms of the disease, don't they?"

Yeah

"And your teachers?" There's a glint in Paretta's eyes, an eagerness to her voice. "Do they present those symptoms the same way you girls do?"

I guess I don't know for sure. But something tells me

neither Welch nor Headmistress is hiding a spine like mine under their clothes. They're sick, I know that. I've seen the sores on their skin, seen their eyes glassy and gone when the fever hits. But not like us.

Not the ones left

"And they would be your headmistress and who else?"

Miss Welch

And they're the ones closest to normal, aren't they? They're the ones who should be here, and I should be back in my room, Hetty next to me, holding on so tight it steals my breath.

I gesture to the room around me, let some bitterness into my smile. *You should use them for your cure*

Paretta reads the board, and I watch a frown furrow her brow. "We do want a cure, Byatt," she says after a moment. "But there are so many more questions to be answered. I'm sure you understand."

I don't

She keeps going like I didn't write anything at all. "I have records of only one person on the island having been assigned male at birth. A Daniel Harker?"

Reese's dad. I nod. I'm not sure what else she wants from me. If she wanted to know about Mr. Harker, she should've picked Reese.

"How did he react? Like you girls?"

And the thing is at first he did. Angry, like some of us. Violent, like some of us. But most of us keep hold of ourselves, and he was on the way to losing it when he left.

No

That's the most I can pin down.

"Interesting," Paretta says. She fumbles with the pad of paper, and I watch her jot something down. Most of it too hard to read, but I see the word "estrogen," and above it, "adrenal," a word I think I remember from some lecture on puberty in sophomore bio. Maybe that has something to do with the way the teachers died, instead of giving the Tox a home like we do.

"This might sound strange," Paretta starts, after staring a beat too long at her notes, "but is your headmistress . . . past a certain age?"

Like we can't just say "menopausal." Headmistress canceled at least two assemblies during my first year because of her hot flashes.

Yes

"And I'm correct," Paretta continues, "that none of you were receiving hormone replacement therapy, yes?"

As far as I know yeah

But I remember one of the lectures Welch gave us when she found a condom in Lindsay's care package. Be prepared, she said, and know your options, and an IUD might be right for some but for others—

Wait is the pill

She's flicking through the stack of files before I can finish writing. "Charlotte Welch, twenty-six. Ah, I see. Prescribed birth control for hormone management." She glances up at me, smiling wryly. "I'm guessing she's had limited access to that medication, which could definitely play a role."

Why are you smiling? I want to ask her. *That limited access you find so funny is your fault.*

"Right," she says, closing the medical file. "We'll have to look into that. Now, as to the rest, I'm here to learn as much as I can from you about the outbreak. The more I know, the easier it will be for us to figure out how to treat it."

Do you know what it is

A hundred questions, but that one's the most important.

"We're not sure," Paretta says. "Our tests haven't turned up much. We've never seen anything quite like it. You girls have such varied symptoms."

You girls, she says, like it's not something worth talking about. I keep my face blank, file it away. Let her think I haven't noticed. Better yet, let her think I don't care.

"We do know, at least, that it's not airborne," she goes on, "and it can't be contracted off contaminated surfaces, which has helped with containment. But we need your help to know more. So, Byatt. Let's start with before it happened."

Before what. Before I got there, before Raxter changed, before I ever found it on the map.

Here is Boston in my hand, spilling between my fingers. Brick and stone and a handful of streets eating their own tails. I walk and walk and lose my way and always come back.

And in the other hand, Raxter. No ferry on the horizon, mainland far and farther. Water and shoreline born new every day. Everything what it wants to be. Everything mine.

I'm buried there no matter where I go.

"Is there anything you can think of in the lead-up? Anything off, different?"

I shrug. *It was normal I guess*

Hetty told me something, though. *Some girls had a fight at breakfast the day it started*

"What kind of fight? They argued?"

No like hair pulling

But I didn't see

"Okay. And who got sick first?"

Mostly seniors I think and then teachers

Your age

Paretta snorts. "I won't ask how old you think I am." I start to write, and she laughs outright, holds her hand up over her eyes.

Born yesterday

"How kind."

For most of the teachers, the end came quick. Our nurse was ancient—I think she died even before the Tox got to her—and a few of the others went out into the woods and never came back. To spare food for the rest of us, that's what the note they left said. But the rest, women my mother's age, gray just starting to thread through their hair, they died like it was a fever. Just dropped, their fingers not even turning black like ours.

"And how many of you girls would you say are left?"

The stack of files is looming. So many names, so many girls long gone. I stopped counting after a while, pulled the borders of the world in tight so only the three of us were inside.

Maybe 60 but not sure

"Your friends? Hetty and Reese? Are they okay?"

I never said. I would never say. I let the warmth drain away, jaw set, eyes narrowed.

How do you know them

She waves a hand. "We know all of you."

There it is again. Said lightly, like it's nothing, but the pill she gave me was labeled "RAX009." And if I'm 009, will one of my girls be 010?

No. They're mine, and I'm not letting them go.

She's fine

We're all fine

I know Paretta wants more. She can't have it.

You've asked questions my turn

Paretta shifts on the bed, almost uneasily. She looks like the therapists my mother used to send me to when they realized I wasn't going to open up the way they wanted. "Sure."

Why me

I'm watching her closely, and when she smiles at me, I can spot the sadness underneath.

"I'll tell you the truth, Byatt," Paretta says. "There's really no reason at all."

I think she expected me to be hurt. But it's a relief more than anything else. I'm not special. I'm not immune. I'm not better at fighting this off, and that's good, because I don't want to.

Right place right time?

"Sure." She gets up. "Something like that."

It was Mona who started it for me. She came down from the infirmary and I couldn't believe it. Couldn't believe she was still alive. I asked how she was and I asked what had happened, and she barely said anything.

I was going to leave when she laid her hand on the inside of my arm. And then, in a wry voice: "They'll ruin it."

When I turned around I saw Headmistress talking to Hetty. Watching me.

That night, after Gun Shift, after Mona's flare-up, I snuck out of the bunk I share with Hetty. When I came back I told Reese I'd gone downstairs, and she was Reese, and she didn't ask, and I needed it that way because it wasn't true.

Really, I went to Mona's room. Her friends had moved in together and left her alone, so she was sleeping in the single at the end of the hall. Her door was unlocked. I went in. There was barely any light from the window, but I could see her prone on the bottom bunk.

"Hey," I whispered. "You still alive?"

She didn't answer, so I went over, shook her until her eyes opened. She looked awful, the gills on her neck fluttering slowly, their edges frayed and bloody.

"Go away," she said.

Instead, I knelt down in front of her. I wasn't going until I got what I wanted. "What did you mean? In the hall this morning."

She sat up. So slowly, like it was the hardest thing, until at last she was looking at me, her legs crossed underneath her, red hair shining so dimly I almost didn't notice. She took a long breath, and by the end of it, I thought she'd forgotten I was there. But then she reached up, ran one shaking finger over the scalloped lips of her gills.

"You'd keep it," she said. "If you could. Right?"

I couldn't pretend I didn't know what she meant. Hetty cried when she lost her eye, and I even caught Reese sometimes looking at her scaled hand like she'd rather just cut it off. Me, I never minded. Bled, and screamed, but that's the cost of sleeping easy.

"No," I lied. "Would you?"

She looked so tired. I almost felt bad for her. "Go to bed, Byatt," she said.

But I couldn't face my room and my bunk, so I went downstairs, wandered the length of the main hall, walking the cracks between the boards. And I thought about Mona, and I thought about me, and of course I would keep it.

Because I think I'd been looking for it all my life—a storm in my body to match the one in my head.

That's where Welch found me. I told her I had a headache, and she felt my forehead, led me up to the infirmary, and took my blood—for good measure, she said, just in case—and then sent me back to my room. And when I got there, I climbed into bed with Reese, Reese who wouldn't force a lie out of my mouth.

If I hadn't spoken to Mona. If I hadn't left my room that night. There are a million ways coming here doesn't happen, but none of them feel possible. I was always on my way. This has always already happened.

CHAPTER 12

"**A**nd how have you been feeling?"

I shrug.

"No stress? Anything you felt a particularly pronounced emotional response to? Because you've been through quite a lot."

I've never seen this woman before now. She came in after Paretta. Didn't tell me her name, just pulled a wheelchair over to my bed and sat down like the room was hers.

"Is there something you're uncomfortable with?" she asks.

She's dressed the way Paretta usually is, that same protective suit and a surgical mask. Only her mask is clear plastic. So I can feel connected to her, I think, but it only distorts the bottom half of her face.

"Byatt?" she says, leaning forward.

I look away, hunch over the whiteboard. *I'm not uncomfortable,* I want to write. *I'm just bored.*

Instead I settle for   *No*

"No?"

Not uncomfortable

She nods, sits back. I stare down, at where the covers are pulled up over my legs.

"Do you know my name?" she asks.

No

"Would you like to?"

I point to the whiteboard.

"Why not?"

I keep my mouth closed, just blink at her slowly, and she nods like it means something.

"What about what I do?" she asks. "Would you like to know that?"

You're a therapist

"How do you know?"

I roll my eyes.

"Have you been to one before?"

What do you think

"Let's try something else," she says. I know her. Brand-new, but I've met her a thousand times. This is how they look at me when I don't give myself away.

She lifts up her clipboard, hands me a thin, bound book she's been holding underneath. Navy, with gold embossed lettering. I recognize it. A Raxter yearbook. The last one we made before the Tox, the only year I had whole.

I fumble for the whiteboard.

How did you get that

181

She doesn't answer. Opens it, flicks through it slowly. "This was your first year at Raxter, yes? The year before the Tox?" I shrug. "You're not in here very much."

Don't like pictures

"Oh, look. Here's one." She holds the book out to me, and I take it, rest it on my lap.

It's me, Hetty, and Reese, sitting in a row on the couch in the main hall. Hetty's facing me, telling a story or something, and Reese is perched on the arm of the couch behind me, in the middle of braiding my hair. She's smiling—only a little, but it's there—and I have my eyes closed, my head tipped back as I laugh. It could almost be Raxter the way it is now, but the couch is plush and full, and in the background a vase of Raxter Irises sits on the windowsill.

"Who are they? Your friends, I mean."

I bend closer to the page. Hetty's eyes are warm, wide with joy. I'd almost forgotten what she looked like with both of them working.

"That's Hetty, right? Hetty Chapin? And that would be Reese Harker."

I shut the book as the therapist leans in, tuck it under my whiteboard. Another of Paretta's crew, asking questions about my friends they have no good reason to ask. I won't let Hetty or Reese be the next girl in this bed.

Why do you want to know

She tilts her head as she sits back, folds her hands in her lap.

"You're protective of them. I understand. It's all right, though, Byatt. They're safe. Miss Welch and your headmistress are taking care of them."

Something inside me snaps its jaws. I lunge out of bed. Too fast, head reeling. The therapist is watching, one hand on the call button at the end of my bed. For emergencies.

"Byatt," she says, "I need you to sit back down."

The world winnows down. Blurred, shifting, except for the pulse in her neck. I can see it beating. Blink and I'm braced over her. Blink and she's pressing the call button and an alarm is blaring. Blink and my knee is wedged under her ribs, her forearm gripped tight in my hands, the suit ripped open. Blink and my nails bite through.

"Byatt!" somebody yells. "What are you doing?"

Somebody's arms lock around my waist, and I'm hauled back, into the air. Slammed to the floor, head aching. The therapist is clutching her arm to her chest, blood streaming from it in ribbons. Marks, twin curves, buried deep in her wrist. My mouth is wet and sticking.

I start to smile, everything around me so bright and new, and then it's gone, and I'm alone again. Someone's hand comes down across my mouth. A prick in my shoulder, and then black.

The crack of a slap to my face, to bring me back. I gasp hard.

"Get her out, let's go."

Above me, light and flicker. I'm in my bed, my arms strapped to my sides again. My eyes are starting to clear, shapes turning to people, and Paretta's is the first face that forms, leaning over me with a snarl.

"Get her legs."

Somebody presses down, binds my thighs together. I convulse, something in me thrashing desperately as the straps notch tighter. Another strap at my hips, another at my ankles. My wrists. And for the first time, one at my shoulders, and they're reaching up to my forehead and my jaw.

I squirm, try to slide down so there's more slack across my hips, and Paretta reaches down, slams me back onto the bed.

The strap hasn't come down over my chin yet, and I throw my head from side to side. I'll scream, I'll do it, and it'll hurt all of us, but better that than only me.

"Don't let her talk!" Paretta shouts. Somebody behind me grabs my head in both hands, and then it's Teddy, Teddy's face, and he's stroking my hair.

"It's okay," he says, over and over. "Relax. I've got you."

It's almost all right. But I know what to look for, and I can see it coming. The heat in his cheeks. The way, just for a second, he looks afraid.

It starts with a heave in his body. Rolling up through him, sweat breaking fresh on his forehead. And then a shiver that won't stop, and he crumples over me, drool dripping down his chin. He rips off his mask, spits something out, and it lands on my chest. A chip of something white, shining. Bone.

"Teddy. Oh my God." Paretta is with him in a second, helping him stand, but his limbs are collapsing one by one.

"Teddy, can you hear me? Teddy!" And they've forgotten about me, they've left me on the bed with the restraints loose enough that I can twist over and see where he's on the ground. Eyes all the way white now. Little tremors running through his body.

And then he's on a gurney, and they're taking him away, and me, I'm still here.

HETTY

CHAPTER 13

I wake to the sound of my name and Reese shaking me lightly. My skin is damp, sweat soaked through the back of my shirt, and my throat hurts, like I've been trying not to scream.

"It's time," she whispers. Around us the house is quiet, no sliver of sound from the other dorms to puncture it, and the moon is so high I can't see it out the window. We must be past midnight. Sun won't hit the sky for a few more hours this time of year, but the lawn is glassy and bright with frost. We should be able to see well enough in the woods without a flashlight.

We get up, moving slowly to keep our footsteps soft. I hesitate at the door to our room. Right now, Byatt's alive. That's what I know. If I go out there, I'll be taking that thought in my hands, bending it to see if it breaks.

"Ready?" Reese says behind me.

Byatt's alive. She's alive and she needs me now, like I've always needed her. "Yeah."

Out the door and down the hall, Reese with her hood drawn up over her hair to keep the light in, and walking so close I can feel the backs of her fingers brushing against mine. Nobody else is awake, or if they are, they're being quiet, so we make it past the other dorms and out onto the mezzanine free and easy.

We crouch at the top of the stairs, my eye straining to find the girl usually stationed guarding the front entrance. I wonder if she'll help Welch take Byatt out to the Harker house or if Welch will do it alone.

I can't see anybody, even with the silver light streaming through the stacks of windows, but maybe it's just my blind eye, so I nudge Reese. "Where is she?"

"I don't know," Reese says. I look back, and she's frowning. "Someone should be on duty."

"She must have changed the schedule." We both know why, even if we're not saying it—Welch doesn't want anybody seeing what she's about to do. An advantage for her, but for me, too, and I'm not about to pass it up. "Let's get outside."

I stand and take the first few stairs slowly, my eye struggling to make edges out of the dark. Step by step, Reese at my elbow, until we hit the ground floor. And still nobody—no guard girls to catch us, no sign of Welch. Are we too early? Or too late?

Reese opens one of the double doors, and I slip outside

after her, hesitating under the porch as the chilled winter air burrows into my jacket. I have a feeling the Gun Shift girls have been pulled off duty just like whoever was supposed to be guarding the door, but I can't be too careful.

Gun Shift always keeps a lantern lit after sundown. I wait as Reese tugs her hood tightly over her hair and ducks out into the night, peering up to the roof deck.

"Nothing," she says, clouds of her breath drifting in the dark. "We're good."

All of this happening in secret. I can't think about what that might mean for Byatt.

Out, then, along the flagstone path and to the spruce copse by the fence. Reese waits for me as I dig for the shotgun with numb fingers, frozen dirt clumping under my nails. Right where we left it, and I should be glad, but I never wanted any of this. Not a gun in my hands, not the life of my best friend on my shoulders.

For a moment I wait, think of the note pinned to the bulletin board in the main hall. Keep the quarantine, they said. Follow the rules and we'll help you.

A knife in my belt, and the shotgun in my hands. A year and a half of empty sky, of not enough medicine, of bodies burning behind the school. We have to help ourselves.

At the gate I go first, open it as gingerly as I can to keep from cutting my fingers open on the shards of glass we've bound to the bars. Anybody can open it from the school side of the fence, but it will lock behind us when we leave, with the key hanging from Welch's belt the only way back in.

"You sure about the north edge?" Reese says. She means my plan for getting back home. Not really a plan so much as our only option, but I'm pretty sure we'll be able to boost ourselves up over the fence where it hits the cliff on the north side of the island.

"As sure as I'm getting," I say, and it has to be good enough. There's no other choice.

Reese leads the way as we head out into the pines. Trees clustered close, needles a carpet of green rot, wet and sweet. Even though the island's changed, even though I'm the one who's been out in the wildwood since it turned strange and cruel, I think she still knows it best. We're all Raxter girls, but not like Reese.

Sometimes she'd tell us about the island. About the secret places she'd found—the beaches you could only get to at low tide, the trails through the spindlegrass. She'd tell us about her father waking her up in the middle of the night and taking her down to the rocky shore, to see the waves glaze the stone with a bioluminescent glow, a cool white like the light of her hair. Those first few days back at school after summer break she'd stare out the window, still freckled and tanned, a look in her eyes like she was trapped.

If only it were like that for me out here. Instead, everywhere I look, there's something to be scared of.

Every noise an animal coming up behind us. I shoulder the shotgun and remind myself I only have two shots to take.

We're in deep enough that I can't see the fence if I look back. Above us, the canopy letting only the barest stripes of moon through. I want to ask Reese to take off her hood, to let the light off her hair show me the path, but we can't risk being seen by Welch, or by whoever she's heading to meet. So I stick close to her, trust that her eyes are making more sense of the dark than mine.

In the distance a branch cracks, and we stop, press ourselves behind a pine and wait. Welch, maybe. Or something else, something worse. My heart racing, nerves alight. Whatever it is, we're safer in the dark than I was that day on Boat Shift. We must be.

"Hey," Reese whispers. She's crouched low, leaning around the tree trunk. "I think it's okay."

What could be okay out here? "Really?"

"Yeah." She stands up, beckons to me. "It's just some deer."

I peer around her shoulder, and there, ambling toward us through a patch of moonlight, a pair of bucks. From here they look fine, almost normal, but up close, I know I'd see their veins raised out of their skin like patterns of lace. And I know if we sliced them open, their flesh would twitch like it's still living.

When I was on Gun Shift we'd shoot them like the other animals, like anything that got too close. To be safe, that was what Welch told us. But they are only deer, and I always wondered what they could really do.

"Let's go," Reese whispers. "They look harmless."

I shake my head. "Not until they pass."

"Fine," she says too loud, and their heads swing around, considering the shadows with eyes washed over white. I hold my breath. Maybe they're blind.

We're not that lucky. One of the deer takes a hesitant step toward us, and as it opens its mouth, I gasp. Incisors long and gleaming wet, sharp like a coyote's.

"The gun," Reese says, trying to sound calm, but she's hitting my arm, dragging me out in front of her. The deer cocks its head. "Shit, Hetty, get the gun."

"Someone might hear the shot."

She scrambles back. "It was your idea."

Just like on the roof, I think. Like I always used to do. The shotgun snug against my shoulder. My eye squinting through the sight. Even in the dark it's not a hard shot, but the deer's moving now, coming closer, and I only have the two shells.

"Reese," I say. "We should've stolen more ammo."

"What?"

I take the shot. The recoil sends me stumbling back, but I hit home, the shell striking deep into the deer's flank. It wails, back legs collapsing, and behind it the second deer darts a few yards into the trees, fur bristled and raised.

The deer thrashes weakly, crumpling with a whimper as the wound begins to ooze, blood pooling thick on the frost-covered ground. I step closer to its prone body, and it lifts its head. I swear it's looking right at me.

"What do you think?" Reese asks. "Put it out of its misery?"

"No," I say. There's no room to feel bad. If I feel that, I have to feel everything else.

We continue on into the gloom. When I look over my shoulder, the second deer is back in the moonlit clearing, standing over the first with its head bent. I watch as it rips a bite out of the wounded deer, coming away with a mouthful of flesh, blood staining the white fur on its throat.

I should be surprised. But I only feel a flicker of recognition. We're all like that on Raxter. We all do whatever it takes to survive.

I balance the shotgun on my shoulder and keep after Reese. We're not far from her house.

It took until spring of my first year for Reese to invite us over. We'd spent third-quarter break on campus, all three of us together—Byatt didn't want to go home, so I didn't either—and when school started up again Reese was easier somehow. Still never smiling, still quiet and closed, but at lunch she started letting me cut ahead of her in line. In English she lent me her copy of *The Scarlet Letter* when she saw I'd lost mine, said she'd read it already even though I knew she hadn't.

One night she showed up to dinner and she wasn't wearing her uniform. We were supposed to wear skirts and collars from sunup to sundown on weekdays, but there she was, jeans and a ratty old sweatshirt, and she said, "Thought we'd eat at my place."

We followed her out through the double doors, down the walk to where two bikes were leaning against the fence. I never had one, never learned to ride, so I waited and tried not to look anxious as Byatt climbed onto hers. I remember wondering if they'd leave me behind. Reese hadn't technically invited me. She hadn't named names.

"Come on," Byatt said. "Get on the handlebars."

"People only do that in movies," I said. But I straddled the wheel, eased myself onto the bars.

It was starting to stay light out in the evenings, and as we flew down the road there was sun everywhere, glare reaching in off the ocean. I wanted to be the girl who closes her eyes, tips her head back. Instead, I asked Byatt to slow down.

Reese's house backed onto the beach, low-slung and weathered, like it grew up out of the reeds. As we got nearer I could see a dock behind the house, stretching out into the waves, and two rowboats bobbing at their mooring. And on the front porch, waving to us, Mr. Harker. Tall, broad. Hair trimmed neat, like my dad's Navy cut.

"You made it," he said, and came down the steps to help me off Byatt's bike. It made me nervous, I remember, seeing him so close up. We saw him through classroom windows, and we saw him across the grounds as he mowed the lawn and cleaned the gutters, but this—a man, his calloused hand on my arm. I forgot I could be afraid of them.

It's only a moment, though. A prick in the cloth. We went inside, to one long room, the whole of the house right there at our feet. And the food smelled good, better than the dining room food, and there were photos of Reese on the wall. Reese learning to swim. Reese halfway up a tree, grinning down at the camera. I couldn't take my eyes off her the whole night. It was like she made sense, finally, in her father's house, with mismatched furniture and the back door thrown open.

"I hope the place looks okay," he said to us when Reese took the plates to the kitchen. "We don't have much company over."

"It looks great," I said, and I meant it. I never missed my house much, but that night I did.

Afterward, Byatt and I waited at the end of the driveway while Reese said goodbye. She was leaning in, saying something I couldn't hear, and then Mr. Harker laughed and laid his palm against her forehead.

Byatt looked away, but I didn't. I watched Reese smile, watched her roll her eyes. "Still fits," I heard him say.

My own father, tour after tour, day after day of being gone. We never knew each other like that.

Sky streaked rose, stars faint and new. We were quiet the whole ride home.

I have that day fresh in my mind, the image of her house so clear. Pale green siding and white trim, windows only just installed. New shingles on the roof—repairs after that year's hurricane.

We crossed the road a while back, to the north side of the island, and I can tell we're getting closer to the shore. Under our feet the ground is damp and full of give, and I can just catch a whiff of salt in the air. I adjust the shotgun where it's balanced on my shoulder, flex my fingers to work the feeling back into them, and we keep going.

As the trees start to thin out, the light builds, moon gilding everything silver. Still no sign of Welch. We pick our way through the pines as they turn slender and leaning, until there's a break in the tree line, and the shore opens in front of us, a wide plain of reeds. Out past the end of them I can see something skimming low across the water.

"Is that—"

"The dock," Reese finishes. "Yeah."

No boat moored there, and nobody on the horizon. For now, I think we're the only ones here. Surely we'd have heard something if we weren't, or seen some sort of light. After all, Welch has nobody to hide from, and neither does whoever she's meeting.

It's easier to follow the tree line than to fight through the brush, so we walk the edge of it, cattails snagging on our clothes. I'm thinking, still, of that first day, of the house as

I remember it; that's why I don't understand when Reese stops, why I stumble into her. We aren't there yet.

But I look again, and we are. Moonlight bouncing off the water, a haze of sea spray as the waves crash in that settles on my skin in a fine, freezing mist and steals the breath from me. And there's the house, or what's left of it, twisting up out of the reeds.

The porch, listing to one side like it's taken a punch. Floorboards cracked, a hole yawning, lichen crawling up the walls. Siding covered in moss and trailing ivy. And in the middle, out of the heart, roof splintering around it, a paper birch, growing on its own. Trunk broad and splitting, branches reaching high.

I glance at Reese. Her whole face open and bright, a softness to it that I almost remember from the first days I ever knew her. "It's beautiful," I try. And I mean it, I do. "I've never seen a birch that big."

But then, everything grows faster after the Tox. And everything falls apart faster, too, the Harker house practically in pieces after a year and a half alone out here. I wish I were surprised. I wish any of this were still strange to me.

Reese doesn't say anything. I don't think she's blinked since we saw the house. I tuck the shotgun under my arm and nudge her elbow with mine.

"Do you think they're here?" I whisper. "I don't see any light." Not to mention there are so many gaps in the wall that I can practically see straight through the house to the other side.

She still doesn't answer me. Just stares at what's left of her house. I'm wondering if maybe it was a mistake to bring her, if this is too much for one girl to take, when she breaks for the porch.

"Wait," I hiss, but it's no use. I hurry after her, adjust my grip on the shotgun. Only one shell left, and only my knife for backup. I have to be smart.

Termites have gotten to the house. Their trails run labyrinthine across the doorframe, so deep it would've collapsed by now if it weren't for the way the birch has hooked one of its limbs underneath. Reese is already inside, so I duck through after her, part of the frame crumbling to dust under my hand.

Above me the birch splits and blooms, throwing down bouquets of silver light. Most of the roof is gone, slabs of it probably lost to the storms we get come spring. Instead, the branches soar like rafters, and roots weave through the floorboards, and I keep thinking of the cathedral I went to in Naples, on vacation with my dad during his leave. How the whole place felt like it was lifting me off my feet.

A voice, suddenly, and a flashlight beam comes lancing through the shattered walls, splashes across the ground. Welch is here.

Fear breaking over me like a sweat, the shotgun slipping in my numb grip, and I grab Reese's arm, drag her out the back of the house. We stumble, trampling a patch of Raxter Irises under our feet. Ahead of us, a thin strip of beach, and the dock off to the right. Welch is meeting someone, and they could come from anywhere. We could be caught any second, thrown onto our knees and shot.

Get it together, I think. We're here. There's no going back.

"Come on," I whisper to Reese. There's a clump of pines back in the tree line that should keep us hidden.

We get there just in time. I crouch down, my muscles stiff and hurting. Lay the shotgun across my knees and peer between the tree trunks at the house laid out in front of us. The flashlight beam is getting stronger, catching some of the reeds, turning them translucent. I squint, my blind eye throbbing. I think I can make out the shape of a person, but whoever it is they're bent over, moving slowly. Is that Welch?

"Lift your end higher" comes Welch's voice. I jump. She sounds so close. But who is she talking to? Byatt?

It feels like forever, but finally Welch steps out from the last of the trees, into the moonlight. She's hunched over something, and there's someone else with her, their face in shadow until they straighten, and it's Taylor. Taylor, who left Boat Shift, and I guess this is why.

And between them. Carried between them, a body bag.

I clap my hand over my mouth, muffle the whimper that slips out of me. No. No, no, no. This isn't how it's supposed to go. We're gonna make it, she said. She promised.

Maybe it's not her, I think wildly. Or maybe they

knocked her out and she's alive in there, waiting for me to save her. I can't give up until I know.

"This would be easier with a third, you know," Taylor says as they set the body bag down among the reeds. It's not moving. Whoever's inside isn't moving, and I can't let myself think about what that means.

"Oh?" says Welch. "And who are you going to ask? Carson's a pain in the ass, and Hetty's not an option."

But before I have a chance to wonder what that means, Taylor says, "How's she working out?"

I go rigid. This is it. If Welch knows I'm on to her, everything's over. My life here, this new thing with Reese that I'm nervous to name.

Welch just shrugs. "Well enough," she says, and I muffle a shaky sigh of relief. "But not well enough for this."

"What about Julia, then?" Taylor says.

"I'd rather not." For a moment Welch sounds as young as she is. "I don't think she likes me very much."

Taylor lets out a laugh. "If you don't like Carson, Julia doesn't like you."

"I missed you out there," Welch says. She turns off the flashlight, shoves it into her jacket pocket. I watch her pause to spit out a mouthful of what must be blood. "It's not the same without you."

"I can do more good this way," Taylor says. I want to shake her for it. There's nothing good about this. "After what happened to Mary . . . She deserved better, you know? They all do."

Mary, Taylor's girlfriend, who went vicious and wild like the animals. Taylor was the one who had to kill her, and the rumor was it broke her. But now I know it didn't. It just made her into something worse.

Welch steps back to the body bag, and for a second she stops there, hands on her hips, looking down at it. Moonlight skittering off the ocean, throwing her face into shadow, and I can't make out her expression, but there's a slump to her shoulders, almost like defeat.

"I really thought we'd got it right this time," she says at last. "You know? She seemed like she was okay."

"Well," Taylor says, "evidently she wasn't."

I knew, of course I knew, the body bag motionless in the grass, but it's something else hearing it out loud. The pines around me hemming in, closer and closer, and Taylor joking like it doesn't matter, like she hasn't just torn the whole world down. Reese pulls me against her chest, holds me tight. It's the only thing keeping me together.

"All right," Welch says. "Let's finish up."

They pick up the body and Reese grips my hand as we watch them carry it into the house. Pain shoots up the inside of my arm, a sparking and twitch, and I try to pull away until I realize it's me, holding on to her so tightly her scaled fingers have cut deep into my skin.

"Come on," Reese says, her voice cajoling in my

ear. "She's alive, right? She's Byatt. She gets through everything."

I nod, but there's somebody in that body bag, and I don't know how much longer I can do this. How much longer I can keep hope burning in my heart.

I lose sight of Welch and Taylor as the house swallows them up, and then I catch a sliver of Welch's face through the gaps in the walls, the beam of the flashlight bouncing off the white bark of the birch.

"Let's put her down," Welch says, "before my arm falls off."

I bite my lip to keep myself from calling out. *Her*. This is real.

"Where are they?" says Taylor. She must mean whoever was on the other end of that walkie call.

"They'll pick her up," Welch says. "We can leave her here."

"What about—"

There's a fizzing sound, and then the house bursts with red. Through the holes torn in the wall I can see Welch holding a flare, the bloodlight harsh and sparkling. "This should keep the animals back," she says. I shift to one side to get a good look as she wedges the flare into the branches of the birch.

I hear Taylor's voice from inside the house. "Is that it, then?"

A pause, and I squint into the dark. Welch is facing the birch, peering at something on its trunk. She's quiet for a beat too long, and then she turns back to where Taylor must be standing.

"That's it," she says. "Let's get back."

"Wait," Reese whispers, like she knows I'm only a few seconds away from dashing into the house and tearing open the body bag. "Just a little longer."

Welch comes tramping out of the house, with Taylor close behind. Taylor looks like she's about to be sick, and against my will I feel a pang of pity. Maybe she didn't ask for this. But then neither did I.

They head off down the path, and I track their flashlight beam through the trees. Smaller and fainter, until I can't see it anymore. I stand up, branches cracking underfoot. I don't wait for Reese, just snatch up the shotgun and make a break for it across the reeds. I don't know how long we have before the others show up. I won't lose my chance.

Into the red light of the house. There's the body bag, tucked at the base of the birch, black plastic and rubber. I stop short, the shotgun falling to the ground.

This is it. The end, or something starting.

Carefully, I step around the edge of the body bag and kneel down next to it. Think of the last time I saw Byatt, how I bent over her just like this. How she looked at me like she needed me.

Please, I think, and I reach for the zipper.

The plastic peeling back. The zipper catching, my hands shaking, and there, there—pale, sallow skin, ink-dipped fingers, and curling red hair.

Mona.

A sob shatters out of me. I pitch forward onto my hands, gasping. It's not her. Not her not her not her.

"Hetty?"

Reese comes up behind me, lays a hand on my back. I close my eye. My whole body trembling with relief, and I think if I stood up, my legs might collapse under me.

"It's Mona," I say. As sorry as I am, I can't hold back a smile, and I don't want to.

"Shit," Reese says. "Where the hell is Byatt, then?"

She crouches down next to me and starts zipping Mona back up. But I'm not watching Mona's bloated face disappear. No, I'm looking at something else. There, on the trunk of the birch tree, where Welch was looking before she left.

I stand up, step over Mona's body. The bark is curling, light from the flare casting long strange shadows, but I can see it. Carved faint and unsteady, but I recognize it. *BW*. Byatt Winsor.

"She was here," I say. It's the best thing in the world, relief sweet and soothing. "Look. She was here, and she was alive."

I wait for Reese to tell me I'm wrong, to remind me how things usually go, but she doesn't. Just rests her chin on my shoulder, her cheek tilted against mine. The birch bark is smooth, and my fingers leave trails of blood behind from where Reese's silver hand punctured my skin.

"Do you think she misses us?" I say. I'm aching for it, for the day I'll hear Byatt tell me she wanted to come home as much as I wanted to find her.

A moment, and then Reese steps away from me, into the shadows. I turn to face her. Of course she misses us— that's all Reese has to say. But she only looks at me and doesn't say a word.

I raise my eyebrows. "What?"

The flare light catches on the curve of her mouth as she smiles. "You don't really want an answer to that question."

"No, come on." Maybe I'm goading her. But I can't stand the way she's looking at me, like she knows something I don't. "Say it."

"I just . . . I guess you know a different Byatt than I do," Reese says, shoving her hands into her pockets. "Because I'm not sure she ever missed anything in her life."

"We're her best friends, Reese." I blink back the sudden sting of tears, feel them catch and freeze on my eyelashes. She can't be right. What has all this been for if Byatt doesn't want to come back to us? "Her best friends. Don't you think that matters to her?"

"Well," Reese says, and there's an edge to her voice, a warning, "let's not pretend. It was the two of you and then me, and that's fine. Because people are messy and that's how it goes. But let's not pretend."

Shame curdling quick, because she's right, and I hate that I'm proud of it, proud of how much closer I got to Byatt than she ever did. But I'll never tell her that. "I think it's pretty selfish of you," I say instead, "to be pissed about that when Byatt is God knows where, suffering through God knows what."

"I'm not pissed." She shrugs. "It's just true. That's all."

I should never have brought her. I should have known she wouldn't understand. "Why are you even here?" I snap. Around us, the patchwork walls of the house pressing in, the birch looming, Byatt's initials traced in blood. "Why did you come at all?"

Reese doesn't answer. But I can hear it all the same. Everything about her—the sorrow buried in her eyes, the tightness of her mouth—all of it screaming the same thing:

For you, Hetty.

It's too much. I can't even say I never asked her to, because I did—I did, over and over again. I'm doing this for Byatt, and Reese is doing this for me.

Fuck.

"I need some air," I say.

I stumble out the back of the house into what used to be a small square of yard. Around me, Raxter Irises, their stems crumpling underfoot, and I think of the vases full of them that we kept everywhere at school, their petals blackening as they fell, of the dried bouquet tucked up among the pictures on the mantelpiece of the Harker house. Her parents' wedding bouquet, Reese told me that first day we visited. Even after her mom left and they cleared out all the pictures, she kept that.

Was it really so clear to her? That it was me and Byatt first, and her second? Even with how badly I've always wanted Reese closer, that didn't change the fact that Byatt was the one who waited for me at breakfast every morning. Byatt was the one who cut my hair and showed me which side to part it on. Byatt was the one who put the bones in my body.

I drop down onto the porch, cradle my numb hands to my mouth, and breathe the feeling back into them. Byatt is what matters right now. She's the only thing. Soon the people on the other end of the walkie will show up to collect Mona. Wherever they take her, that's where Byatt will be. And I'll find a way to get there.

I'm expecting Camp Nash, where the Navy and the CDC are headquartered. And it turns my stomach to think of Byatt taken off Raxter. I never knew her off the island. The closest I ever got to it was that day on the ferry across from the mainland, when I first saw her, sea laid out behind her, and Raxter on the horizon, her hair unfurling in the wind. When I find her on the mainland, will she still be my Byatt?

A noise from inside the house. I leap to my feet, grab the shotgun. Somebody's talking, somebody who isn't Reese.

I barrel into the house. Nobody here but us.

"You heard that?" Reese says, and I nod.

"Welch coming back, maybe? Or someone from Camp Nash?"

"It sounded different," she says. "Familiar. I don't know."

"There." I point out through the shattered walls into the trees, where something else is moving, coming our way. The shape of a man.

CHAPTER 14

I raise the shotgun. Too dark to see a face, but there's something familiar about the build of him, something that stays my finger on the trigger.

"Hello?" I call.

No answer, but he's closer now, almost to the house. I can imagine it as he steps up onto the porch. The shape of him warped by the old glass in the windows at Raxter. The sound of his voice over the hum of a lawn mower. And then he's through the doorway, a soft creak as he crosses the surviving floorboards, and he's lifting his head and there's a tear in his shirt and a cut on his cheek, but I know him. Even in the dark, I'd know him anywhere.

"Dad?" Reese breathes.

It's Mr. Harker.

Until he eases into the red glow of the flare light, and it isn't anymore.

"Oh God." My voice sounds strange, muffled and far away. "Reese, Reese, I'm so sorry."

Because it's his face, and it's his body, but I don't think anything else is left. His skin bleached and pulling, his mouth sprouting roots. Branches burrowing in ears and under fingernails and slinking down his arms. And unblinking, eyes still his, pupils blown wide as he watches us.

More than a year out here, alone with the Tox. What did we expect?

"No," Reese is saying. I grab hold of her arm, haul her back a few steps. She's barely on her feet, and she stumbles, collapses to her knees. "No, no, Dad."

But he's not here anymore. "We have to go," I say. "Come on, Reese. Now."

He looks at me, cocks his head as he opens his mouth, takes a long, rattling breath. Black, splitting teeth, and a nest of green at the back of his throat. The air musty and sour, so pungent I can taste it.

I lift the shotgun, get ready to aim, but Reese shoves me away, looks up at me with a feral light in her eyes. Behind her, Mr. Harker advancing, step by step, vines unspooling from his mouth.

"Don't you dare," she says, and her voice breaks open, raw underneath.

"Please," I say. "We have to run."

It's too late. A vine writhes up Reese's legs, along her spine, and another curls around her arm, jerks it back. A cry, and a crack of bone. Her right shoulder pops, hangs wrong in its socket.

I lunge for her, grab my knife from my belt. Slash once, twice, at the vines holding her. Mr. Harker shrieks, rears back and drags her with him.

"Hetty!" Reese yells.

The shotgun. But when I fire into the heart of him, it makes no difference. He only roars and pulls tighter on Reese's arm, winds a vine around her throat and starts to squeeze.

I could run. I could save myself and get back past the fence, back to the house. All I've got is my knife now. And what good is that against Mr. Harker?

But there's no choice to make. I break for him. Duck the thickest vine as it swings around, feel the thorns rip down my back, and there he is. I crash into him, and we tumble to the ground. Dirt in my mouth, the scrape of bark against my skin. My knife knocked from my hand, and I scramble for it across the damp earth.

A vine locks around my ankle, yanks me onto my back. I graze my knife with my fingers, but it's too far—I can't—and he's pulling me away.

"Reese," I call. "Get it!"

But I can't find her, can't see anything but the looming dark as Mr. Harker bears down and his bruised hands, spongy with rot, close around my throat. I thrash, try to throw him off me, and his grip only tightens. Branches snake around my waist, holding me down. And one slithers up my neck, wrenches a scream from me as it hooks around my jaw and pries my mouth open.

It's bitter on my tongue, and I'm choking, scrabbling at Mr. Harker's bloated face. His skin peels off like strips of paper, gathering under my nails, soft and pulpy.

"Hey!" I hear Reese yell. For an instant the pressure lessens, before Reese's silver hand flashes above, the knife deep in his shoulder, and she slams into her dad, sends him reeling back onto the ground.

"Quick," I say. "Pin him." But Reese is just looking at him, her mouth open. She's no use, not anymore.

I throw myself down, trap Mr. Harker's ribs between my knees and pin him to the ground. He roars, muscles straining, and he's looking at me, I know he is. Me and Reese's dad, face-to-face.

I cry out as his body surges up. The bristle and spray of branches, thorns scoring a gash down my arm. I get a good grip on my knife. Pull it out of his shoulder and plunge it into his chest, flesh splitting and rising like foam. Bile bubbles up between my lips, trickles down my chin as I work the blade, widen the rip in his skin.

"Don't," Reese cries from behind me.

But I can't listen. It's not him anymore. I lean hard, brace my hand on his elbow as I wedge the knife deeper and deeper and start to lever it up. There's a heart to all this. There has to be.

Blackened blood weeping down over my fingers, knife blade duller than I thought, but I've got a seam opening in him, and he's getting weaker. Smaller roots are snapping, breaking away. At last I rip the knife out, toss it aside and dig through his shredded skin.

He's rotting from the inside out. Tissue mottled with mold, the smell so sour and stinging that my eye is watering. Something scuttles up my jacket sleeve, first one and then another, and another, and in the red light of the flare I make out the gleam of a hundred wingback beetles crawling out of the wound.

I choke back a yell, and before I can move, a vine slinks up my back and knots around my neck. Squeezing tighter and tighter, splinters jabbing sharp, pain spilling across me in waves. But he's weak now, blood pouring out of him. I grip the vine and break it in two. Fling myself back at him, his face pulling apart as his mouth opens wider and wider.

I shove my hand deep into his chest again, bear down with my whole body until I hit what I think is bone. But a glimmer of the flare light, and they're not bones. They're branches, spindled ribs curving and cresting. I hook my fingers underneath them. Wedge my knee under his chin and pull, inch by inch.

Until finally. A snap. And inside his rib cage, I see it. A beating heart, glossed in blood. Built from the earth, from the bristle of pine, and inside, there is something else, something more, something living. I don't think twice. Just claw at it with both hands, and it comes screaming out with a wet tear.

Mr. Harker's eyes close. Everything goes limp. I let the heart fall from my shaking hands and bend to one side to throw up.

When I'm finished I sit back, spit slick down my chin. I wait for the guilt, wait for the gnawing in my stomach. After all, I know that feeling. Since Boat Shift, since Byatt, I'm starting to think I'm built for it.

But Mr. Harker is dead, and I'm not, and the guilt doesn't come. I did what I had to. I kept us alive.

I get to my feet, my legs unsteady, hands numb as I find my knife and slip it back into my belt loop. We made it. If this was the worst the wildwood could throw at us, it might be okay in the end.

When I turn, Reese is there, her right shoulder hanging at an angle that makes me dizzy. "You okay?" I say. "We should fix that."

She's looking past me to the wreck of her father. "You killed him," she says. Her eyes hollowed out, her face drawn and pale. "You really did."

She's in shock. That's all. She'll come back, realize there was no other way. "I had to save us," I say as gently as I can. "I'm sorry, but—"

"He's dead." Voice flat, everything that's her stripped out of it.

"It was us or him." She doesn't answer, so I step in close, push her braid off her injured shoulder. It doesn't look all the way dislocated, but when she tries to move it out from under my hand, the color drains from her face and she gasps. "We should take a look at this, yeah?" I say softly.

"I'm fine," she says, even as she sags against me, and I watch her close her eyes, feel her shaking. "I had him back," she whispers. "I thought he was gone, and then I had him back."

"It wasn't him."

"He knew me." She opens her eyes, and when they meet mine the accusation in them is clear and sharp. "You took him away."

"He was going to kill us," I say, frustration building. I had to save us. Why doesn't that matter to her?

"Better me than him," she flings back at me. "Better us than my father."

I don't know this version of her. Even at her angriest, Reese is always contained, always whole. But this girl, this Reese in front of me, is in pieces. Edges torn, heart scattered.

"That's ridiculous," I say. "I was supposed to let you die? I was supposed to sacrifice myself? Reese, that wasn't even your dad anymore."

She pushes me away, injured arm hanging uselessly by her side. "No. It was him. He was here."

"He wasn't." And my patience is gone, bled out of me. "Look, you don't get to put this shit on me just because you're angry at yourself."

"For what?" A stillness, suddenly, about her, and I know she's waiting for me to make a mistake, to say the wrong thing. Well, fine. Have it.

"Angry at yourself for helping me kill him." She looks stricken, but I don't stop. "I'm not the only one who held that knife."

Nothing, for a moment, and then she smiles and says, "Fuck you, Hetty."

My mouth drops open. She's hurt me before, but until right now, she's never seemed like she wanted to.

"If this is what I get for saving your life," I say, "I should've let him take you."

She laughs, a horrible flatness to it, and I wait for her to stop. But she doesn't. She bends over, braces her silver hand on her knee, and the sound keeps coming, ripping out of her like Mr. Harker's heart from his chest.

"Reese," I say, because I need this to stop before it turns to something worse, but before I can say anything else, a noise rumbles through us. The growl of a motor coming nearer, and fast. We both startle, Reese's laughter cutting off. It must be whoever Welch was supposed to meet.

I make for the back door and peer outside. There's a boat drifting in at the dock, motor idling, and in it the ballooning shape of a person, proportions strange and obscured by a hazmat suit. Like the doctors who came that first week of the Tox, who took our temperatures and took our blood and disappeared into their helicopters and never came back.

"Shit," I say, hurrying back to Reese. I grab the shotgun, tuck it under my arm. "We have to get out of here."

Through the gap in the wall I can see a billow of plastic

as the person in the hazmat suit climbs out of the boat. If we don't move now, they'll see us, and they'll know we've broken the quarantine. And everything will fall apart.

Reese shakes her head, stumbles away from me. "No," she says. Stubborn like always—at least that part of her is together. "I'm not leaving him."

"Someone's coming," I say, and she's being so unreasonable, and I'm talking too loud but I can't help it. "We have to go."

"I can't." She's looking at her father, laid out on the ground, his chest open, heart still oozing next to him. Black teeth gleaming darkly in the red light. "He's all I have. I can't just—"

I snap. Lock my arm around her waist and drag her away, back toward the door. At first she fights, scratches at my hand with her scaled fingers, and it hurts, but we have to go. Doesn't she understand? We have to leave.

We stumble past the birch tree, past Byatt's initials carved there, and at last she finds her feet, and we're running—out of the house, into the woods. Through the pines growing tight and narrow, pushing farther and farther into the green. I can hear something behind us, but I can't look, can't do anything but keep on, the shotgun jabbing me in the ribs as we stumble forward. Crashing through the brush, loud and leaving a trail. Branches catch on my hair and pull at my clothes, and we'll look like a mess when we get home, but we'll get there. We will.

Eventually, we hit the road, the broad stretch of it a

familiar relief. It's still dark, and we're far enough from the house that nobody can see, so I stop, and turn to scan the woods behind us. No waxy gleam of the hazmat suit. No sound but us.

"I think we're okay," I say. Reese doesn't answer. When I look down she's dropped to her knees, clutching her injured shoulder and biting so hard on her lip I'm surprised it hasn't split. "I thought you said you were fine."

"I am," she grits out. Her breath coming slow and labored, her face paper white in the moonlight.

I don't try to help her. The sting of her words is still fresh, and I got her out of that house, after all. That's enough for now. "Get up. We have to make it back over the fence."

We can't go through the gate, so we're heading for the north edge of the island, where the fence ends in great brick columns at the lip of the cliff. We'll have to scramble up them and over the fence, back onto school grounds.

I know where we are now, and Reese is in no shape to be leading anybody anywhere, so I shoulder the shotgun, bend down, and pull her to standing. I'd carry her, but even if I could, I don't think she'd let me.

"Come on," I say. She's heavy against me as we stagger down the road.

There's light snatching at the sky by the time we hit the fence. I can't bring myself to look up at the roof deck. If somebody's on Gun Shift, let them shoot us now and get it over with. But nobody does, and we follow the tree line where it presses up against the fence, branches yearning and straining through the iron bars, follow it to the edge of the island.

Sea spray whipping at my skin. Pines pressing close on one side, the fence on the other, and out ahead the earth falls away. Just the cliff, granite worn by the wind, and a twenty-foot drop to the water below. I glance up at the house. Every window dark, no lantern on the roof deck. Nobody's up looking for us. And nobody out on the horizon, either—the ocean empty and endless, waves breaking in ranks.

The fence ends right at the lip of the cliff, forming a T with a thick brick column so big, so close to the edge, that there's no way around it. Not for us, not for the animals. But there are scratches and teeth broken off in the mortar. It's not like they haven't tried to get through.

Slowly, I drag Reese over and prop her up against the brick column. She's pale, her eyes glazed and staring.

"Hey," I say, shaking her lightly. I smooth my hand along her cheek, her skin too cold, too pale. Shock, maybe. I remember the sound her shoulder made, the way she screamed. She needs more help than we can afford to get her. "Come back," I try. "Reese, it's me."

She blinks, slow like it's the hardest thing she's ever done. "I'm so tired," she croaks.

"I know. One last push, okay?"

Here, the iron bars and the brick hit at a right angle,

and there are enough breaks worn into the brick that we should be able to find a few footholds to boost us up and over. I help Reese stand and turn her around.

"See?" I say, pointing to one spot on the column, about knee-high, where some animal's torn a chunk out. "Climb up. I'll spot you."

Her right arm limp by her side, useless and wrong, but Reese is stronger than anybody I've ever met. And even after everything, she braces her injured shoulder against the fence, wedges her foot into the crack in the brick, and levers herself up with a muffled scream. Her scaled left hand scraping the mortar loose, and I watch with a strange sort of pride swelling in my chest as she pulls her body over the fence.

She's left scoring in the brick, and that makes it easier for me to follow her. Soon I'm jumping down from the top of the column and landing with a groan on the battered lawn. School-side, this time. We're home.

Reese staggers to her feet with a whimper. Even the glow of her hair seems dimmed, like the whole of her is draining away.

"You go upstairs," I whisper. "I'll put the gun back in the barn and meet you there."

She nods, and I think she's about to say something—an apology, maybe, for what she said at her house—but then she's turning around and drawing up her hood, the shape of her disappearing into the dawn.

It was so easy sneaking to the barn that I kept looking behind me, waiting for Welch to step out of the shadows and press her pistol to my forehead, yet nobody came. But if that was easy, this, Reese—this is the hard part.

She's in our room when I get back, sitting on my bunk, clutching her injured shoulder, and for a second I just watch her, watch the play of light on her skin. It was her life that fell apart out there, not mine. I have to be the one to put us back together.

"Hey," I say. "You okay?"

She chuckles, shakes her head. "Okay?"

"Sorry. Stupid question." At least she's talking to me. I come farther into the room, shut the door behind me. "Let me do something for your shoulder."

She doesn't answer, so I step around her and reach for my pillow. It still has a pillowcase even though most of the others got stitched into makeshift blankets. I peel the pillowcase off and start ripping down the side seam.

"I don't think it's popped all the way out," I say, but that's not why she's angry, and we both know it. "I'll make a sling, and you can just rest it for a bit."

I help Reese cradle her right arm against her chest and loop the pillowcase around. I bend over her to make a knot in the sling, and freeze when I feel her let out a shaky breath, her forehead leaning against my chest.

"What the hell happened to him?" she whispers.

"I don't know," I say. "He was out there a long time."

And, I want to say, he's not like us. The Tox swallowed him whole the way I've never seen it touch a Raxter girl.

I take one more moment, brush my thumb against the nape of her neck, and then I drop onto the bed next to her. "Maybe we can get you a real bandage tomorrow. Or some painkillers."

She doesn't answer. I'm not even sure she's breathing. I can't let her disappear into herself. I can't let the Tox win.

I reach out, rest my hand on her knee, and squeeze. Just to reassure her, just to remind her I'm with her. But she flinches away from me.

"Reese?"

"Don't," she says, and I jerk back as she lurches to her feet, scrubs at her face with her silver hand. "Don't do that."

"I'm sorry. I should've asked."

"I mean all of it," she says, and when she turns to look at me, it's like I can see it, the mask of calm she's wearing and the anguish underneath. "You have to stop, Hetty."

"Okay," I say, holding up my hands. We just need to calm down, and we will figure out a way to fix this. "It's okay."

"It's not," Reese snaps. "It's not fucking okay." She sounds so resigned, so close to giving up, and I feel a bright flare of panic, because I can't lose her too. "I don't know how any of this is supposed to work after what you did."

And no, I can't lose her, but there are only so many ways I can explain this. Only so many times I can justify keeping us alive before I lose my grip.

"There was no other solution," I say. I'm struggling to keep steady, my fists clenched so hard I can feel my fingernails biting deep. "It was him or us, and I made the only decision I could."

"So, what," she says, acid dripping from her voice, "I don't get to be mad that my father is dead? That the Tox ripped him apart so badly you had to put him down?"

I shoot to my feet, and I don't know what it is—anger or pure desperation—that has me so wound up I'm shaking. "No, actually," I say, "you don't get to be mad that I saved your life."

Reese narrows her eyes. I brace myself for whatever's coming next. I've never met anyone who likes fighting the way she does, never met anyone so good at it. But the silence beats on. At last she lets out a long, slow breath, tension draining from her shoulders.

"Do you think I want this?" she says. She sounds hoarse, and I can barely pick out one word from the next, every ounce of exhaustion crashing down on both of us at once. "We don't get to choose what hurts us."

My heartbeat thundering in my ears, the slow coil of dread tightening in my chest. Please, please don't be doing what I think you are.

"Reese," I start, but she shakes her head.

"I understand what you did. I think you did the right thing. And I'm still angry about it." She shrugs her good shoulder. "What else is there to say?"

For a moment I'm back there in the dark, my life in my

hands. There was no other way. It was kill or be killed. And it feels like tearing my own heart out of my chest the way I did Mr. Harker's, but I say, "Nothing, I guess."

She nods. My stomach clenches as I see a tear wind down her cheek before she swipes it away. "Right. That's what I mean."

The past few days I've seen her break open. Watching her now, I can see her closing back up. There the familiar remove, there the way she never quite looked me in the eye. All of it put back together as she says, "You can have the room. I'll bunk in one of the empty dorms."

She's waiting for me to argue. And if she were Byatt, I'd know what to say. I'd know the gap in her armor. But Reese doesn't have one.

"Okay." I'm proud when my voice doesn't break. But I can't let her go without making sure she understands. "I'm sorry," I say. "You have to know that."

Her hair the only light, features strange and unknowable like the day I first met her. She's gone. She's here but she's gone.

"Yeah, I know." And the door shuts behind her as she walks out.

BYATT

CHAPTER 15

They open the curtains and they wheel him in
	Gurney across from me both of us strapped in tight and I know who it is I do it's just I'm not here anymore
	A fog in my head I'm awash I'm at sea and I can't feel anything except when they stick me and bleed me
	Teddy that's who I forgot

No boys allowed I told him I kissed him I did I did I ruined him and I wasn't even trying to
	When will you learn my mother says to me
	She is by the window again she is watching me and she is wearing scrubs just like the doctors do as she winks in and out
	There are more important things than what you want she says

————

How are you feeling

Me and Hetty on the roof she's got a bandage covering her eye and we're pretending like she doesn't and I say how are you feeling and she says

Doesn't hurt so much

And I'm glad and then she looks over at me and it's taking a little to get used to her new face but she's used to it so I have to be too and she says

You seem all right Byatt

All right like not just all right but something more except I don't know what so I just shrug and

I guess

That's what I say

Light   my eyes tearing up they always do they're too sensitive I could never get my pupils dilated when I went to the eye doctor and somebody bending down over me blinking and sharpen and

Paretta

Shake my head try to get away but she says something I can't understand and then

Test they're doing a test

My arm is moving .

Try to put it back come back I didn't but no good   a hole   a tube and bright yellow hands pushing

Open my mouth to scream and scream but nothing comes out just a whisper of air and what is that in my IV it's clear it's coming down it's going in

I can't stop it

Pull tighten stretch and Teddy where is Teddy there is something in me cool and sweet

He is not here

I am not either

A soft wash

Waves

The beach at Raxter at the Raxter before the Tox

I'm alone but the kind of alone where you aren't where you can feel the other girls behind you running laughing chattering and it's okay that you're by yourself on the beach because all you have to do is turn around and there they'll be

But I don't turn around

In the water there's a crab still and bright and I bend down so my knees break the surface no canvas and denim just the plaid skirt all soft like I never stopped wearing it

The crab looks at me

I look at the crab

It floats up floats out of the water and lands in my
hands and it's dry

I'm dreaming I'm not really there and I know it but
I hold the crab up and I look in close at the gleam of the
shell and there I am reflected in tiny pieces

a hundred little versions of me

and they say "welcome home" and then

The crab twitching and its claws turning black slowly

Slowly and then the whole shell until the body black
the legs black my hands black my arms black

I try to let go but I can't and around me the water black
the shore black and if I let go I will disappear

If I lose this I will disappear

I know it the way you know things in your dreams

everything black everything everything and   oh

Awake

It's quiet at first. My head finally clear, the ward empty.
Nobody is coming. Maybe they have what they need, or
maybe they know they will never get it.

"Hey."

I try to lift my head, and there's Teddy, propped up in
bed. Skin dull and drained, but smiling, wearing a pair of
scrubs so white it hurts to look at him.

"They tried another cure," he says. "A virus that might
kill whatever you have, but your body fought it off."

I'm staring at the ceiling again when he says, "Whatever *we* have. I mean, whatever *we* have."

After a while he gets up. Crosses to my side of the room and undoes my restraints. No need for them now. We both know that.

"Okay?" he asks.

I nod. Open my mouth and tap my throat.

"Hang on." He finds the whiteboard in the cabinet. Gets in bed alongside me, helps me wrap my fingers around the marker, and we ask questions we will never have time for.

What's your last name

"What?"

You know mine

"It's Martin."

You know what they say about men with two first names

"No."

Me neither

It takes about an hour, I think, for the signs to come back. And when they do they turn him sweaty and make him shake. They draw dark lines under his eyes and they empty him out.

What hurts

He groans. Rolls up onto his hands and knees and vomits over the side of the gurney. Black liquid, something grainy to the texture. I put my hand on his shoulder.

"I'm fine."

But he isn't, and he never will be, and I reach under the gurney, press the call button with shaking fingers.

"It's no use," he says. "They won't come."

I don't ask how he knows.

It gets worse. He goes limp like his bones aren't in him anymore, like Gaby from the youngest year who never survived her first.

I kneel, help him take my spot propped up against the pillows. When I lay my hand across his forehead he pulls away.

I didn't think it would happen to you

He shuts his eyes and leans his head back. The skin of his throat is new and young, soft when I press my fingertips to the crest of his collarbones.

"Sure," he says, and it's the last thing for a long while.

I write them while he's sleeping. Over and over across the whiteboard.

I'm sorry I'm sorry I'm sorry I'm sorry I'm sorry

When he wakes up I show him, and I take his hand, press his palm over my heart. Beat and beat and at last he relents, and shuts his eyes, and slumps against me.

What I meant, what I wanted. They don't matter anymore. We're here, and that's the rest of our lives.

The second flare-up ties him in knots, and when it's over I can't touch him without feeling a static shock. He is crying. I feel like crying, too, but I know it would turn into a ragged kind of laughter.

I can see faces in the windows. Sometimes Paretta, sometimes a nurse whose face seems familiar, even behind her mask. They are watching. Waiting for it to end.

"Tell me something," Teddy says, the last of it wringing him out.

What

"Anything."

I think back to the day I met him. The questions he asked. I write down the price of milk. He tries to laugh.

"Something else," he says.

By the time the third flare-up comes, I have torn the bottom of my hospital gown to bits and used it to wipe bile from the corners of his mouth.

Someone is in the window and Teddy is lying down and I am next to him and my hand is cramping as I write out a joke I heard my father tell once. I notice his finger first. The index finger. A twitch, a pulling so small you wouldn't see it if you hadn't spent almost a year and a half on a roof looking for it. But I did.

It makes me scramble away and I wish it didn't, but I huddle at the far end of my bed, try not to make any noise. I remember how it can go. I remember what it makes you do when it doesn't want your body anymore.

His eyes flick open, glassy and bright. Beautiful, and for a moment he's just Teddy. Just a boy, but then he speaks.

"Hello," he says. Empty. No recognition waiting underneath.

He's trying to get up, trying to crawl his way over to me, and if he does, he will hurt me without meaning to. I am worried I will let him.

It is the strips from my hospital gown that do it.

They are long, and he knots them together, makes them longer. Smiling. His mouth open, something starting to move behind his teeth. Shadowed, delicate, and there—there—a vine crawling out from inside him to curl around his lip. Like the kind that slink across the fence at Raxter. Like the kind that drape from tree to tree.

His hands tying a rope like they aren't his anymore. And more vines, another and another, branching and winding in a black tangle, blood leaking from his mouth, from his ears. Reaching for me, like they're looking for a new home. I start to know what the rope is for. But I don't do anything. I sit so my legs are tucked under me. I watch the Tox go to work.

On his knees. A rope into a noose.

His eyes never close. His grip never changes. He is pulling right until the end.

CHAPTER 16

There is not enough difference between the white of the wall and the white of the floor. I am having trouble keeping them what they are.

There is a stain on what I think is the floor and it is a little ways away from my foot. I am watching the edges of it come and go.

There is a sound in the room. I am having trouble telling what it is.

This is with my eyes closed.

A cut on my left ankle, about as long as my thumb. A bruise rotting down from my right kneecap. Nothing on my thighs, only a tenseness inside them.

At my hips three indents in the skin where the strap has pressed. A patch rubbed pink on my ribs. The IV marks on my hand.

My wrists are clear since they started using the softer restraints. More bruising up by my throat. A red welt on my cheek from the branches in the woods at Raxter.

With my eyes open there would be more.

They come in to move the body. The body, that's what I'm saying instead of   you know.

Three people, their faces covered. They pick the body up. They put it in a bag.

"Did she do that to him?" one of them says.

"Nah," says the other. "You should've seen it. Kid did it himself. Not sure there was anybody home anymore, if you know what I mean."

That's what the Tox does when it doesn't want you. Like the twins, Emily and Christine. Like Taylor's girlfriend, Mary. *You were watching,* I want to say. *You must've seen.*

"How come she hasn't done it yet?"

"Dr. Paretta says it's her hormones. Says they help her get along with it a little better."

They carry the body out. I stay. I am sitting, and there is red on the soles of my feet. I'm not looking at anything. No, no, I'm not looking at anything. I will never look at anything again.

I expect them to move me. I expect them to put the IV back in my arm, to do up the restraints again. But nobody comes and nobody minds when I move to the empty gurney next to mine.

When I sleep, he is there.

When I wake, he is there too.

When it's my turn it is only Paretta. I roll over, close my eyes, but she uncurls my limbs and sits me up. An oxygen tank waiting by my bed, tubing and mask bright yellow.

"Well," Paretta says. "I'm awfully sorry."

Nothing to say to her. I just stare, and stare, even when she puts the whiteboard in my hands.

She sits down on the edge of the gurney. Teddy gone, and she is covered from head to toe, skin showing only around her eyes. When she reaches out I let her. Let her push my hair off my face, wipe the crusted spit from the corner of my mouth.

"I brought you something," she says. From one of the pockets in her plastic suit, she pulls out a Raxter Iris. A little bit crumpled, the stem splitting, but the petals are still blue. It's still alive. "You liked them downstairs, I think, so. Here."

She gives it to me, and I cradle it in my palms. Indigo drape and the barest spots of yellow hidden at the center. Hetty used to pick them for me during the summers and tuck them in my hair.

"Listen," Paretta says. "We can't stay here anymore.

There's Teddy, and something happened at your school, and our study's been ended. I'm sorry I can't help you."

I think she's waiting for me to absolve her. Instead, I close my eyes and hold the iris up to my nose. Sweet, and something of salt, of Raxter.

"All right," I hear her say, and the wheels of the oxygen tank squeak as she rolls it closer. "You just have to breathe, okay? It's as easy as that."

I keep my eyes shut as she slips the oxygen mask over my nose, tightens the straps so it stays in place. Doesn't bother strapping my hands down, keeps her touch gentle and soft. She knows there's no fight left in me.

A moment, and then a hiss, a valve releasing. I look at Paretta, and I make sure she's watching as I breathe deep, and I let it in.

It's like when you drink water for the first time in a long time, how you can feel the cold in your veins. Except it isn't cold, it's a fizzing kind of heat, catching and growing.

I won't mind ending this way.

Paretta gets up, and I think she's leaving when she stops at the foot of my bed. "Tell me one thing," she says. "If you can. I've been trying to understand how Teddy got sick."

I manage a shrug.

"Because nobody else did," she goes on. "And I can't think of anything he did differently."

Oh. I can.

Teddy taking off his mask, Teddy with his hands in my

hair, Teddy disappearing and something else taking root inside. I pick up the whiteboard, and I write:

I kissed him   *would that do it*

For a moment Paretta just stares. And then she laughs, only it sounds like something else.

"Good luck," she tells me, and turns quickly so I can't see her face. A click, and the door is shut.

Over the announcement system a woman says it's time to begin evacuation procedures. I can hear people moving, talking, all calm and measured. No panic. No rush. They've known this was coming.

A twitch in my legs, and a thrum running through me. Like a plane engine before flight, like the moment before a flare-up but bigger, so much bigger. My body shaking, my body pulling apart at the seams, and I close my eyes, but it doesn't matter. I can still see. I am still here.

Sweat across my forehead, and this is too much, I wasn't built for this, I can feel something moving in me, behind my ribs, up to my heart, and the air is squeezing out of me

I can't

Not like before not like the glitter and the calm   this is fracture this is breaking

this is an ending   I wasn't supposed to let go

The tips of my fingers they're turning black   a

Raxter Blue   and it all disappears everything until out
of my chest   like a column of light   a scream
   I'm nothing
   I'm
   I'm done.
   And now, now it hurts.

I sit up, the iris falling to the floor, and I hold my fingertips under the light. Black, like I dipped them in ink. It reaches all the way to my knuckles.

This is what happens to things when they're from Raxter, when the island's knit itself into their bones. This is what happens to them when they're dying.

I push the oxygen mask off my face. It's done its job.

I get out of bed and stay close to the wall as I make for the door. My legs are steady enough, but I can feel the weakness in them. They'll give out before long. I take a short rest at the gurney next to the door and lean close to the window looking out into the corridor. My reflection stares back at me. The skin under my eyes is mottled blue and yellow. Even through my hospital gown I can tell my ribs are pushing out, and my hair is matted, stiff with sweat.

And then I see it. In my arm, there, a flicker in the mirror. A bulge in the flesh, a shiver in my skin. I can feel a pulse in my wrist, patterned like a heartbeat. I am dying, and the darkness inside me is trying to flee. I press my finger against the burning skin and feel something recoil. A tendon, maybe. But maybe something else.

Leave it alone, part of me says, keep it for yourself, but if I am dying, I won't do it as anybody but me.

I find a scalpel under the bed by the door. Trace a light line down the inside of my arm. The blade is cool against the heat of my skin, blood beading faintly.

The same line, but I press this time, drag the blade slow. Blood like this is rich and dark. It wells up until it spills over, trails down to my elbow. Again, and again, until a tingling spreads through my wrist, until I know I've hit something deep. Pain, gripping and everywhere, and a scream through my body, but I am always hurting and I know what to do.

Put down the scalpel, pry my skin apart with slick fingers. A flash of bone, and the world is swimming around me, vivid and blurred. I slide my thumb and forefinger in, swallow a whimper, and spread the sides of the cut.

I don't know until I see it, but then it moves. Glistening, thick like a muscle. Twitching softly and radiating heat. A worm.

I try to pinch it between my fingers, but it's too slippery, so I keep trying, keep wishing somebody had left a clamp lying around. It's writhing now. It knows what I'm doing. And finally, I get a good grip and yank it out of me.

It's like ripping out a fishhook. A tear in my flesh, and blood springs up fresh. But it doesn't matter now. I have it in my hands. It's dead, or dying, not moving at all, and I can get a good look. The color fading, a milky white showing through underneath. Ridged and segmented down the length of it. And it's long, could run maybe from the tip of my middle finger to my wrist. A parasite. It was inside me and I didn't even know.

A violation, but a gift too. It let me find a reason for everything I felt, at Raxter, in Boston, and every day in between. It let me match my body to my mind. I can thank it for that, at least.

I look back at the window to see my reflection, to see if I look different. But I don't. Same me, same old   same old   but I think   I think maybe something is missing

It doesn't matter anymore. I tear up my sheet, bandage my arm   stain spreading and I get to my feet. I don't want to be where they put me when it happens.

My clothes are in the cabinet behind my bed, sealed up in a biohazard bag. I rip it open with my teeth and take them out   jacket, shirt, jeans, and in their own bag, my torn-up boots.

I clutch them tight against me, breathe in the cold salt smell. This is enough to make me my own again.

By the time I get everything on, my legs are trembling. I find the iris where it fell, hold it tight, and hobble to the door, push it open with my shoulder. There's a wheelchair just outside. I manage a few last steps over to it, let my body collapse into the seat.

The lock is manual, a catch I have to release and a handle I have to bear down on hard. And then there's some maneuvering, and I almost throw up because I'm so tired and my stomach is so empty, but I get it moving. Down the hallway. The way   the way somebody took me when we went outside.

Something drips down over my upper lip. Slow, like syrup, with a taste almost like blood, but sour. I wipe it off   don't look at where it stains my hand.

My right leg numb, my vision darker and darker. Won't be long.

It's just the way I remember it being.

Through the lobby all emptiness and disarray and familiarity   think   think Byatt don't you know

and then around   around around corners and there to the dented door

To the outside

To winter sweet   and cold   and just for me

I make it as far as I can

Stick close to the wall I scrunch down at the base and press my back against it wrap my jacket around me tight   clutch the iris to my heart

I can see it coming like a wave cresting like the sun
rising like a train down the tracks like a bullet like
  like home or
  won't it be better this way   won't it be better

Sun rising in the trees
  Slanting through in pale streams
  I've done what I could I've tried   how I've tried

Breathe in breathe out
  Keep my eyes open as long as I can I want to see I want
to look I want
  the woods to fall away
  the ocean to crawl up to my feet
  the island to come drifting in on the tide
  Raxter don't forget   Raxter
  It will be like sea glass I will bend down I will look
into the rippled surface of it I will see myself suspended
inside   I will know exactly where I am
  I will cradle it in my palms until it dries   until
the edges have worn off   until it has stopped being
beautiful
  (Roaring a roaring a rush it is coming)
  I will keep it anyway

HETTY

CHAPTER 17

"Time. Come on."

I sit up so fast my head slams against the top bunk. I'd laid awake all night alone in our room, and when I did manage any sleep, it was fitful with nightmares of Mr. Harker, of him turning into Reese.

"Seriously." It's Julia, leaning in the doorway. I peer behind her, looking for Welch—she's supposed to be the one who wakes us—but Julia's alone. "We don't have all day."

"Where's Welch?" I ask, trying not to sound as nervous as I feel.

"Busy. Get up."

I breathe deep. It's just Boat Shift as usual. If Welch knew I broke quarantine and followed her out, I'd be in trouble already.

I rub the crust from my blind eye, take a second to let my vision adjust, and follow Julia down the hallway, half in gloom with the sun not up yet. Somewhere behind me Reese is sleeping in one of the empty dorms.

I keep my gaze resolutely ahead, ignore the pang in my chest. She made herself clear.

We step out onto the mezzanine. Below us I can see Carson standing by the door. She's got her coat on—she's always so cold—and she waves when she sees us. But Julia pulls me aside at the top of the stairs.

"Welch and Headmistress were down in the main hall when I came to get you. They're pissed about something." She leans over the railing to see the rest of the hall. "I'd rather not get caught in the crossfire."

It could be about a million things, I tell myself. About dwindling supplies, about managing schedules, about the broken generators. But then Headmistress comes striding out of the hallway leading to the office, Welch on her heels, and it's clear that it's not any of those things at all. They look too wrecked for it to be about anything but our most important rule—they must know someone broke quarantine. Maybe they don't know it was us, but they know it happened.

Welch catches up to Headmistress and they stop, talk in low, strained voices. Headmistress's hands, shaking so hard I can see it from here. A flush spreading down Welch's neck.

"Looks intense," Julia says.

"Headmistress probably found out we weren't saving her any of the chocolate delivery," I say, smiling tightly and pushing past her. "Aren't you the one who said we don't have all day?"

Headmistress is gone by the time we get downstairs. Welch is a mess in her wake, French braid loose and wispy, blood leaking from the corner of her mouth. Usually, she likes to look as neat as Headmistress, but today there's a pink stain ringing her lips.

"Let's go," she says.

Julia clears her throat. "Hetty and I need our stuff."

"Well, hurry up, then." She's not even looking at us. It should be a relief, proof she doesn't know it was me, but all it does is set my teeth on edge.

Julia grabs my sleeve and hustles me down the hall to the closet, where we store the jackets and supplies. She pulls open the door, checks the clip in her pistol, counts the bullets while I do up the clasps across the front of my coat. I'm yanking the red hat down low across my forehead when Julia reaches deep into the closet, under a stack of blankets, and fishes out a pistol twin to hers.

"Here." She holds it out to me, eyebrows raised expectantly.

"No, I didn't have this last time."

"I know. Nobody did."

I eye the pistol warily. Is this a trap somehow? "Did Welch tell you to—"

"Look," Julia says, "you were on Gun Shift, right?"

"Yeah," I say, "but we didn't use pistols."

Julia barrels on. "And I've seen you out in the barn. You're a good shot. I need a good shot out there today."

"What for?" I press, Mr. Harker's face hovering at the edge of my sight.

"I mean, did you see her?" She must be talking about Welch. "She's gonna lose it. Maybe she already has."

I swallow hard, look down. Bite back the urge to explain. Julia's right. Welch is on the verge, and what if she finds out it was me who broke quarantine? What'll she do then?

I take the gun. Grip ridged into my palm.

"Hide that under your coat," Julia says. "I don't want her knowing you have it."

On a different day it would be a strange thing to say, because we don't do that—we don't keep things from Welch, and we don't defend ourselves against her. But it's today, and I've seen her leave Mona's body in the woods, and I don't think anything surprises me anymore.

Back in the main hall, Carson is shifting from foot to foot while Welch paces in front of the door. Julia beckons to Carson, who comes rushing over, a grateful smile on her face.

"Okay?" says Julia.

"She hasn't said anything," Carson says, nodding at Welch. "She's been doing that the whole time."

She doesn't know. I keep repeating it to myself. She doesn't know it was you. You have no reason to be afraid.

But I'm still grateful when Julia takes her spot next to Welch and leaves me to walk with Carson.

We pass the bulletin board, tap the note from the Navy for luck, and then it's out the front doors and onto the path. Through the gate, with Carson just behind me, Welch and Julia ahead, and as we follow the road deeper into the woods, Julia looks back at me. The gun skin-warm. I feel the press of it with every step.

We reach the pier before midday. The whole way I kept my eye on the road, afraid any glimpse of the woods would put me back there with Mr. Harker, his heart still beating in my hands. Here, it's blessedly open, sky stretching above us, endless and gray. Caution tape snapping in a brisk wind, waves smacking hard against the boards. Carson's tucked her hair down her jacket to keep it out of her face. I take my hat off, stuff it into the bag I'm carrying so it doesn't blow away.

"They better come soon," Julia says. That exhaustion from yesterday is back, leeching the life from her voice, and when she coughs it's a horrible, hacking sound. "It's freezing today."

"We could wait in the trees. For shelter." Carson's teeth are chattering. I think of how her lips felt against my cheek our first trip out. I wonder if her blood still runs as warm as mine or if the Tox took that from her.

Julia shakes her head. "Safer out here. This way we can see if anything's coming for us."

Welch hasn't moved since we arrived. She's staring out at the horizon, squinting at the nothingness where the mainland sometimes is. It's too gray today to see anything, but she's trying anyway.

She didn't say a word the whole walk across the island. I was grateful at first, but now it's making me uneasy. I want to keep watch, try to get a read on what she's thinking, but I can't look at her too long. I'm worried she'll see the guilt all over my face. Instead, I step back so I'm even with Carson, and press in close.

"Warmer this way," I say when she looks taken aback.

Welch has started pacing again. Back and forth, back and forth. The last time we were out, she had a gun. I can't see one now, but if there's one hidden on me, there could be one hidden on her. Julia shuffles a few steps away from the pier, closer to me and Carson.

Sharp, breaking, a seagull's cry in the air. I look up, draw in a quick breath. One is circling above us, wings dark against the sky, and soon there are two more. Just like last time, how they showed up just before the tug. They know it's coming.

It's a minute or two before we hear the foghorn, muted and almost hollow. Welch stops pacing, whips around to face the horizon. There's a wildness in her eyes I've never seen before, one that's all her own.

"Get ready, girls," she says.

Another bellow of the foghorn, and the tug appears through the mist. The seagulls are collecting now, cries overlapping. I want to cover my ears, but Julia nods to me and I follow her up to the start of the pier, Carson trailing behind.

It's the same as before. The long, slow turn and the familiar markings. There's nobody on the tail, and the closer the tug gets, the more we can see the emptiness. No high stacks of cartons. No pallets of canned food. Just what looks like one box, with bright markings on the sides.

I look over at Julia. She's chewing hard on the inside of her cheek. "Does this happen sometimes?"

She shakes her head, says something, and the tug motor is so loud I can barely hear her, but the grim line of her mouth is enough.

A grinding and screech as the crane starts up. Hooks a crate—the only crate—and swings it out over the pier. Last time they let it drop, but today they lower it all the way down and only release when it's settled. The crane reels back in, chain rattling, and then the final foghorn blast, ringing in my ears long after.

We watch the tug kick up a big wake as it moves away. Last time we could barely keep ourselves back. Now nobody wants to be the first to move.

I peer around Julia at Welch. Jaw clenched, a tear streaking down her cheek, its track glassy and freezing, and she's shaking her head. I've never seen her like this before, not when the Tox started, not even when a girl broke her arm during my first semester and had the bone poking all the way through her skin.

"Well?" She wheels around to stare at us, and I can't help a quick step away from the redness of her eyes. "What are you waiting for?"

Julia smiles. "After you."

A beat, the air so quiet I can hear Carson's shaky breathing, and then Welch brushes past us, knocking against Julia as she goes. We follow her onto the pier. Boards whining underneath us, and the wind picking up.

We walk three abreast behind Welch, and I look down over the side of the pier, into the ocean. It's a vivid, sick green today, layered with foam. I shift closer to Carson, safe in the middle.

The carton is smaller than the ones from my last trip, and it's not wood, like the others were, but something else. Plastic, maybe. Smooth, gray, and curved at the corners, with two sets of buckles holding the lid down. There's a symbol on the lid that I don't recognize. Bright orange, a little smudged, like it was spray-painted through a stencil. Almost the biohazard symbol—that set of interlocking near-circles we all know by now—but not quite.

"Okay," Welch says, holding out one hand. "Wait here."

I'm happy to stay away. That box is too polished, too manufactured. Nothing like that belongs here, and I almost don't want to know what's inside. But Julia is stepping forward alongside Welch.

"Let me help," she says, and looks over her shoulder at me as she and Welch head for the box. I touch the waistband of my jeans, where my gun is, and nod. Bad enough when it was just Welch to worry about, but this is worse.

Near the end of the pier the boards are weathered black, algae creeping across them in green webs. Carson and I hang back, and I swallow my unease, undo the bottom clasp on my jacket to make it easier to reach my pistol.

"Should we take the whole box back?" Julia says. The wind is carrying her voice back to me, thin and skittering.

"No." Welch crouches down and lays her hand flat on the top, like she's feeling for movement. "We'll open it here."

Julia stays standing, and we watch Welch's shoulders heave as she unlatches the last set of buckles, tendons straining in her arms.

The light on the rim of the lid blinks green. The lid springs up an inch or two, like a catch has released. Welch lifts it gingerly, her face turned away.

I can't see inside. I can only see Julia's frown deepen, can only see the way Welch slumps forward to rest her head in her hands.

"What is it?" Carson asks.

Nobody answers, so I step closer. Inside the box is a

bed of black foam. And nestled snugly in the center is a small canister, glimmering chrome, maybe the size of my fist. It looks like a miniaturized oxygen tank, the kind you see people wheeling around in hospitals, but the valve is sealed shut with bright red tape, the same symbol from the lid emblazoned in a repeating pattern.

Something inside me recoils, and I swallow, my mouth suddenly dry.

"I don't understand." Carson is peering over my shoulder, her cheeks so pale it makes me nervous. "What is that?"

Julia doesn't take her eyes off of Welch. "A cure, maybe?"

"I doubt it," I say. Wouldn't they tell us if it were? Wouldn't they come?

"Where's the food?" Carson says, louder now. "Where's—"

Julia cuts her off. "It's obviously not coming."

Welch's whole body is shaking, and I can hear a muffled sound, a strangled kind of sob from deep in her chest, the cold air cutting a ragged edge to her breathing.

"We don't have enough food at home." Carson steps around me. "What are we gonna do?"

And before I can stop her, she grabs Welch's shoulder.

Welch rears up and swings around fast, her arm knocking Carson's. She backs away from us so fast I worry she might go over the side. "Don't," she says.

"I'm sorry." Carson's chin trembles. "I didn't mean—"

"Do you understand?" Welch is looking back and forth between us and Julia, and as the wind pushes her hair back, I see blood trailing down her chin from where she's bitten her lip.

Julia smiles easily and says, "Sure we do." I know that tone, know a lie when I hear one. She's trying to keep things calm, but she's got her hand in the pocket of her coat where she's stashed her pistol.

"No, you don't. That's—" And Welch's voice snaps in half, comes back low and rough. "That's the end of it. The food, us, everything. They're never coming back."

"Don't be silly. Of course they are." Julia's getting closer to Welch, one hand outstretched, and she sounds like somebody's mother. Patient, and controlled, because someone here has to be, and we're children, but we stopped being kids a year and a half ago.

"Not after yesterday," Welch says. "Somebody broke the quarantine."

I can barely hear the wind over the roaring in my ears. This is it. She knows, she knows, and I'm about to find myself with her gun pressed to my temple.

I would do it again, I think. To be sure that Byatt's alive.

"Who?" Julia asks. Surprise widening her eyes, stopping her in her tracks. I hold my breath. "Who did it?"

"I don't know," Welch says, and relief is thrumming sweet in my veins. "But it doesn't matter." Her face is wet, tears blown back across her cheeks and a long string of spit stuck to her chin. "Camp Nash has always been clear. We're too high-risk. One strike and it's all over."

One strike. Me and Reese, we're the reason the dock is empty. We're the reason we have no food, no supplies, no nothing. Shame burns hot on my cheeks, and I duck my chin behind my collar.

"They're not gonna just disappear," Julia says.

Welch shakes her head. "That canister? It's the end. Whatever's inside is designed to kill us."

No. No, she's wrong. They wouldn't do that to us. They said they'd help. They promised.

"How do you know?" Julia says. Carson is starting to crumple, leaning heavily against me, and I push aside my own panic, take hold of her forearm and give it a reassuring squeeze.

Welch nods at the box. "The symbol."

I glance at the canister quickly, afraid to look for too long.

"You could be wrong." Julia is doing her best, but the defiance is leeching out of her.

"I'm not. I'm really not." Welch scrubs at the tears scudding down her cheeks. "They gave it a shot, right? Gave it the good old college try. And now they're calling it. No matter what I do, I can't protect you girls."

Protect us from what? From the Tox? From whatever's in that box? I look to Julia, but she's just as lost as I am, my rising terror mirrored on her face. This is more than we can handle. But the only person who could help us is Welch.

She laughs, hitching and broken. "Blood's already on my hands, isn't it? They wanted to experiment with that fucking food and I wouldn't let them, and they wanted to test all of you but I wouldn't let them, and I paid for it. I paid; I made choices and I sent you to die."

The food, I think. Is that why we tossed half of it out? "Wait," I say, and there are so many more questions I have to ask, but I don't have a chance before Welch's feverish gaze swings to me.

"Hetty," she says. "You can't trust them. Okay? You have to remember that. The CDC, the Navy—"

"Hey," I say, and it's easy to pretend everything's fine when you don't know what's wrong. "My dad's Navy. There are good people there." It doesn't matter if I believe it. It doesn't matter that Mr. Harker showed me what a good man can become, that I've seen what a father can do to his daughter. "They will help us. It's not over."

"Your dad?" She sighs. Pity, but more than anything, impatience. "Hetty, honey, your dad thinks you're dead."

"What?" She has to be lying. I push back a swell of nausea. She said not to trust the Navy, but it was her in the woods last night handing over Mona's body. She's the one we can't trust. "I don't believe you."

"It's all of you," Welch says. "Your families, your neighbors. You don't understand. It's been over for a long, long time."

I don't believe you, I repeat to myself, I don't. It's not working, though. Because it makes sense.

Oh God. Nobody worrying about us, nobody waiting. And we couldn't talk to our parents anymore, and it was for security, but it wasn't. It was just another lie, and we believed it.

"Hang on," Julia says. "You have to explain." But Welch is looking at Carson now, and her face has turned soft.

"Carson," she says. A whisper, the wind slipping it into our ears, and she holds out her hand. "Come here a minute. I need your help."

I grab for Carson's sleeve, but she's already moved, stepping carefully across the wet boards to take Welch's hand. My stomach drops as Welch pulls a knife out from her jacket pocket, the blade fire-bright and thirsty.

Julia yells, but it's too late. Welch has her grip tight around Carson's wrist, and she leans in. "It's okay, Carson," she says. "I just want to end it my way. The only thing you have to do is slide it home."

I look to Julia. She nods. I draw the pistol from my waistband and hold it by my side. We can't lose Welch. She knows where they've taken Byatt, and if she goes, the answers go with her. And even with all the lies she's told me, all the things I think she's done, everyone knows the whole place will fall to pieces without her. We need her. I need her.

"You can help me," Welch is saying. She presses the knife handle to Carson's palm, the blade glinting like ice in the winter sun. "It's easy. It'll be so easy."

"Don't," Julia says, her gun coming up in a blink.

Aimed true at Carson, not even the smallest shake to it. Welch knew what she was doing when she asked Carson. Of all of us, she's the easiest to maneuver, the one most likely to say yes. She might do this for Welch, and we can't let her.

"You can do it," Welch says, her smile growing. "You're strong enough, Carson. I know you are."

I can't see Carson's face, but with the way her shoulders straighten, I can tell. Nobody's said that to her before. I lift my gun, level it at the base of Carson's neck. I'm close enough that I won't miss.

"Let her go," Julia says to Welch, a quiver in her voice turning it to a plea. "Come back to the house with us. We can fix this."

Carson is staring down at her hand, holding tight to the knife, and I can see her knuckles whiten.

"This is it." Welch closes her eyes, presses her forehead against Carson's. "You're the only one who can help me."

"Drop the knife, Carson," I say. "I'll shoot. You know I will. We need her at the house. We can't hold it together ourselves."

Nobody moves. Just the wind and the ocean spray, and above us the sun is starting to break through the clouds. I blink hard, refocus my aim.

"I'm sorry," Carson says at last. "I can't, I'm sorry."

I let my gun drop, feel my breath rush out of me. A shaft of sunlight slips through to bounce off the water, and as Julia turns to shield her eyes, I watch it happen. Welch's hands clasping tight around Carson's, keeping the knife in her grip. Welch's chin lifting, and a smile breaking as she looks up. The last flex of her arms as she pulls Carson in and buries the knife between her own ribs.

CHAPTER 18

She goes down slowly. To her knees first, and then she slumps forward onto the pier as Carson lets go and staggers away.

"I didn't," Carson is saying. "I swear I didn't."

Shock, numb in my nerves. The blood dark and sticking, seeping out to the edges of the pier. Soon it'll blossom in the water. I can picture it spreading across the surface like oil, shiny and slick and red, red, red.

Julia steps around the box, canister still gleaming inside, and bends to press her fingers against Welch's neck.

"Nothing," she says.

She's dead, and she's taken her secrets with her. I can't work out how to feel. Thankful that she can't hurt me. Angry that I'll never find out what she knew, that my chances of finding Byatt are slipping through my fingers.

And under it all, under everything, so familiar it's like breathing—guilt eating away at my heart.

I tuck my gun back into my waistband, bend over, and brace my hands on my knees. Welch had to be telling the truth about our families. There's no reason for her to lie. And that means my mom is out there, and she isn't counting the days until I come home.

"Do we tell the others?" I say. I sound hoarse, like I've been screaming for hours. "About our families?"

When I straighten up, Julia is shaking her head. "I'm not breaking that news," she says. "I wish I didn't know."

Me too. But there's no time for any more about it. The day's passing, and we can't be out here after dark, especially not without Welch.

I take a quick glance at her body. Her fingers haven't turned black. Her and Headmistress, sick but not like us, and there's my proof. "What do we do with her? Carry her back to the house?"

Julia looks past me, to the trees. Blood heavy on the air, a tang like copper in my mouth.

"No," she says. "The body'll slow us down. Attract attention we don't want."

There's only one option. Carson is starting to cry, so I take her shoulders, urge her away. Julia and I will do this ourselves.

She takes the feet, and I take the arms. Welch's body is still warm, limbs still loose, and when I move her hair off her face, I'm looking into her still-open eyes. I want to close them like I've seen people do in movies, but when I reach down, her lashes brush against my fingertips, stiff with cold, and I recoil. Mr. Harker felt like this. Soft, with no tension left in his body.

"Let's do it quick," Julia says. She's crouched by Welch's knees. "Grab her keys, and then we'll just push her in."

It's nothing, I tell myself. It's what has to be done.

The ring of keys is clipped to her belt, and my hands shake as I work it free. There, the key to the gate, long and iron. There, the key to the barn even though we never lock it. And there, at the end, a key to her old classroom. Still on the ring, like she was hoping for those days again.

Enough. I hook the keys to my own belt and then bend over again, rest my hands on either side of the bloody slice in Welch's chest. "On three."

The first push gets her right to the edge, and Julia sits back, clenches her fists. She's working up to it, but I can't take any time, I can't wait because the more I wait, the louder Carson's crying gets, and it has to be now. I wedge my shoulder against Welch's and shove against her hip. It's slow and scraping, but finally, legs first, she tips off the pier.

A splash. Water clinging to my face, chill seeping into my skin. I wipe myself dry.

"Thanks," Julia says quietly.

Welch floats. Hair drifting out, blood leaking.

I let myself feel it all—the hurting, and under it, a small part of me violent with satisfaction—and then I stand up and turn away. Sooner or later something will come from the woods to take the body. I'd rather not be watching when it does.

After that there's just the question of the canister. We gather around it, face resolutely away from the water.

"What the hell is in this thing?" I ask.

"I don't care about that," Julia says. "I care about what we're doing with it. And I vote we toss it. Don't mention it to anybody. It'll just make a mess. I mean, look what it did to Welch."

Carson flinches. I expect her to crack, crumble, but she draws herself up, sets her shoulders. "It's coming with us."

I watch Julia's face go slack with surprise. I've never seen them disagree before.

"Why would we do that?" Julia snaps. "Why would we take it back?"

"We'll bring it to Headmistress." Carson shrugs. "She'll know what to do."

"*We* know what to do," Julia insists. I nod, but they're hardly paying attention to me. "It's meant to kill us. Why would we want that in our house?"

"We can always get rid of it later. Without Welch," Carson says, "Headmistress is all we have left. I don't see sense in hiding things from her."

Julia reaches for Carson's hand. "I know you're shaken up, but—"

"And what if Welch was wrong, huh?" This is the

loudest I've ever heard Carson. Her eyes are glassy, and her bottom lip is trembling, but she's holding her ground. "What if it's the cure? Headmistress will know." She swipes a stray tear from her cheek. "I'm so tired, Julia. We keep so many secrets, and we make decisions we shouldn't have to, and I can't do that right now. I had the knife in my hands, okay? Not you. We're giving it to Headmistress."

Julia looks stricken. "Sorry," she says roughly. "Of course. Yeah, we'll take it back. Hetty, is that—"

"Whatever Carson wants," I say. I'm tired, and if Carson starts crying again, I think I might too.

I look away, drift a little farther down the pier to give them a minute, but I still catch a glimpse of Carson slumped in Julia's arms.

The box turns out to be too heavy for any of us to lift by ourselves, and nobody's saying anything, but we're all reluctant to take the canister out.

"We'll take it," Julia says to Carson. "You go on ahead."

I crouch down, shut the box, and run my hand over its smooth surface. It's cool to the touch, with tiny ridges I couldn't see from farther away, and there's a handle built into the side. Julia finds a matching one opposite. Together we lift it, Julia wincing as it knocks against her hip.

"When Headmistress asks," she says as we start to walk, "Welch did it all herself. Carson was behind you."

"Of course she was," I answer.

My jeans are sticking, soaked through, and an ache is setting in behind my eye. The glare off the ocean's making it work too hard. All I want is to be home again. Somewhere quiet, away from memories of Welch and Mr. Harker. Somewhere with Reese to tell me that everything will be okay.

We're only just into the trees when I feel it, a thrum in the ground, distant movement in the branches. Julia speeds up and I keep pace. Try not to look back. But there's a bend in the road, and I see it, over my shoulder. The shape of something giant and void-dark, prowling through the trees in the opposite direction. It's a bear, drawn by the blood, by the lure of the body in the water.

I'm too worn out to feel afraid. Too tired to do anything but keep moving. Face front, Hetty. Think about something else. But all that comes is yesterday, the way Mr. Harker's skin flaked away under my touch. And before that, Mona in a body bag. And before that, and before that, and before that.

The things I've done here, the bodies I've felt under my hands. They're for nothing if I don't find Byatt. Welch can't give me any answers now, but I'll find them anyway.

We leave the pier behind. Since the Tox, calluses have grown thick on my hands, and I'm grateful now as we keep on, Carson in front of us, the box getting heavier and heavier. I wish we'd stuck the canister in one of our bags and left the case on the dock.

"Nearly there," Julia says as the road starts the last long curve before the house. I keep my eyes on the treetops, wait for the roof to poke through. "People will be in the hall," she continues. "Carson should go in alone. Get Headmistress and bring her to the gate so we can figure out what to do."

The food. I've been beating it back, but it's no use, and I bite hard on my lip to keep tears from welling up. Please, let Byatt have been worth it. Please, let her life be worth all of ours. "Will it be that bad, do you think?"

"It certainly won't be pretty."

"Yeah," I say, hope it sounds like I'm agreeing, and then I call out to Carson, try to ignore the churn in my gut.

She turns around, stumbling a little on a divot in the road. "What?"

"We're gonna send you in first."

"Just find Headmistress," Julia says. "Bring her to meet us."

"I—"

"You don't have to explain," I say gently. "You can just tell her we're waiting. Doesn't have to be more than that."

She nods, turns back around, and we keep going, until the railing of the roof deck is visible through the trees. The sight of it releases a catch in my chest, and I exhale long and slow. The sooner we're there, the sooner this box is out of my hands and I'm back to the danger I'm used to.

We round the last corner and start up the straightaway to the gate. Carson waves to the Gun Shift girls on the roof. I know what they must be feeling, the fear that must be rising as they count our number and count it again.

Things will change without Welch. The order we built

for ourselves is already shaky. Without Welch at the center, there's nothing binding it together.

We put the box down, and I unclip the ring of keys from my belt, sort the iron one out from the others. It's cold against my fingers, sticking and pulling at my skin. I slot it home and twist, the metal ringing as the lock slides back.

Carson holds the gate open for us. Julia and I carry the box through, setting it down again on the other side. Julia groans as she stretches, the bruise from yesterday visible as her shirt rides up. I wince—it looks even worse than before—and I flex my numbing fingers before pulling the gate shut behind me.

"I just tell her to come out here, right?" Carson is picking nervously at a hangnail. I reach out, take a light hold of her wrist, fight back a flinch at the cold bite of her skin.

"Just tell her it's important. And put on a good front, yeah? For the girls. Everything's fine." I say it as much for me as for her.

She nods, takes a deep breath. "Everything's fine."

"Give it five minutes, and everybody will know what happened," Julia mutters as Carson heads off for the house.

"We can at least avoid a panic," I say.

"For now." Julia squints up at the girls on Gun Shift and steps in front of the box. "I'd say we're due for one eventually."

It's only a minute or two of waiting, but it feels like longer, every gust of wind pulling a shiver from my body. At last the front doors bang open, and when I look up, it's Headmistress barreling toward us.

Her hair's coming out of the chignon she always wears, and she's as close to running as I've ever seen her. Tan slacks stained with dirt, like she's been digging around in storage somewhere, and one side of her shirt almost untucked. Behind her, Carson is barely keeping up.

"What happened?" Headmistress says. "Where's Ms. Welch?"

I cast a reassuring glance at Carson. "There was an incident at the pier."

"An incident?" Headmistress looks from me to Julia. "Speak clearly."

"They delivered something unexpected," Julia says. "Welch didn't take it very well."

Carson cringes, and I can't fight back the memory of a body still warm against my palms. But Headmistress doesn't move a muscle.

"Are you telling me . . . ," she starts. But nothing more comes out.

"She killed herself," I say, voice trembling. "She bled so much, so fast. We couldn't do anything. We had to leave her behind."

"Of course," Headmistress says faintly. "Of course you did." She sways a little and then rights herself, plants her feet firmly. "Thank you, girls, for telling me. Go on inside and get the food sorted out."

"Actually," Julia says, shrugging. And Headmistress looks at our empty hands, at the bags hanging loosely from our shoulders.

"Did you leave it with Welch?" she asks. "Go back out. There's time before sundown."

"No, we didn't." I clear my throat. I have to say this. It's the only responsibility I can take. "They didn't send any."

Headmistress stares at me for a moment, her face electric with surprise. "What?"

Julia steps aside to show her the box. "All they sent was this. It's what . . . upset Welch."

Headmistress crosses to crouch in front of it. I can tell the second she recognizes the symbol painted on the lid. Her mouth drops, and a frown creases deeply at her brows.

We wait for her to open it, but she doesn't, and Julia clears her throat. "She said it was designed to—"

"I know what it does." I wait for her to tell us, but she stands up quickly and brushes off her slacks. "Get inside."

Julia looks at me, baffled. "What are we gonna do about—"

"I said get inside." Headmistress is veiled with a deadly sort of calm. "Send Taylor out to me. And not a word to anyone. And, Hetty, I'll have those keys."

"Okay." I drop them into her outstretched palm, and then I'm hurrying away from her. Julia's not far behind. I snag Carson's sleeve as we pass. Together the three of us move quickly up the walk, file through the double doors.

We forgot. Or at least, I tried to. About the girls who would be waiting for us. They're clustered in groups around the main hall, and as the doors shut behind us, they fall quiet, the easy hum and chatter dying down. I remember that feeling. The excitement, the hunger gnawing bone-deep. And the dread too. The worry that one day there won't be enough.

Well, today they're right.

I look to Julia. Don't pass this weight to me. I can't bear it.

"Food's in the kitchen," she says. "Gotta make do with what we have."

Nobody moves. I'm not sure if anybody believes her. Julia isn't exactly known for her sense of humor, and we've had a lot happen to us, but I can see girls start to smile nervously. One of the youngest ones in the corner giggles before she's hushed by her friends.

"Well?" Julia says, her voice filed sharp. "I'm not your goddamn waiter."

There's a flurry of movement as girls get up and head for the kitchen, to claim food for their circle just like always. Except now there's no Welch to claim it from, and Reese isn't here waiting for me.

I take the pistol from my waistband, push it into Julia's hands, and go upstairs, back to my room. Stretch out on my bunk. Try not to see Welch's body when I close my eye.

CHAPTER 19

Dinner here and gone, evening coming in. It feels like years since Reese and I snuck out to follow Welch. But it's only been a day. A day, and everything's fallen even farther apart.

If Byatt were here, I keep thinking. She'd know how to fix it. She'd know what to do to make it right. But she's farther away than ever. Welch dead, answers slipping out of reach.

It's late, now. Nearing morning. I thought maybe Reese would sneak back in once she thought I was asleep, but nothing. Just silence in the hallways, and the nightmare sounds we're used to now—a scream here, a whimper there, and under it a girl crying herself back to sleep.

And then, faint and on the wind, a low, jagged moan. It comes in stuttering pulses, the sound so deep I can feel it in my body. I've never heard anything like it. Not machinery, not man. That sound came from the wild.

I get up, go to the window. The light is blue and rising, but from my window, all I can see is the courtyard and the north wing of the house. Nobody else is stirring. The whole house is quiet. Probably just something out in the woods, then. Or maybe I imagined it.

But I didn't. It comes again a minute later. Clearer, longer, with an echo to it, a space inside.

Somebody else has to have heard it by now, so I head for the door and step out into the hallway. It takes a bit for my eye to adjust, and at first I think I'm alone. And then, farther down the hall. Reese, her hair creating strange shadows.

"Oh," I say. I haven't seen her since we ended things. She looks like she's fine. Of course she does.

Reese doesn't answer. She has her head cocked, and when I open my mouth to say something else, she holds up her hand. She's taken off her sling, but from the pallor of her skin I can tell she's still in pain.

That's when we hear it a third time. Loud enough now that I can hear it trail off into a low growl. Whatever this animal is, it must be close.

"Should we get Headmistress?" I ask.

She won't meet my gaze, but she sounds normal when she says, "Not sure."

We haven't seen Headmistress since this afternoon, when Julia, Carson, and I got back. She must be dealing with whatever's in the canister, dealing with losing Welch.

Cat pokes her head out from her room near the mouth of the hallway, Lindsay lingering in the shadows behind her. "Hey. You guys heard it too?"

"Yeah," I say.

"What is that?" She rubs sleep from her eyes. "Has anybody heard from Gun Shift?"

I come farther out into the hall. "Nothing yet."

"Some kind of animal. I think," Reese says, and then she breaks off, nods toward the mezzanine overlooking the main hall. "Let's take a look."

We walk together, Cat and Reese ahead, me trailing behind with Lindsay. Lindsay's watching me, I can feel it—she must know something's wrong, with Reese sleeping all the way down the hall, but luckily, she doesn't say anything. I don't think I could stand it.

Across the mezzanine, and down the stairs. Ali's on guard at the door.

"Hey," she says when she sees us coming, her face relieved. "What's that sound?"

"We were gonna go take a look," Reese says. "It's coming from outside, over that direction." She points to the south corridor, toward Headmistress's corner office. "You want to come?"

"No," Ali says quickly. "I'll go up to the roof, check with Gun Shift." She hurries up the stairs, leaving us alone in the main hall.

We head for the double doors, and Cat and Lindsay ease back, waiting for Reese to open them, deferring to her in that way all the girls do, equal parts fear and awe. But she can't, not with her shoulder like that.

"I've got it," I say. With two hands I heave one of the doors open. I glance at Reese, hoping for anything. Just a smile. Just a look. But she ducks through, her head turned away. Cat and Lindsay follow, and I check to make sure the door will stay unlocked before I slip out after them.

We collect on the porch, doing up our jackets as the cold steals into our bodies. The air is heavy, with a charge to it like a storm's about to break. It's sweet and sharp, and I breathe it in, look out to a clear sky and whorls of stars. For a moment we're all still, and I hear one of us sigh softly. And then it breaks. The sound again, a juddering groan. It's coming from over by the fence.

I squint into the night and head a ways down the walk, the other girls behind. We should be able to see it by now. By the sound of it this animal's big. It should be hard to miss, even through the trees.

A wide, flat stretch of frost, the flagstone walk slicing through. The fence holding strong, and above the trees, above everything, the first hint of sunrise. But there's something else, too, something dark and moving by the gate, and I can't quite pull it out from everything else. I blink, look away and back again, and Cat gasps, and Lindsay says "Holy hell," and suddenly the lines are clear.

Black, glossy fur. Huge, as tall as me on all fours, with hulking shoulders and a low-slung head. A bear. What I saw on my first trip out on Boat Shift, what I heard in the woods as we left Welch's body behind. Only now it's on this side of the fence.

It moans again, and we stumble into one another, hold as still as we can, the winter air ripping ragged breaths from our lungs.

"What the hell is taking Gun Shift so long?" Cat whispers. "How did it get through the fence?"

"There," Lindsay says, pointing into the dark. "That's how."

Dread burning in my gut, but I know it already. And sure enough. Behind the bear, swallowed up by the dark: the gate, swung all the way open.

I should have paid more attention. I should have checked. But I came back in from Boat Shift, and I just pulled it closed. Welch, and the canister, and the wake of the night before, but that shouldn't have mattered. How could I have put us at risk like that? How could I have been so stupid?

I did this. I brought the end of everything. I'm sorry, I think, I'm so sorry.

The bear is closer now, on all fours with its nose to the ground as it lumbers toward the house. Every so often it huffs loudly and bites the air, the pop of its jaw sounding dully across the lawn. I can see its ears twitching, can see patches of skin ripped bare and raw all down its spine.

A yell from the roof and then a gunshot. It skims in over our heads, hits the stone of the front walk, and the bear rears back. I yelp in surprise. Someone's hand clamps down over my mouth, but it's too late.

The bear's head swings up and around to look right at me. I let out a muffled scream. One half of its face is bare to the bone.

Make noise, Mr. Harker told us. Fight. But this is the Tox, and I don't think those rules are true anymore.

"The shot didn't scare him off," Reese says. "But Gun Shift could still hit him."

Next to me Lindsay is trembling. Pressed in against the other girls, my body feels like a live wire. Tension running so strong you could snap me in half, my heart racing.

"Give them one more chance," I whisper.

Another shot, and the bear roars. I think maybe they hit it, but it's still coming toward us.

"We're going to move backward," Reese continues, her voice even and low. "Slowly, on three."

I grab Cat's hand as Reese starts to count. We're all of us linked, and I feel somebody shiver as the bear snorts and shifts its weight. It's not far to the house, but if we run, it's sure to catch at least one of us.

Our first step takes us back enough that I can't smell the hot stink of its breath. It watches us, and I'm trying not to blink, trying not to break eye contact, but my blind eye is aching, the strain and the dark and I'm so, so tired.

"And again," Reese says. Together, another step. Shivering nerves, clenched fists.

For a second everything is quiet, and I feel my shoulders

relax. And then a growl, rumbling up out of the ground, so loud it shakes me to my core.

"Okay," Reese says. "It's time to run."

Cat breaks first, pushes away from us and takes off. I crash onto my hands and knees, dirt rough against my palms, cold scrape tearing skin. Shadow thickening, and when I look up it's coming, bone glistening, mouth open and wet. A calm settles over me. All I have is my knife tucked in my belt, not good for much in a fight like this, but I can buy the others time. I'm the one who let it in. I'll die keeping it out.

But Reese hooks her silver hand under my arm and hauls me to my feet, eyes wild, a flush high on her cheeks.

"Move."

Feet pounding, air whipping against my face, blood pumping, and I can hear it—the bear, steps shaking the earth as it sprints after us. The crack of a gun, but it misses in the dark, and I can't look back, can't look back. Cat waiting at the door, Lindsay just ahead of me. Past her, and into the open. Every breath harder and harder, the cold closing my lungs.

"Hurry!" Cat yells. Reese hits the door and disappears inside. Cat reaches out to me, and the control leaves my limbs, breaks my stride as I crash into her, let her shove me into the main hall.

"Come on, Lindsay," she calls. And Lindsay was right behind me, I swear she was, but I hear her cry out and then a scream, fractured and hoarse. The sound rakes down my back, terrible and scraping. I don't think I'll ever forget it.

Cat braces the front door, and Reese fumbles with the lock, throws the deadbolt across. Over it all, wet snarls and pops of bone. Lindsay whimpers once, and never again.

"You okay?" I say to Cat.

She's got no color left in her, and her eyes are bright, but she nods. Stoic and strong, the way they teach Navy daughters to be. "For now."

We wait—thank God the room has no windows—and pray the bear won't try to break through the door. The lock is strong, but it won't hold for long against something like that.

"Let's go," Reese says, "while we can. We have to warn Headmistress."

Ali comes dashing down the stairs, the two Gun Shift girls at her heels. "Shit," she says. "Where's Lindsay?"

"Where's Lindsay?" Cat pushes past Ali and grabs the nearest Gun Shift girl. It's Lauren, the one who took my vacant spot. "Where the hell were you?"

"I'm sorry," Lauren says, stumbling over her words, and the other girl, Claire, steps between Cat and Lauren.

"It's not her fault." She swallows, a blush visible on her cheeks even in the dim light. "We were taking shifts and it was my turn. I fell asleep."

Cat releases Lauren's jacket. "You fell asleep?"

Claire won't look at her. "It was an accident."

"Tell that to Lindsay," Cat snarls.

Light, then, showing at the mouth of the north corridor, and Headmistress comes hurrying into the hall, her head down. I can't think of any place in that direction where she could keep the canister, but she knows the house better than I do.

"Hey," Reese says, and she jumps. Stares up at us with wide, nervous eyes.

"Girls. What's going on?"

Reese explains it all. The sound we heard, the bear, how it broke through. She leaves out Lindsay, leaves out that Gun Shift fell asleep. It doesn't matter anyway.

Headmistress's mouth opens and closes, a sore flashing vivid red on her tongue, and finally, she clears her throat. "How did it get through?"

Me, always me, bringing this school crashing down. Reese is angry, and I know she's thinking about it, about telling Headmistress my half of the truth. I won't fight it—I'll deserve it if she does. But she shakes her head. "We don't know."

"Okay," Headmistress says, more to herself than to any of us. "Okay, okay." And then she looks at me, and she looks at Reese, and disappears into her office.

"Well, shit," Reese says. "What do we do now?"

CHAPTER 20

What we do is wake everyone up. The house won't hold on its own, and it's only a matter of time before the bear breaks through. Too many doors, and the dining room windows, so tall and spreading the whole length of it, but we can at least stay alive as long as possible.

Cat and I go upstairs, march down the hallway room by room, knocking on doors and shaking the littlest girls out of sleep. There's Julia, there's Carson, and without prodding they start herding the others into groups and down the stairs. Candles light and girls start trickling into the hall, bleary-eyed and frowning.

Without Welch, though, we need somebody to take charge. Not Reese, but somebody the littlest girls aren't afraid of. Somebody like Taylor.

I'm not sure exactly which dorm is hers, but I know some of the girls in her year bunk down at the end of the hallway, separated from the others by a few empty rooms.

This one used to be Emily and Christine's, that one Mary's. I walk past them, try to ignore the rising chatter coming from the main hall as the girls assemble downstairs.

At last, a few doors before Mona's, there's a room with a small flicker of light and the rustle of movement inside. I knock, step back, and Taylor wrenches the door open, her hair mussed as she finishes pulling on her shirt. There, set into her chest, a cord of muscle the width of my thumb, running down to disappear past the waist of her jeans. Pale blue and twisting, almost braided, with a pulse to it like it's alive.

"Seen enough?" Taylor snaps.

I look away quickly. Is that some kind of vein? "Sorry. I didn't mean to—"

"What is it?"

I clear my throat. "It's just . . . we need you down in the hall." I tell her about the fence, about the bear, and watch her face drain of color.

"Where's Headmistress?" she asks.

"She went to her office, but I—"

She pushes past me, one of her broad shoulders knocking mine. I can feel my body relaxing as I follow her toward the mezzanine. If she's in charge, we'll figure it out. She'll know what to do.

Down the stairs, past the last few stragglers joining the others in the main hall. I catch Reese's eye, watch relief sweep across her face as Taylor wades through the crowd. But it's jumping the gun. Just like Headmistress, Taylor ignores the girls gathering and breaks into a jog as she heads for the office.

"It's fine," Cat says, coming to stand next to me. "We'll handle this ourselves."

The first and most important thing to do, we decide, is to shore up the front doors. Claire and Ali lead a group to the classrooms to raid them for leftover desks and chairs, anything we can use to build a barricade. Julia and Carson head for the kitchen, looking for tools to pry the dining room tables up from where they're bolted to the floor. Landry even pitches in, takes some of the younger girls to the dorms to tear the ladders off the bunks.

And me, I'm rooted to the ground, stuck there in the middle of the hall. For a year and a half we've been as safe as we could ask for. The fence, regular supplies. Welch and Headmistress to hold us together. A year and a half, and in a week I've torn it all apart.

Sarah and Lauren are dragging the couches over to the front door. Cat's nearby, looking adrift without Lindsay next to her, and I think I can see Julia in the dining room wrestling with the bolts on the long tables. I start toward the dining room, but before I can get far, a door slams down the corridor, and Headmistress comes sweeping out of the office, Taylor at her heels.

She looks better than she did at the gate. Clothes smoothed—sharp lines and folds fresh, like she's got an iron hidden somewhere—her hair back in its neat gray bun.

"Up," she says, clapping twice. "Everybody up."

There's a pause, the whole room still. We're not used to her like this—she's usually removed, distant, her words spoken by Welch. But I guess that's not an option anymore.

"Well? Now," she barks, and we scramble to our feet. She winds her way through us and climbs up to the middle of the staircase, where we can see her. "All right, everybody line up. By year, please, and last name."

It takes us a minute because it's been a long time since we broke ourselves up like this into seven lines. Back before there'd be fourteen or fifteen girls in each line, but now it's like some of them never existed, and we used to start when we were eleven, but now the youngest of us is thirteen. So many girls are ghosts now, and the lines are short and ragged, and this is why we don't stand like this anymore, because it hurts too much.

I'm Chapin, so I'm first, then Reese. Beyond her, Dana Kendrick, Cat Liao, Lauren Porter, and Sarah Ross. I can't help looking at the space at the end of the line, empty, where Byatt would be.

"Thank you," says Headmistress when we've finished shuffling into place. "Now, as you all apparently already know"—and I can hear a crack widening in her voice—"early this morning the fence suffered a breach. Nobody is allowed out onto the grounds until further notice."

I close my eye. I have to get used to it, to this guilt twisting inside me. I don't think it's ever going away.

"To work on our emergency preparedness," she

continues, "we'll be conducting a safety drill this morning. Follow me, please."

It's ridiculous. Of course it is. But we follow her down the north hallway, past classrooms and faculty offices, around the corner and all the way back to the music room. It's big, high ceilings and no windows, with risers built in along one wall. We reform our lines across the wide, empty floor.

There were music stands, before, and a piano. Some girls had violins they brought from home. But everything's long gone. Only the teacher's desk left, bolted to the floor at the front of the room. Next to me, Cat shivers. It's cold in here, where the sun never reaches.

Once we're inside, Headmistress counts us and counts us again. I wait for her to explain, but she stands in front of us with her lips moving silently, and if I didn't know better, I'd say she was shaking. And then she nods to Taylor, who takes a step out of line.

My stomach drops. I should have known. I should have seen it coming. She was the one carrying Mona to the Harker house. I thought she was ours, but she's not. She's theirs.

"Take her," Headmistress says.

Taylor pushes toward me, and it must be me, it must be—they know I broke the quarantine. Headmistress must have found out. But Taylor strides past me, her eyes fixed on someone else.

"Wait," I say, but it's all I have time for, and then Taylor is wrapping Reese's braid around her fist and dragging her to the ground. Reese cries out, but Taylor wrestles her onto her front, pins her arms behind her back. It jerks her injured shoulder, and she screams something that sounds like my name.

Somebody yells, and I'm pushing past Cat, fighting to get to Reese through a crowd of confusion as Taylor cuffs Reese on the back of the head. I see her go limp, blood blooming fresh as her eyes flutter. Before I can blink, Taylor has Reese heaved over her shoulder and she's making for the door. What the hell is going on? Where are they taking her?

"Hey," I call, and lurch after them. I'm almost to Taylor when somebody grabs my collar and yanks me back, tosses me to the floor. Headmistress stands over me, her outline blurred as my vision swims and clears.

And then they're out of the room, Headmistress shutting the door behind them. I struggle to my feet, pull at the handle, but there's the heavy click of a lock being turned.

"Reese!" I yell. "Reese!" But they're moving down the hallway, quick footsteps until they're gone. Why would they take her? What will they do to her?

Julia comes up next to me, worry written clearly on her face. "What's going on?"

"I don't know. I don't know, shit, I—"

Suddenly, a hissing noise above us, and with a sputter the safety sprinkler system turns on.

It's a fine sort of mist, light and clinging. I squint up into it, feel my hair getting heavy with the damp. Too thick to be just water, the scent too clean, too chemical.

What the hell is this?

But I know. It's whatever was in that canister. Carson and Julia and me, we carried it back in our own hands. We signed our own death warrant, laid our heads on the chopping block and handed Headmistress the ax.

Around me girls are covering their heads with their jackets as the mist thickens to fog, chatter rising. Somebody starts coughing, and it's getting harder to see, harder to think. Droplets stick to my lashes, scattering light across my vision, and I run my hands over my face. They come away almost sticky, the pale, sickly cast of skin muted and flattened underneath the clinging fog. My chest thick, stuffed with cotton, and the deeper I breathe, the less air I can find.

We have to get out of here. We have to get out of here *now.*

The door is brand-new, built a few years ago, with a big square of glass set into it, run through with security wire. I know Headmistress locked it, but I test the handle anyway. Throw my whole body against it, and no give.

"Here," Julia says, "my knife." I step aside, and she crouches in front of the door, slides her knife out of her belt, and starts working it into the keyhole on the handle, trying to get it to turn.

It's panic now, electric. Not just in us but everywhere,

and whipping us into havoc. I can barely think over the shouting, can barely see through the fog. I tug my shirt up over my mouth and breathe through it. It helps at first. I can feel my head clear and my thoughts come whirring back, but there's too much of it, still spraying out of the sprinklers, and there's no place for it to go but into us.

That's when the first of us drops. Fast, there one second and down on the ground the next, angled all wrong, eyes open and staring.

"Oh my God," Cat says, and then she's out too.

"Julia," I say, "you have to hurry."

Sarah bends over Cat, shakes her shoulders. On the other side of the room somebody short and rail-thin is cradled in Landry's arms. Someone crying, someone screaming, and if we stay in here much longer, there won't be any of us left.

"This isn't working," I say. Breath too short, too shallow. "Can we break the glass?"

Julia stands up, looking faint. "With what?"

And she's right. There's nothing in here, not even a music stand, and the security wire in the window would shred the hand of anybody who broke through it. But that may be the only choice we have left. My head is clouding, my vision going. I don't have long before I pass out. This has to be quick.

I take off my jacket and wrap it around my left hand, grip the fabric tight in my fist. I know this will hurt, but the fog is burning in my lungs, and it's now or never.

I hit the glass, hit it hard, once, twice, and again.

It smashes open. There's a second after the break where I don't feel anything, just the cold rush of new air, and then the pain slams into me, explodes up from my hand and knocks me out at the knees. I slump forward against the door, work my other hand through the gap in the window, and fumble for the lock. The metal turning in my slick grip, and I think I'm gonna be sick.

I lean against the handle. The world tilts wildly. Door swinging open, and above me a gray plain, wavering, blurring. I can't feel my hand anymore, and I close my eye, sink to the floor.

"Hey, hey. Come on, now."

I fight awake. Julia is kneeling over me. "Did it work?" I croak.

"It's okay," she says. "The air's clearing. Here, lift your arm. I think you're supposed to keep it elevated. You're bleeding pretty bad."

She hoists my arm up by the elbow and peels my jacket from around my shattered hand. It feels like skin ripping off me, but it's nothing, just more pain, and I have enough of that already.

The rest of the room is coming back into focus, and around me, I'm starting to see. All of us girls, collapsed and sprawled out where we fell. Julia and me by the door, the others spread out across the room. Every one of us, some more awake than others and starting to stir, but all with the same hazy nothingness behind our eyes.

"Outside," I say. "We have to get out of this room."

Slowly, the sprinklers stop spitting down, and Julia helps me cradle my arm across my chest as I get to my feet. Glass scattered, blood staining the checkered floor. I watch the girls left living drag the bodies past me, out into the hallway, and I stagger after them.

How could Headmistress do this to us? After all this time, after everything we've survived, how could she give up on us now?

CHAPTER 21

Sixteen dead. We take stock in the main hall, away from what's left of the gas, Julia binding up my hand with strips of cloth ripped from a dead girl's jacket. It's mostly the little ones, only Emmy left from the youngest year, but Dara from my year is gone, and so are three from the year above. We line up their bodies and close their eyes.

When we've finished, everyone's quiet, just the sound of muffled crying breaking the stillness. About forty of us left, and we feel so small. I see Emmy sitting by the bodies of the girls in her year, combing their hair out with careful fingers, and my heart catches in my chest.

"This is Headmistress," Cat says, her voice cracking. "She did this to us. We can't let her get away with it, with killing our friends. With trying to kill us."

"What is there to do about it?" Lauren says, and I look

over to where she's standing by her friend Sarah's body. "She's gone."

"I can find her," I say, ignoring the throbbing pain in my hand. I have to. If I find her, I find Reese. And Reese is depending on me.

"And then what?" Lauren laughs harshly. "We kill her?"

"Yes," says Cat. "That's exactly what we do."

There's a murmur of agreement, starting low and building, but Lauren shakes her head. "There's still a bear outside. The gate's open. This house is done for and so are we. Isn't that what we should be worried about?"

Cat starts yelling, and the room fractures into sound. I look to Julia, who hasn't said a word. She's got her arm around Carson, whose head is tucked in the hollow of Julia's neck. She has her girl. I'm missing both of mine.

"Hey," I say softly. "What do you think?"

Julia looks at Cat and Lauren as they argue, and then back at me. "Go find Reese," she says. "She doesn't have time for this."

I smile gratefully, give her hand a squeeze with my working one before backing up slowly, inching toward the door. When nobody gives me a second glance, I duck through, and step out into the corridor. Hurry back to the main hall, my gait uneven, head still clearing from the fog. My left hand is pulsing in time with my heart, blood still seeping through my bandages, and I know it'll never straighten and bend the way it used to.

Through the windows the day is bright, full of sun, and

if I listen close, I can hear the bear, huffing sharp breaths just outside the door. It must have finished with Lindsay's body. And now it's coming for the rest of us.

There are only a few places secure enough for Headmistress to use to hold Reese. One of them is her office, but I can see from here that the door is open, and so I don't bother checking. Just hurry up to the second floor, every step stronger than the last. Headmistress tried to take me down and she couldn't—I'm not letting her take Reese, either.

There, the door to the infirmary staircase. It's ajar, swinging slightly like somebody just went through. But I don't hear anybody up on the third floor. Maybe Taylor and Headmistress are lying in wait, ready to lock me up just like Reese. Nothing for it, though, no plan to make. I don't have anything left. I start up the stairs, leaning heavily against the wall as the pain in my hand gets worse.

The infirmary is dark, shut doors blocking the morning's sun. The last time I was here I was looking for Byatt, and it felt like the answers were just out of reach. Now I have them—I know they've taken her off the island, and I know Welch was tied up in all of it—and it's drained the fight from me. I don't need the truth anymore. I just want to live.

Nowhere to hide down the narrow corridor. I think I'm alone up here. I stumble from door to door, listening for something, anything. Until there, the last door in the corridor, to the room where I found Byatt's needle and thread. The locks done up, and a muffled sound from inside, like the springs of a mattress.

Reese.

Easy, I tell myself. If she's there, someone else might be too. I lie down on the floorboards, my left eye to the ground. I can see under the door, through a gap maybe an inch or two tall. There are the legs of the cot, and what looks like a stool pulled up next to it. No Headmistress and no Taylor.

I start at the top, undo the deadbolts one by one. They're driven deep into the wall, and with only my right hand working, it takes all my strength to slide them back. I've just finished the first one when I hear it. Soft, hardly there.

"Hetty?"

I press my forehead against the door. It's her. It's really her. "Hey. Are you okay?"

A beat of silence and then: "I think so."

"What did they do to you? What did they want you for?"

"They wanted . . . ," she says, trailing off, and she sounds woozy. "They wanted a way off the island."

The blow to the head she took back in the music room must have her dazed still, and the way she's talking is strange, like she's not all there. I pull at the next deadbolt, and it barely moves. "Hang in there," I say. "I'm getting you out."

I hear her take a catching breath, and I think she's about to say something when somebody, somebody not Reese, says my name from down the hall.

Taylor.

I turn around slowly. The edges of her are smudged in the darkness of the hallway, but there she is. Watching me.

"Back up," she says. "Get away from the door."

"Taylor?"

She takes a few steps toward me, and I can see her face now, can see the stubborn set of her jaw and the knife in her belt. I turn more fully toward her, make sure the makeshift bandage on my hand is visible. If she thinks I'm not a threat, maybe we can find a way out of this.

"I just wanted to talk to her," I lie. "Just to make sure she's okay."

"I don't believe you." Taylor's voice is flat, harsh. "I said get away from the door."

"Is she all right? Can you tell me that, at least?"

"Back up. Right now."

Taylor used to be one of us. Underneath everything, she has to care at least a little. If I can just keep pushing, maybe I'll get her to crack. Maybe I'll get myself another chance. "What did you do to her? What did you want her for? Tell me that and I'll go. We can pretend I was never here."

Taylor shakes her head. "You know I can't let you leave, Hetty."

I put on my best smile. "Sure, you can. You can do whatever you want."

"I am." She takes another step closer. "Headmistress and I are getting off this fucking island. And if anybody knows how, it's your friend."

I remember what she said at the Harker house that night. How she said she left Boat Shift because we deserved better. What kind of bullshit. This is what she really did it for, why she knocked Reese out, why she left us in that room to die. To get away.

"You really think they'll just let you leave? The Navy and the CDC?" She can't be that naive. I used to be, and look what happened.

She shrugs. "It doesn't matter. We're not about to stay here."

"But what about the rest of us?"

"I am so sick of that question," Taylor growls. "What about me, huh? What about me?"

I can't argue with it, can't push past the guilt sitting in my stomach. "Listen, you can't just kill me," I say instead. Taylor scoffs, but I smile like Byatt would. "You want a way off the island. So come with me—we'll find it together."

Another step closer. "You're lying," Taylor says.

"I'm not, I'm not. I promise." But Taylor isn't listening to me anymore, and she reaches for the knife stuck in her belt.

"Put that away. Come on, you don't have to," I say, sugar

words already crumbling apart. My hand is trembling as I hold it out, try to ward her off.

"Yes, I do."

I have to go now. But she's blocking the way, and there's no escape, and Taylor, she lunges to grab me.

CHAPTER 22

Fast, so fast it blurs. I see her reaching, I see the white of her hand and the white of her knife, and I don't know which is which so I grab the one that's near me, force the other one away. Stamp down hard on her foot.

Taylor smashes her elbow into my nose, and I'm staggering back against the wall, pain exploding in my injured hand, my hair in my eye, blood in my mouth and smearing everywhere, up over my cheeks and into my ears.

Her knife darting out, and I yank her in closer, press the blade flat against me so she can't use it, and she's trying to turn it, she's trying to drag it across me, trying to open a canyon in my chest so I—it doesn't take much, I just—I tilt and push—and it goes in easy. Like she was waiting for it.

"Oh my God," I say. "Oh my God."

She slides off the knife. She falls. The knife does too.

She's leaking everywhere, and I don't know how to make her stop.

"Hetty."

I don't know if anything could make her stop. Taylor's eyes are fluttering. There are choking noises in the air as she twitches and shudders, one hand grabbing at nothing, the other pressed to her ribs. And Taylor is Welch, and Welch is Mr. Harker, and everything is always happening over and over again.

A voice from behind me, from somewhere else. "Hetty. Hetty."

I can't move. I can't breathe. The blood is about to touch the toes of my boots. Maybe if I stand here long enough, it will sneak through the seams and my socks and touch my skin too. This stain I will never wash out.

"Come unlock the door," Reese says.

Reese.

My boot makes a squelching sound as I lift it out of the blood and step across Taylor's legs. Reese is saying my name again, steadily, covering up the sounds, covering up the sputter and the burble of blood rolling out of Taylor's mouth.

At the door it takes a few tries to get each of the deadbolts undone, and my shoulder is aching, but I lift the latch and swing it open.

The cot is bare, mattress stained with streaks of blood. On the stool sits a walkie and a shortwave radio, and next to them a knife gleams in the sun coming through the window. Its edge is dulled down with blood, and I almost don't want to look, because what more could anybody do to her? But there she is, waiting off to the side. Reese, with her moonglow hair and torn-up shoulder, a bruise starting to wake across her cheek.

"Okay," she says, and cups my cheek with her silver hand, her thumb pressed to the corner of my mouth. "Okay."

"I didn't mean—" I start, but it's all I can get out.

"You had to," she says. It's supposed to make me feel better, I know it is, but bile stings the back of my throat. "Right now we have to go."

"And do what?" There's no way out of any of this.

"Step by step, okay? For now, we just gotta get downstairs. That's it. And then we'll figure this all out."

"Yeah," I say. And then because she's still looking at me, still waiting, I try again, stronger. "Yeah."

She lets me close my eye on the way out, to keep from seeing Taylor's body, and she tells me to hold on to her, leads me into the hallway.

"What did they do to you?" I ask. I can't stop seeing that knife.

"Nothing," she says, and she almost sounds calm, but she can't keep the tremble out of her voice. I feel a sick churning in my gut.

"What did they do after they did nothing?"

Reese doesn't answer. But when I open my eye I can see blood leaking through the rips in her boots. And every step she takes is tentative, like she's favoring one leg and trying not to let it show. Like they took the knife to the soles of her feet.

I push it out of my head. If I let this burrow too deep, it'll wreck me from the inside out.

We hesitate at the top of the stairs, noise from below drifting up to us. Down on the main floor the girls are back to barricading the door. Headmistress tried to end it, but they won't let her. And we're not saying it, but I know we're both wondering where she is. Have the girls found her? Or will she catch us and lock Reese up again? She won't care about me, but Reese knows the island like she's Raxter turned to blood and bone. Headmistress will never let her go if she can help it.

Somewhere down in the main hall there's a crash, and somebody yells. A rising clamor of panic echoing up to us. Another horrible slam. It's a heavy sound, like something hitting hard against the door. Suddenly, that pulsing moan ricochets through.

The bear, battering its way in. With the Tox inside it, it won't stop until it gets what it's after.

"Come on," Reese says. We jog down the stairs, and I try not to think of the footprints I'm leaving behind, the treads in Taylor's blood. My pulse is pounding in my ears as we burst out onto the mezzanine. The main hall laid out under us, girls yelling, Julia barking orders. Somebody crying in soft, airy gasps.

It's chaos as we hurry down the main staircase. The front doors shudder as the bear throws its weight against them, battering its way in. Two girls follow us down from the second floor, carrying a filing cabinet between them. A handful of girls are crouched where the couches have been pushed across the doors, bracing them to keep them from giving way.

"Hetty," Julia calls when she spots us. She's standing near the barricade, overseeing the whole thing. "You found her."

We join her, step hastily out of the way as the girls with the filing cabinet barrel by.

"What's going on?" Reese asks. "It wasn't doing this before."

Julia nods. "It must've caught the scent. Hetty's blood in the music room."

My bandage stained red, but that's nothing compared to all that blood upstairs, I think.

"Shit," Reese says, "look." I follow her gaze to the front doors, where they've started to buckle. The industrial lock, restored and secure, giving way as the bear crashes into it again and again. The noise coming like a heartbeat, and the doors quiver, strain against their deadbolt.

"Get back," Julia says. And then, yelling as the doors rattle against their hinges, "Everybody get back."

The lock breaks and the doors blast open. Cold sun,

wind whipping in. Bone jaws snapping. The couch, the desk, they split, scatter like shrapnel, and the doors rip off their hinges, come crashing down and bury girls underneath. Screaming, I hear screaming, and there, the colossal silhouette, the growl shaking the sky as the bear advances.

"South wing!" Julia yells. "Get to the south wing!" Anybody still on their feet makes a break for it. I'm rooted to the ground, watching the bear watch little Emmy crawl out from the ruins on bloody hands and knees.

This, at least, I can do.

"Hetty," Reese says. "Don't."

But I'm running, pushing past Cat and vaulting over what's left of one of the couches.

"Emmy," I call.

The bear looks up, fixes its rotting stare on me, and Emmy scrambles toward me, her elbow cracking hard against my shin. I throw my good arm around her waist, haul her up.

"Go," I say, "go. I'm right behind you."

"Hurry!" I hear Reese yell. I take a slow step backward, keep myself between the bear and Emmy as she breaks for safety, but the bear snaps its jaws, and instinct sparks to life. I turn, sprint for the south wing, adrenaline clear and cool, and I feel like more than myself. Moving fast, Reese waiting at the mouth of the hallway. They kept the doors open.

"Get in, get in," she says, and I chance one look over my shoulder as I take my last few steps. The bear is nosing at the body of some girl who took a spear of wreckage through the eye.

Reese ushers me farther down the corridor, into the waiting crowd as Julia and Cat shut the double doors, closing the south wing off from the rest of the house. Already girls are tearing through the classrooms and offices, shoving desks out into the hallway to build another barricade.

How much longer can we do this? How long until the next set of doors breaks open? What then?

The hallway doors don't do much to muffle the sound as the bear huffs out a quick breath and moans, calling to us. Emmy's crouched by the wall, nursing a split lip and pinching her ripped palm shut. And around her, more girls hurting, more girls hungry and alone and dying. This is my fault. I made this world for us.

"Is there a way out?" I say. "You didn't tell Headmistress, but tell me, Reese. Can we leave here?"

She looks at me for a long moment, and then she sighs. "I think so, yeah."

Is she serious? I pull her even farther away from the others. "Why the hell wouldn't you use it before now?"

"At first I didn't think I could get past the fence," she says, avoiding my gaze. "And then I could, but this place is my whole life."

I swallow hard, blink back a flicker of Mr. Harker's face in the dark, empty eyes and blackened teeth. "And now?"

She shrugs. "You asked me to."

CHAPTER 23

Nobody notices as we ease away from the others, down the hallway toward the corner where it turns toward the kitchen. There's a door there, an emergency exit that nobody uses, just in case the alarms still work, but there's no sense in worrying about that anymore.

We're passing Headmistress's corner office when I stop dead in my tracks. The door was open before, but now it's mostly shut. Through the gap, I can see a box of food, and then somebody moves past, blocking my sight. It has to be Headmistress. And she's hoarding supplies, supplies we'll need if we're leaving Raxter.

The door isn't locked, but as I try to push it open, it hits up against something inside and stops. "Excuse me," someone says inside, sounding indignant. Definitely Headmistress. "You're not allowed in here."

I almost laugh. Like that matters anymore.

I try again, give the door a shove with my shoulder, and

slowly it scrapes open. I blink, adjust to the sun flooding through the tall office windows, and there's Headmistress outlined against them, her shoulders slumped, her chignon coming undone.

She's standing over a carton of water bottles, and next to her, piled alongside her ancient, mammoth desk, are stacks of boxes I recognize—food, supplies, all stolen from the pantry, all stolen from us. Mixed among them are packets of medical tools, the kind the Navy used to send us. Small first aid kits, stacks of paper, records from the infirmary, and coolers, too, like the one I found in the woods.

How long has she been hoarding all of this? How long has she been only looking out for herself?

I move in front of Reese, because I'm not letting her go again, I'm not, but she bats me away, and after another look at Headmistress it's clear why. Bloodshot eyes, trembling fingers. A crumpling, nervous laugh as she fusses with the hem of her shirt.

"Girls, I'm going to have to ask you to leave," she says, and I can hear the fractures in her voice. She's afraid. Afraid of *us*.

"What's going on?" I ask. "What are you doing with this stuff? This belongs to us."

She brushes her hands off on her slacks, picks at a fleck of dried blood under her nails like she doesn't have glossy pink pus spilling out of her mouth. "Nothing. Just taking inventory."

The anger comes back in a flood, rushing over me until

I'm drowning in it. "Nothing?" I say. "Like what you did in the music room?"

Reese reaches for me, but I shrug her hand off, surge forward. Headmistress reels back against the wall, and it takes everything in me to keep myself in check, to keep from going after her.

"You locked us up!" I yell. "You tried to kill us."

"No," Headmistress says, eyes darting back and forth, "no, no. That's not it. I was just trying to help you." She smiles weakly at me. "That's what this is all for."

Behind me Reese lets out a bark of laughter. "Don't lie. If you wanted to help us, you would've started a long time ago."

"I don't know what you mean."

"Oh, come on." I step back, let Reese ease in front of me, her face lit with a cold kind of thrill. "It's just us girls here. You can be honest." When Headmistress doesn't answer, Reese nods. "I'll tell you what I think, then. I think you were always planning to get out. I think you had your escape set from the start. Just in case they couldn't cure us, right? But they left you behind, and that's why you needed me."

"It wasn't like that."

"Explain it, then."

"We knew something was happening years ago," Headmistress says, babbling now. "It was staying so warm in the winters, and the irises kept growing, and they asked—the people from Camp Nash, the Navy, and the CDC—but it was only access they wanted. Just to test a few things here and there. But we weren't expecting something like the Tox. I promise you: we never thought, I never thought, that would happen."

It's a lie and we can both tell. She knew. She knew something was wrong, before the Tox started. And she kept us here anyway.

"You mean you never thought it would put *you* in danger," Reese says. "But the rest of us, we were a risk worth taking, right? My father always said you wanted the wrong things, he always said not to trust you, and now I know why."

Person after person collapsing under the weight of this place, lie after lie, and I've had enough of this. Enough of these confrontations, of secrets spilling out of us like blood. I reach out, grab hold of Reese's jacket, and tug until she looks back at me.

"Come on," I say. At first I'm not sure she's heard, and then something changes in her face, softens, like she's coming back from somewhere else. "Let's leave her with the mess she made."

Reese shakes her head. "She could've saved us. She could've tossed that gas into the fucking ocean."

Yeah, I know. I could've too.

I take a deep breath, ignore the sick turn of my stomach. "But right now we can save ourselves. Please, Reese. Let's go."

She glances at Headmistress, who's quivering,

314

watching me with wide, helpless eyes. "If she moves a goddamn muscle, I swear—"

"She won't," I cut in. "Right?"

"I won't," Headmistress says, nodding frantically.

Reese sighs, and some of the tension drains out of her. Shoulders slumping, head tipping forward. "Look for some food," she says softly. "I'll grab water."

"Thank you," I say. "We'll be quick, I promise."

Headmistress is pressed against the wall, her palms splayed open and empty, so I turn my back to her, leave Reese to keep watch if she likes. There's a canvas backpack by the bookshelves that line the wall, already half packed with a pistol and a few boxes of ammo. I grab the pistol, check the safety, and hand it to Reese. Her shoulder might be injured, but I've never fired a pistol before, and she'll be the better shot. With any luck she remembers what I taught her about switching her stance.

She sticks the pistol in the waistband of her jeans and crouches by the carton of water bottles. The plastic wrap has been slashed open, and a few bottles have toppled onto the floor.

"You take those," she says, nodding at the box next to me full of jerky and packets of crackers. "I'll take a few marine flares. And one of those first aid kits too."

I load as much of the food as I can into the backpack. It's strange—at the bottom of the box, there's a layer of paper, like Headmistress has packed some of the school records. I pull them out and skim through them, Reese looking over my shoulder, but the print is small and my eye is aching, desperate for some rest, so I just shove them deep into the backpack. We'll get to them later.

Reese goes back to the water, but a few moments later she says my name, and I squint up at her. She has one of the bottles in her hand, the cap undone.

"What?" I ask.

"It's already been opened. The seal's broken."

I picture Headmistress as we came in, how she was standing over this case. There was something in her hands. I look up at her now, try to catch her eye, but she's staring straight ahead.

"Is it just that one?" I ask.

Reese takes another from the carton, twists the cap off. "This one too." I scramble over to her, and we pick through them. Every bottle, the cap opening easily, the seal already snapped.

"Shit," I say, but Reese is already on her feet, advancing on Headmistress.

"What," she says softly, "did you do?"

Under my knees the floor is damp, seeping up into my jeans. Headmistress must have tampered with them somehow. But what for?

I hold one of the bottles up to the light. At first I don't see it, but then . . . there. Grains of fine black powder, collecting at the bottom.

Reese breaks off as I push past her. Headmistress shies away, but I hook my fingers in the pocket of her slacks and drag her toward me. I'm right, I know I am, and I wish I were surprised, but this is just the same thing over and over. Everything is the same thing over and over.

"Hetty," Reese says, "what is it?"

Headmistress is struggling away from me, but I wedge my shoulder in against her chest, pin her as flat as I can.

"Check the bullets," I say to Reese. "You'll see."

"I didn't mean to hurt anybody," Headmistress pleads. "It was only to help."

"Oh," Reese says behind me, and I know without looking what she's found. Some of the bullets already cracked open, emptied of gunpowder the way the older Gun Shift girls taught us to do. I never knew how we first found out what a little powder could do to a body with the Tox. Nobody would ever tell me when I asked. But I know it's a slow death, like sleep if sleep lit you up with pain.

"You put it in the water, didn't you?" I say, leaning so close my spit flecks across Headmistress's cheek.

She takes my face in her hands before I can back away and looks down at me, her expression soft even as her grip tightens. "You have to listen to me," she says. "This is the best thing for you right now."

"Let her go," Reese says, but Headmistress ignores her.

"They're on their way, Hetty. Jets off an aircraft carrier." Her voice drops, hoarse and barely more than a whisper. "You know what they can do."

I do. It's not that I heard things when I was living on-base. It's that I didn't. And that said more than anything.

I push her hands off me and step back. "Why now? They've had a year and a half. What's changed?"

"There was a contagion on the research team," Headmistress says, "and then one of you girls broke the quarantine."

It takes everything I have to stay standing, the guilt pressing down on me, and it's like drowning except I can't show it. I can't let Headmistress know it was us.

"Too great a risk for too small a payoff," she continues. "They can't cure this. Maybe if they'd been able to do a broader range of testing—"

"A broader range?" It's knocking at some memory I can't quite find, and I shut my eye, filter through the last few days until it comes burning back. Welch, on the pier that day, right before she died. They wanted to test all of us, to experiment on the food, she said, but she wouldn't let them.

"Welch was on our side," I say. "Wasn't she?"

Headmistress frowns. "I'm not sure what constitutes your side, Hetty, but she was adamant that we not subject the whole student body to testing, that it would lead to unnecessary suffering." She smiles nervously. "Personally, I think it's clear she was mistaken."

"She killed herself." I'm shaking, and Reese presses in closer, lays her hand on the small of my back. "She did that because of your plans."

"Let's not forget," Headmistress says, a flash of annoyance crossing her face, "she was a grown woman capable of critical thinking. She made her own choices. I won't be held responsible for them."

She's right. Welch did choose—she chose us every time she threw out the contaminated supplies, every time she had us lie to Headmistress about it.

And I was wrong. I had her wrong the whole time.

I can't be here anymore. Every mistake I've made, digging us in deeper, and the whole place will be better off without me, even when the jets come.

"Hetty," Reese says behind me. Out in the hallway I can hear talking, louder and louder as the other girls raid a nearby classroom for desks and benches, anything they can barricade the doors with.

I look back to Headmistress. "How long until the jets?"

"They'll be here by dark."

That's it. A day. That's all Raxter has left until a squadron of jets blows it off the map. I can hear my father in my head, and he's telling me to run, as fast and as far as I can. I will. But there's still one thing left. "Why bother with the water, then," I ask, "if we're all dead anyway?"

Headmistress coughs delicately. "It's more humane."

"Humane?" I nearly laugh. I can't believe her. "Where was that when you tried to gas us?"

"Gas?" Reese says from behind me, shock tight in her voice. I'd forgotten she didn't know.

"It should have worked," Headmistress insists. "I don't think your dose was concentrated enough. It worked on your friend, after all."

For a second I'm not here anymore. I'm on the ferry that first day, watching Byatt watch me. Her smile like something I'd been waiting for my whole life, her smile like I was something special.

"No," I say. "No, I don't understand. What are you talking about?"

"Your friend. Miss Winsor."

My breath catches. Reese swears softly.

But Headmistress keeps on. "From what I hear she was very helpful."

"'Was'?" I say. But I know; I know what's coming.

"She's dead." Headmistress shrugs. "The CDC administered her dosage of the gas sometime yesterday."

I feel hollow, like the center of me has vanished. Ripped clean out of me. She can't be gone. Tears pricking at my eye, and my whole body shuddering. "I don't believe you," I say. "I don't, I don't."

"Well, that hardly matters."

I'm across the room before I realize it, my hand clawing at Headmistress's face. She cries out, and blood streaks over her skin as my nails tear a stripe down her cheek. Reese grabs me around the waist and hauls me back, my legs kicking wildly as she drags me away from Headmistress.

"She's lying," I say. "She doesn't know Byatt. She doesn't understand."

"I know," Reese says in my ear. "You're right. You are. But we don't have time. Like you said, okay? We have to go."

"Yeah." I swallow hard, force my body to relax. "Just one thing first. Dump the bottles. Except one."

"No," Headmistress says, "no, no, wait." Reese lets me go, lets me press my forearm against Headmistress's neck.

"It's over," I say. Behind me Reese starts pouring out the water. The floor turns dark and slick, and Headmistress is crying.

Byatt isn't dead. I won't believe it. Headmistress has lied before, and she could be lying now. I'll find Byatt like I promised I would. And when I do, I'll be able to tell her I did this in her name.

I drop my arm from Headmistress's throat. Reach back toward Reese, and she presses the last water bottle into my working hand. For Byatt, for Mr. Harker, and for us.

"We were supposed to drink this?" I say, holding the bottle up to my lips. She nods.

"It's what's best for you," Headmistress says. "You don't want all that pain. I promise, it'll be the easiest thing in the world."

"Yeah." I stare down at the water and lick my lips. When I look back up at Headmistress, she's watching me with warmth in her eyes, and she reaches up to touch my shoulder.

"It won't hurt," she says softly.

I lean in close. "Prove it."

She gasps, and I shove the bottle into her mouth,

throw all of my weight against her jaw, holding it open as the water tumbles in.

A muffled yell, and a whimper as she thrashes under me. Water spilling down over my hand, drenching the front of her shirt. She can try not to swallow, but soon enough she'll have to. Her lips are wet against my palm, but I don't give, just press harder, touch my forehead to hers. She did this to us. Now it's our turn.

Snot dripping from her nose, and she starts to choke as spasms rack her body. I'm watching her throat, waiting, waiting, and finally, a moan slipping out of her as she swallows.

I stay there, hip to hip with her, until she goes limp and I can't hold her up anymore. I step away, let her body drop to the floor. On her hands and knees, gasping for air. She looks small. I can see the narrow taper of her wrists, skin sallow and pale. I crumple the water bottle, toss it down next to her.

"Leave her," Reese says, "and let's go. It's getting nasty out there."

I look back at her, confused, and she nods toward the hallway. Hit after hit against the double doors closing off the main hall. If the front doors didn't hold, these don't stand a chance. I can hear Julia, yelling at the other girls, urging them to keep supporting the barricade. But it's no use.

"Okay," I say.

I hoist the backpack up, staggering a little under the

weight of it, but soon it's on and we're heading out of the office. Not a backward glance, not until we hit the kitchen and I check to make sure none of the other girls is following.

Empty space, and the sound of screams. We need to hurry.

Reese crosses to the emergency exit door, the sign above it dark and cracked. I follow, and she goes first, opens the door just a few inches, and looks out.

"Seems clear."

I laugh a little. "Either way, we're going."

She holds out her silver hand to me, and I take it. "Stay with me," she says, "and I'll stay with you, yeah?"

I close my eye. Raxter behind me, and who knows what ahead.

CHAPTER 24

The door spits us onto the south side of the grounds. Strong sunlight through the clouds as the morning fills out. Lawn empty ahead of us, just a few stands of coastal pine between us and the ocean. To my right, across a hundred yards of frost-dusted grass, the fence, and the way out.

"If we get separated," Reese says, "find my house. I'll meet you there."

"And then what?"

"My dad's boat," she says. "More like a dinghy, I guess. It's hidden along the shore somewhere."

A crash from inside the house, maybe one of the doors giving way, and I hear the other girls start to shout. I squeeze Reese's hand. The jets are coming, I think. I hate how it sounds like an excuse.

"Count of three," Reese says. "Break for the gate."

I nod, and together we whisper, "One. Two. Three."

We sprint, so quick I lose my breath, let my mouth go slack as I throw everything into my legs. Overhead the first flurry of snow, stinging against my cheeks. The backpack is too loose, jerking from side to side, and I stumble, but Reese won't let me fall.

"Almost there!" she yells.

The fence coming up quick, but I can't stop. I'm tired, so tired, and my legs go loose, my stride turning wild. But at last, the gate.

We stagger to a stop. My hand is throbbing, and Reese is leaving bloody tracks in the snow, but adrenaline is sharp and bitter in my mouth, the cold waking against my skin. I'm alive. I'm here and I'm alive.

I tighten the backpack straps as Reese slides the pistol out from her waistband. The gate open ahead of us, and she bites her lip against the pain as she lifts the pistol, her stance and firing hand switched like I taught her, and aims it into the shadow coating the trees beyond the gate.

"Just to be safe," she says.

I almost laugh.

We take a different route to her house. Keep out of the wilds, stick to the spidery deer paths that run through the trees, both of us keen to face the danger we know instead of the danger we don't.

The woods are strangely quiet, even for Raxter. Snow speckled on the ground, falling more thickly than it usually does this early in the winter. We scan the ground closely for tracks, but every time we find some they're heading away, toward the school. If we're safe out here, it's at the other girls' expense.

Eventually, the ramshackle shape of the Harker house is visible ahead. I blink the snowflakes from my lashes and hurry forward, eager for a bit of rest.

Reese goes in first, wipes her feet at the door absently, and it makes something clench in my chest. And then she gasps, lets out a sob, and of course, I forgot. Mr. Harker. The body.

I rest my working hand on her shoulder, step up next to her, ready to offer some comforting words. But they won't do anything, because crowded around what's left of Mr. Harker are three gray foxes, their mouths dripping black as they rip into his torso.

"Get away from him!" she yells. Lifts the pistol and fires between the foxes, no aim to speak of, stance in shambles. "Go!"

One darts through a hole in the house wall, disappearing into the reeds, but the other two just lift their heads and look at us. Reese doesn't care, though. She stumbles toward the body, batting my hand away from her as I try to hold her back. Drops to her hands and knees at her father's feet, one of his boots unlaced, the other with a striped sock peeking above it.

The foxes regard her calmly, almost like she's one of them. But when I approach they skitter away with a high-pitched cry and squirm through the wall.

"Reese?" I say. She sits back on her heels, and I catch the trail of a tear on her cheek before she wipes it away.

"Do you mind," she says, "if we get out of here?"

We head farther west along the coast of the island, and it would be easier going on the beach, but Reese keeps us in the trees, far enough back that we're still under the cover of the branches.

Raxter's edge is shifting here, almost porous. Later it'll turn to jagged clusters of rock before easing out into marsh at the other end. When we left I asked Reese where we were going, but she just shook her head and pulled me along. A week ago I would've called it stubborn, but this is Reese embarrassed, because I asked where we're going, and Reese isn't all the way sure.

It's the rocks, now. Reese is frowning, peering down the shore, taking us out of the trees a few steps at a time.

"Almost there," she says, and I nod. Don't press. She'll find what she's looking for.

We keep on, our bodies tense, the backpack heavier on my shoulders with every step. It's quiet, as if everything on the island is hiding from what happened at the house. Once the bear has finished with what's left of us, it'll go after the other animals. We have to get out before this place turns to war.

Reese stops suddenly, points ahead of us.

"There," she says.

Tucked in between two tall spears of stone, there's a path cleared out, and I can just make out a stretch of shore, the waves stranding nests of seaweed on the sand. And laid out on the beach, barnacles and moss growing over the hull, a dingy white boat.

We head down, careful of the rocks oiled over with sea. Reese holds out her arm, and I grab it, let her keep me steady as we pick our way to the shore.

The trail breaks off above the sand, and we have to jump down. My boots sink in, leave disappearing footprints behind me. On the horizon I can see the mainland, empty and black against the sky.

"Here," Reese says, gesturing to one of the rocks. "I should redo your bandages."

I sit down there, hand her the backpack so she can fish out the first aid kit. The bandages Julia gave me are barely enough to cover half the tears in my hand, and when Reese flips open the kit, I let out a relieved sigh at the sight of a pristine ace bandage.

She takes my hand in both of hers, rolling her shoulder to keep it relaxed. The snow, still light but sticking where it lands, sneaks under my collar, hits the back of my neck, and I pull my hood up as she undoes my makeshift binding.

"God, you really messed this thing up," she says, probing my palm softly. "Can you feel that?"

"Only in spots."

She smooths the bandage out and rewraps my hand,

careful to avoid the places where blood is already seeping through the first layer of cloth. "What about moving it?"

I manage a twitch in my thumb, and Reese smiles, lets go of me.

"That's good," she says. "We'll keep trying."

She stands up, packs the first aid kit into the backpack, and I look past her to where the mainland is faint on the horizon. "It looks so far," I say.

"Maybe thirty miles to the shore." Reese squints at the horizon. "And then what, once we get there?"

"I want to go to Camp Nash," I say firmly. "That must be where Byatt is, and I'm not leaving her behind. Not even if she really is dead."

"Hetty—"

"I'm not doing it. I can't leave her like that. You don't understand."

Reese looks away. "I do, though."

Of course. Her dad. I fight back a wave of nausea. "I'm sorry. I didn't mean to . . ." I tilt my head back, watch the snow come down. "I don't want you to think I've forgotten. Or that I think it's all okay. I know you're angry, and I know you will be for a long time, and I can accept that."

"I am angry," Reese says slowly. "But I can barely feel it. And I know it'll come back, but I have things to be sorry for too." She glances at me, at my throat, and I remember the feeling of her arm pressing hard across it. A week ago, but it seems like years. "There are more important things, right now."

I let out a laugh of relief that totters on the edge of tears, and Reese leans in so our shoulders brush.

"One of those important things," she continues, "is a cure. Nobody's looking for a real one. We know that now."

"Maybe we'll find something at Camp Nash," I say. And then I think of Welch on the pier, of what she told me about my parents. Of what I said about my dad. "Or maybe there's somebody else who can help."

Reese frowns. "Who?"

"My dad." I wonder if he's still stationed in Norfolk. What have he and my mother done with their lives now that they think I'm dead? "He's Navy. I mean, not like Camp Nash, but he might know something. And at this point, I think that's all we can hope for."

Reese is quiet, and I look away. I know she's thinking about her own dad, and I wait for her to pull herself out of it.

"All right," she says at last. "Byatt and then a cure."

I zip up the backpack while Reese goes to the boat to turn it over, and in a minute or two she has it righted and dragged to the water. I can see a rusted outboard motor barely hanging onto the stern.

"Will it work?" I ask. "Or do we have to row? Thirty miles is far."

"Should be all right," Reese says. "And my dad always kept a spare fuel can in the lockbox."

I watch as she inspects the oars and lays them across

the seats, just in case. A strong wave jolts the boat, and I dart back a few steps. I'm a Navy man's daughter—boats are bigger than this where I come from. Stable, and wide, holding together without a tar patch on the stern.

Reese laughs, the wind tugging at her braid, and I feel my heart clench. The clouds rippling above us, and the sun dipping below the horizon. The rocks moaning as the wind hollows around them, and I'll never let go of Raxter, no matter how far away I get. It'll never let go of me.

"Get in," Reese says, handing me the backpack. "I'll push us out."

I climb in and sit quickly, facing the shore, gripping hard at the gunwale. Reese starts to shove the boat farther into the surf until she's knee-deep in the water, and I can feel my stomach start to twist as the boat jerks from side to side.

"Okay," she says. "Brace yourself. I'm climbing in."

She takes one last step, pushes off as strong as she can, and hoists herself up onto the gunwale. The boat tips wildly to one side as Reese swings one leg over and then the other. I jerk back as the water hits my face.

"There," she says, dropping onto the bench opposite me. "Okay?"

"You brought half the ocean in with you."

She rolls her eyes. "Besides that."

"Yeah."

The waves are already pushing us back to shore, so Reese adjusts a lever on the engine and yanks the start pull. Nothing happens, but she tries again, and again, and at last it sputters to life, kicking up a spray as we start to hum forward.

"All right," Reese says. I can barely hear her over the engine. "Here we go."

The shore drifts away. Reese never looks back.

CHAPTER 25

We stick close to the north side of the island. Reese is keeping the motor running low to save gas, and we move slowly, the coast slipping by, snow spiraling in gentle gusts. Trees lined up next to one another like matches, and then, as the sun nears high noon, the marshland begins. Just about half a mile before we reach the point of the island where the pier juts out.

The going is tougher here, with sandbars cropping up in strange places. I squint, scan the shore for the visitors' center. Just past it, the ocean floor drops deep, and then it's into open water.

Soon enough, there it is. The center is perched on the north side of the island, cut off from the marsh by a thick band of trees. Built to look like a house, coastal and shingled with a viewing porch, and a boxy addition off the back, from maybe a decade ago when the tourism board decided to try to go modern. But today it looks practically shapeless, draped over in some sort of tent.

I sit up straight. Rub at my eye, blink hard, and look again. There's the radio antenna, poking through, but the rest of the building is tented, its edges catching in the breeze.

"Stop," I say, and Reese flips a switch so the motor idles.

"What is that?" she asks. "That place should be empty."

The tent doesn't seem to cover the whole building, but I can't tell from here. I've seen things like that for fumigation, for keeping buildings isolated. But why would it be here?

And it clicks into place. A boat left the dock that night at the Harker house, but it didn't make for Camp Nash. It came here.

"We always thought they were on the mainland," I say. "The Navy, the CDC. But they weren't. They've been on Raxter this whole time." I turn to Reese. "That's who I heard Welch talking to on the walkie. They're the outpost. Think about it. There's no way they'd bring infected material to the mainland."

"So they send a unit here instead." Reese frowns. "It makes sense. But they're risking their own contamination."

"A trade-off." Their own safety, for access to materials. Access to us. "And when they're ready to test a cure, they ask for a live subject. And they get one." I lean forward, send the boat rocking to one side. "That's where Byatt is. I know it."

Reese takes the boat around the point of the island and aims for the pier. The moorings are all long gone, and we don't have any rope, so she heads for the shallows, noses it into the marsh.

She lets me get out first, says she'll keep the boat balanced while I do. The water's muddy here, and I can't see the bottom, but it can't be that far down. I get astride the gunwale, the boat tipping as I let more of my weight slide over the edge. And then there's the water closing cold over my legs as I push off the boat and land in the reeds.

It only comes halfway up my calves, but it's a wrenching cold, worse than any day we've had so far. I shiver violently, remind myself not to make a break for the shore and to hold the boat so Reese can get out.

She slings the backpack over her good shoulder and slips over the side easy, like she's done it a thousand times, and of course she has. She sloshes around to the stern and pushes while I guide the boat from the bow. Together we get it beached, a foot or two above the waterline.

The ground between here and the visitors' center is mostly marsh, with almost no cover before we hit the trees keeping the center out of sight. We stay off the boardwalk, stay low to the ground, creep through the gnats and the stink only just dusted with white. Safer that way, but I feel hot, my skin crawling, and sweat is fresh on my upper lip. Maybe the jets aren't coming, and maybe they haven't been evacuated, and maybe they're still here.

Things keep shifting in the corner of my eye. I keep hearing the click of a safety releasing. A reed snaps behind me, and I flinch, drop to my knees. They're coming. It's over, it's over.

"Hey."

I just hope they do it quick, put the bullet between my eyes. I won't fight it—I've earned it, I deserve it—but please, don't make me wait.

"Hetty. Jesus, you're burning up."

I feel it, then, a hand on my forehead, and I blink hard. Reese, it's Reese, and she maneuvers me to sit, my chin to my chest, the ground damp and seeping underneath me.

"We should take a break," she says as she roots through the backpack for the first aid kit. "You need rest."

"I'm fine."

Reese throws the first aid kit down, a bottle of aspirin slipping out and into the mud. "It's not enough," she says, anger tearing at her voice. "What will any of this do?"

When she helps me up, we leave the first aid kit behind.

At last we're across the marsh and in the trees, picking our way through them until we come out the other side and see the visitors' center looming, plastic tent whipping in the wind.

The walkway is just ahead, the flagstone path sneaking out from beneath the tent. I know I should have some sort of plan, some special way to sneak in, but my hand hurts, and I'm so tired, and all I can think to do is lift the tent and duck under it. Reese swears behind me, and then she's following. The plastic drops down behind her, sealing us into the stifling dark.

We pause for a moment, in case somebody comes running, but there's only silence, and if the jets are on their way, the research team must have already evacuated. The center's double doors are an arm's length away. I reach out, pull lightly on the handle, and it opens with a squeak.

"Should we just go in?" I ask.

Reese shrugs, her shoulder brushing mine. "What, you want to knock?"

Inside, the main lobby looks the way it did on my first day at Raxter. Faded and yellowing, the walls painted with abstract shapes in shades of green and blue. We cross the room to the reception desk, which is long enough for three or four people. Only one chair behind it, and most of the surface covered by wilting catalogues about the area's recreational points of interest.

"It's so quiet," Reese says. "And so warm. Do you think anybody's here?"

I think of Headmistress, promised a way out and then left behind. "No. They must have evacuated." I lean over the desk, pick through the catalogues, but there's nothing important, nothing to help us find Byatt.

"Where would they put her?" I say, turning to Reese. "They'd need a big enough room."

"There's an event room at the back of the building, in the new bit."

She leads me along the ground floor. We follow signs down a main hallway and then around a room labeled as a chapel to another lobby, this one smaller, shabbier.

There's blood on the linoleum. That's the first thing I notice. Pools of it, drawing a path in either direction away from the stairwell that leads up to the antenna tower. I exchange a look with Reese. It's a lot. More than anybody could really stand to lose.

"Left or right?" Reese says.

We head left, follow the signs for the event room. A bank of windows opens up, and inside, the room is all gurneys and curtains and tears in the linoleum tile. Along the far wall, a small row of cabinets and a sink, a wet bar for the parties nobody ever had here, and above the cabinets, papered over but showing through, posters advertising all Raxter has to offer.

"Where do you think they went?" Reese asks. "The doctors, I mean."

"Back to the base on the coast, maybe. This place is far enough from school that we wouldn't see if somebody came to get them."

The door's open, the trail of blood disappearing through

it, and I go first, take careful steps into the ward. Four beds, three slept in. Across from me one bed is rumpled, the covers thrown off, an IV stand knocked over next to it. Red stains are smeared across the floor.

Reese picks up the clipboard tied to the foot of the gurney and scans it. "This is her. There, see? Byatt Winsor."

She really was here. But I'm too late. I'm always too late.

I turn, scanning the rest of the room for some sort of clue, when I notice the bed to the left of the door. It's drenched, the covers soaked with deep maroon splotches. In the middle of it all there's a scalpel, glinting softly in the flickering light. And there's something else too.

"Hey," I say, and Reese turns. "Look."

"What the hell is that?"

We inch closer. It's not moving, but Raxter taught me not to trust my eyes. Things can be dangerous long after they're dead.

"Is that—"

"A worm," Reese says.

It's caked in dried blood, but underneath I can see pale, translucent flesh. And somehow it looks familiar. I've never seen it before, I'm sure of that, but there's a twitch in my gut; like answering like.

The worm, and the scalpel, and I can put it together now. Byatt here, with the scalpel in her hand, digging through her insides until she found what she was looking for.

"That was inside her," I say. And then, because we're

both thinking it: "There's one inside us, too, isn't there? It's the Tox."

Parasites, living in our bodies, making us their own. Using those who can take it, abandoning those who can't. Protecting themselves at all costs. Inside me, inside the animals—inside Raxter. Making us wild.

I can't keep looking at it. I bend over, convulsing as I dry heave.

"It's okay," Reese says, rubbing my back.

"I want it out of me." Tears spring to my eye, and I'm breathing too fast, I have to slow down, I have to. "Please, get it out."

"We can't do that."

I straighten, push her arm off me. "Don't you want it out of you?"

"We don't know what might happen if we try. We could bleed to death." Reese tucks my hair behind my ears, gives me a shaky smile. She's trying so hard to make it okay. "We'll figure it out," she says. "We'll figure it all out."

"I don't understand. How could we not know?"

"It must've grown. It would've been small to start with. Microscopic."

"But"—and I feel lost, like the whole world's learned a new language and left me out of it—"what about tests? Our blood tests, and physicals. And why now? Why us?"

"I don't know," Reese says. She goes back to the clipboard from Byatt's bed and starts flipping through the papers collected there. I wish I could be like her; I wish I could let go of things when there's nothing to be done.

I stand next to her, read over her shoulder and catch words here and there that I know—"estrogen," "adapting," and over and over again, "failure"—but most of it's all charts and numbers. Are the answers in there somewhere?

More charts, more paragraphs done in unreadable handwriting, and Reese flicks through quickly, barely looking at them, until she stops on one page.

"What is it?"

She folds over the corner, then dumps our backpack out on the mattress, fishes through it for the records we took from the school.

"Reese?"

"I thought I recognized this," she says, and lays out the pieces of paper. Twin graphs, with analysis printed below in text so small I'd need a magnifying glass to make it out.

"It tracks the climate," Reese explains, pointing to one axis where years are listed. The year of the Tox is highlighted on one copy, yellow ink faded and bleeding. "The average temperature on Raxter over time. Look, it goes way back."

One copy in the school records, and another here in a makeshift hospital, pinned to Byatt's bed. And there it is—the climate changing, the temperature rising. I read once about creatures trapped in the arctic ice. Prehistoric, ancient things, coming awake as the ice melts. In Maine, on Raxter, a parasite slowly reaching into the weakest things—the irises, the crabs—until it was strong enough to reach into the wilderness. Into us.

CHAPTER 26

Reese keeps staring at the graphs, and I take the clipboard from the bed, peer at the rest of the documents. Observations made about a patient BW. And on the bottom of every form, the same signature. I can't read it, but there's a printed name underneath, under "Attending Doctor."

"'Audrey Paretta,'" I read. "That was Byatt's doctor."

Headmistress said they dosed her with the gas. It would've been Paretta who did it, who made the decision to kill my best friend. If she were here, I'd tear her eyes out with my bare hands.

"She got evacuated," Reese says gently. "There's nothing we can do about her right now."

I nod, push the thought of Paretta out of my head, and keep flipping through the clipboard. Tests and tests, and none of them working. The Tox too strong to die, and us too weak to live. RAX009, they labeled her. Eight others, then, and I think of Mona in that body bag.

Welch said that night that they thought they'd gotten it right. They must have sent Mona back to school, waited to see if she would last, if the cure they'd found would hold. But she didn't, and it didn't, and I bet she's somewhere in this building, eyes wide and staring, body stiff and sliced open for answers. This story was hers too.

I give Reese another minute to poke through the room, let her gather up the documents from Byatt's bed and shove them back into the bag. When she finishes we both head for the door. There's nothing more we need in here, and the jets will be overhead soon enough. It's time to get Byatt.

We follow the blood back out of the ward, down the hallway and through the lobby. It leads past the stairwell and along a narrowing corridor that twists sharply. The trail gets fainter, but it doesn't give out, and here and there, scattered along the wall, are handprints, as if somebody leaned on it to keep themselves upright.

After a third corner the air begins to smell of the outside, fresh and clean. I speed up, Reese at my shoulder. And then it's there, a door, dented and half open. And beyond it, grass and daylight.

I slam through it, stumble out into a small pockmarked yard. A chain-link fence closing us in, and beyond it trees bristling thick with leaves. This must be around the back of the building, pressed up right against the woods. Above us the sky is vivid blue, uncluttered with clouds.

I almost don't see her. A ways down, propped up

against the wall of the center, body so small and crumpled, jacket wrapped tight around what's left of her.

"Byatt?"

I'm running, feet pounding the earth, and I crash to my knees by her side. It's a mess, it's awful, but I can't look away. Snow scattered across her dark hair. A bandage around her arm, soaked through with blood, her skin so pale I can almost see through it, and a Raxter Iris clutched in her pure black fingers. She's cold. Her body's so cold.

"Byatt. Byatt, hey, come on. It's me, it's Hetty."

No answer. I feel for a pulse at her neck, but I'm shaking too hard, and she's looking right at me, eyes bright and warm, just the way I remember them. Only there's nothing behind them now. No life, no hidden place. I stroke her hair back, and it's a year ago and a month ago and the first day we met all at once. Byatt sneaking me food from the kitchen, Byatt calling my parents for me when I failed a test, Byatt saving me a seat during evening mass, Byatt, Byatt, holding me through nightmares, always walking on my blind side and resting her hand on my elbow until I learned not to need it. My friend, my sister—part of who I am.

"The doctors dosed her with the gas," Reese says, and I drag myself back to the world. "She must've known she was dying."

Byatt, with the end almost on her. Taking her body back. Coming out here, away from where they put her.

A sob shatters me, and I press my face into the

curve of Byatt's neck, give over to the shake of my body. Headmistress told me, but I couldn't believe it. Byatt's too big, too much to ever disappear. How could anybody do this to her? How could Paretta have met her and not seen what she's worth?

"What do you want to do?" Reese asks when I've quieted. "I don't think we can take her."

"What?"

"We can't stay here forever. The school's probably destroyed by now, and the jets will be here soon."

"I'm not leaving her," I say, adjusting Byatt's jacket.

"But—"

"I said I'm not leaving her." And I don't know how we're getting around this, because I'm not giving in and neither is Reese. I can see it in the set of her jaw. Staying here is dangerous, I know that, but after everything I've done to find Byatt, I'm not leaving her now.

Reese sighs, and it looks like she's about to say something when there's a cough, a slight hitch in breathing, and I jump. Turn slowly, almost afraid to look.

She's alive. Byatt, chest barely moving, eyes blinking as she opens her mouth.

"Oh my God." I brace my hand behind her head to support her neck. "Byatt, can you hear me?"

Finally, she tilts her head, and she looks at me, and I can feel the smile slip from my face. Something's off. "Byatt?"

"What is it?" Reese says.

"I'm not sure." I take Byatt's hand in mine, press it against my cheek. "It's me. It's Hetty."

Nothing. No recognition. Byatt's face, but nobody's there.

"I don't understand," Reese says. "They gave her the gas. How is she still alive?"

I look down at her hand, limp and bony in mine. And the bandage on her arm, the edges of a gash peeking out from underneath.

"She's alive because she took it out," I say.

"What?"

"The gas was supposed to kill the Tox. But she took it out. So there was nothing for it to kill." Byatt's eyes unfocus, leaving her staring just over my shoulder. "And it's like she came out with it. Her personality, her everything."

Reese crouches down at Byatt's feet, and we watch Byatt's head slowly swing around to look at her. At first I think there's something, a spark in her, but it's gone before I'm sure I saw it.

"Let's see if she can move," Reese says. "You're not strong enough to help, and I'm not sure I can get her to the boat carrying her on my own."

Too hurt, she means, but she'd never say it. Not even now, after everything.

I get on one side and Reese gets on the other, and together we're heaving Byatt to her feet when a low roar kicks up, soft but growing, in the distance. The jets. My mouth goes dry, fear lifting the hair on the back of my neck.

"Shit," I say. "We have to hurry."

Byatt's steps are halting, like she's only just learning how to move her limbs, but we start heading for the door back into the center.

Inside, then, and down hallway after hallway. I'm fading, strength leeching out of me, and every step we take is slower than the last until we reach the main lobby, noon sun sneaking through the boarded-up windows. We stop, lean Byatt up against the desk so I can rest for a moment. I can feel Reese watching me. She's waiting for me to say it, for me to leave Byatt behind, but she'll be waiting a long time.

"Come on," I say. "Now or never."

Out across the marsh. There's our boat on the beach, and it's so far and I'm losing my will, but Reese says my name once, just once. Stern and strong, and she believes I can do this, so I have to.

A whistle, and a huge rush of freezing air. "Get down," I have time to say before a trio of fighter jets comes swooping overhead. It's so loud I can't think, can't do anything but endure it. They're flying too low. We have to go now.

They disappear then, circling around for another pass, and I hoist Byatt farther up with my good arm. "Come on."

At last, the pier, and we scramble down the shore as fast as we can, Byatt's feet dragging in the sand. Carefully, we drape her body between the seats, and her eyes are closed, but she's breathing. She's alive.

"Get in," Reese says. "I'll shove us out."

The sway of the water, the rev of the engine, Reese at the stern as the boat eases away. A quick turn and we're skimming along, the island blurring until it's lost in the spray. Farther, farther, until I can't hear the jets.

The snow stops and the day grows warm, the ocean throwing shimmer across my sight, the hull of the boat spangled with waterlight. I lose minutes, hours, staring at the horizon, trying to make out the low-slung buildings of Camp Nash. But the mainland blurs and it never seems closer, no matter how Reese steers us against the waves.

We're still miles away from shore when she cuts the engine with a frustrated groan. I start, rubbing at my blind eye. "What are you doing?"

"Current's pulling us away from the inlet. We won't gain any ground like this."

"So we're just stopping?"

"Until the tide changes." She pushes her hair out of her face and gets to her feet, the boat sloshing to one side. "We only have so much fuel. It's a waste to use it now."

Reese steps over Byatt's prone body to sit next to me at the bow of the boat. Byatt looks so strange, her face slack, her eyes closed. There was always something sparking about her, even when she slept. It's gone now, or different somehow.

"What's he like?" Reese asks suddenly. "Your dad, I mean."

"I don't know." It falls out of my mouth before I can stop it. It's true, really, but I know that's not what she's looking for. "He comes home from deployment and he goes away again."

Reese tilts her head. "And you love him?"

"Of course I do. I just don't know him." It doesn't make sense to her, I know, and I want to explain, to tell her how he doesn't live in my heart the way her father lived in hers, but I don't get the chance. My body twists, chest wrenching to one side, and I feel my throat thicken with spit.

"Hetty?"

The fever in the marsh, outside the visitors' center. The one Byatt's body burned out of my mind. I should've recognized the sign. It sizzles through my body and settles in the pit of my stomach, and there's something heavy inside. I gag, lean over the side of the boat, and spit out a watery mouthful of bile. I can feel an object in my throat, but I can't get it out.

"Help," I manage, and Reese is tugging me around to face her, eyes wild. "I have to—" Another racking shiver, blood trickling down my chin. "You have to get it out."

She looks at me blankly, and then I see it click. "Okay."

I sit astride the bench, and Reese mirrors me. My hand

braced on her thigh, her silver fingers gripping the back of my neck.

"Tell me if you want me to stop," she says.

I shake my head. "Not until it works."

I open my mouth. And Reese sticks two fingers as deep into my throat as she can.

I can't breathe. A cough building in my chest, but I can't get it out, can't swallow, and a wave rolls through my body as it tries to force Reese out. My eye waters and the world is hazy, distorted, but something is moving, stuck halfway down.

I smack at Reese's arm, and she pulls her arm back, dragging strings of spit. First one heave, and another, until finally, I vomit, pain everywhere like my insides have been torn out. Something fleshy and pulsing splatters onto the deck of the boat.

I wipe my mouth on my sleeve. Whatever it is, it's covered in blood, but it looks familiar, like I've seen the shape of it somewhere before. In a textbook, in a body, in the woods with Mr. Harker.

"It's a heart," Reese says. "That's a human heart."

This one shrunken, shriveled, and mine still beating in my chest. I look away, collapse against Reese, head spinning. She loops her arm around my waist.

"Doesn't someone at school have that?" she says.

"Sarah," I say. "Two heartbeats." But two hearts instead, and if her body kept hers, why couldn't mine?

I think of Byatt and me, on the beach that day before I

got Boat Shift. The last moment we had before it all went haywire. The crab she found, the Raxter Blue, with lungs and gills both like we learned every year in bio. Lungs and gills both. So it could live no matter what.

The Tox, working in the Raxter Blue, in everything, and in me.

"It's trying to help," I say. "It's trying to make me better, but I can't take it."

Reese pushes my hair off the back of my neck to let the breeze cool it. "Calm down. It's okay."

I cough, blood tangy and metallic on my tongue, and Reese pulls me in so I'm leaning against her chest. The boat sways, salt spice in the air. I close my eye, shut out the glare off the water and the pallor of Byatt's skin. "I'm fine. I just need to rest."

The three of us together, laid out in the quiet. We've been here before. One weekend during my first year at Raxter. Byatt got a run in her last pair of tights, and Mr. Harker drove us to the mainland to get her new ones. We were supposed to meet him in the park when we were done, but he was late, so we stretched out in the dappled shade under a low sprawling oak. The leaves turned translucent in the light, the air fresh and sweet. Byatt in the middle, me and Reese on either side, and it was the first time we let the quiet be. The first time we were ever really us.

"You're gonna be okay," Reese whispers, and I let it

push me further into sleep. "You saved me. Now I'm gonna save you."

I don't know where we're going. I don't know what's next. But Reese's heartbeat is steady in my ear, and I remember—I remember how it was. The three of us together, and I'll make it that way again.

ACKNOWLEDGMENTS

I have been so lucky to work on *Wilder Girls* with an incredible team. Thank you so much to each of you—you saw what I meant and helped me find the right way to say it. I will always be grateful.

To Krista Marino—thank you for your dedication as we pried the girls all the way out of my head, and for your guidance as we laid them out on the page. Your insights have taught me so much, and pushed this book to grow in ways I didn't know it could. I could not have asked for a better editor.

Thank you to my agents, of whom I am in complete awe. To Daisy Parente, for every panicked email you have answered. For your enthusiasm, and your advice, and for seeing something in *Wilder Girls*. To Kim Witherspoon, for your wisdom and level head (and for a whole other set of answers to panicked emails). To Jessica Mileo, for your support and your invaluable feedback. And to the teams at

Lutyens & Rubinstein, InkWell, and Casarotto—thank you so much for all of your help.

To Delacorte Press, thank you for your unending generosity and for the incredible dedication you put into making *Wilder Girls* the best it could be. Barbara Marcus, Judith Haut, and Beverly Horowitz: thank you for believing in *Wilder Girls*. I am so proud to have joined the Delacorte and Random House family.

Thank you to Betty Lew and Regina Flath, for designing such a stunning book, inside and out, and to Aykut Aydo du, for the cover art, which is eerie and beautiful and everything I could have wanted. To the rest of the Delacorte team, I can think of no better people to be working with. Monica Jean, Mary McCue, Aisha Cloud, and the Underlined team—Kate Keating, Cayla Rasi, Elizabeth Ward, Jules Kelly, Kelly McGauley, and Janine Perez—I am more grateful to you all than I can say.

Wilder Girls would never have existed without my cohort at the University of East Anglia. Thank you all for your support, and for giving me that most crucial of early feedback: asking to read more. To the faculty—to Jean McNeil and Trezza Azzopardi—for advising me as I shaped *Wilder Girls* into something readable. To Taymour Soomro, for understanding what I wanted to say even before I did, for all your feedback, and most of all, for your friendship. To Avani Shah, for accompanying me to a variety of breakfasts, for sharing my correct opinions on bread, and for reading version after version of *Wilder Girls*. I am so lucky to know you.

To my mother. Thank you for every Darwin's trip, for every movie, for every dropoff at the train station, and most importantly, for texting me pictures of the dog on demand. Thank you for sticking with me. I will always stick with you.

To those girls I met on the internet: Christine, Claire, and Emily. You know just how much writing this pains me, but I'm awfully fond of you all. You are vivid and you are sharp and you are very, very dear, and I am so thankful to have you in my life.

Thank you to my sensitivity readers for your time and feedback—any mistakes this book contains are mine and mine alone. Thank you to the Yarboros, who generously introduced me to Harkers Island, the original inspiration for Raxter. To Sama's in Middlebury and Sin in Providence, for witnessing the bulk of my *Wilder Girls* breakdowns. To my teachers, for the extra time you put in reading my work, and for the encouragement you gave me. To my friends, for enduring me as I showed you close-up pictures of parasites, and to my family, for your encouragement even as I changed my mind (again, and again, and again).

And lastly, thank you to younger Rory, who decided to stay. I would not be here without you.

ABOUT THE AUTHOR

Rory Power grew up in Boston and earned her BA at Middlebury College and her MA from the University of East Anglia. She lives in Rhode Island. *Wilder Girls* is her first novel.

itsrorypower.com

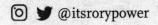 @itsrorypower